RAG AND BOYD

The FABULOUS ZOO

Helen L. Brady

RAG AND BOYD

The FABULOUS ZOO

HELEN L. BRADY

Rag and Boyd The Fabulous Zoo

Published by The Conrad Press Limited in the United Kingdom 2021

Tel: +44(0)1227 472 874
www.theconradpress.com
info@theconradpress.com

ISBN 978-1-914913-33-4

Typesetting and Cover Design by: Charlotte Mouncey, www.bookstyle.co.uk
The Conrad Press logo was designed by Maria Priestley.

Printed and bound in Great Britain by Clays Ltd, Elcograf S.p.A.

For my children, Nick and Sasha –
who always forgave me when I said
'keep quiet, I'm working'.

Prologue

A hand shook his shoulder; callous fingers flicked his ear, hard.

'Wake up! Answer me – do you know where you are?'

He tried to open his eyes, but the light was so bright he had to squeeze them closed to a squint. The voice began again. 'Wake up! Who are you?'

He shook his head. He wanted to reply, but his mouth was so dry… when he opened it to speak he felt the skin on his lips crack.

'Who are you?' the voice insisted. 'What is your name?'

His head dropped – he didn't realise whoever the voice was had been holding his chin up. He tried to think… he had been here for… a long time. He'd lost track after the first week or so, darkness and light did not seem to follow each other in the proper patterns as day and night. He tried hard to think… how long had it been… but gave up.

The calloused hand lifted his chin and a little water was dribbled into his mouth. He opened his cracked lips for more, stuck his tongue out to collect each precious drop.

'Who are you? What is your name?'

The water was taken away, and the hand that held his chin. His head dropped backwards. He tried to squint, to open his eyes, but the light was still too bright for him. He could just about make out some dark shapes, before he had to screw his eyes up again, leaving only a blood-red glow seeping through his eyelids.

'What is your name?'

Why didn't they leave him alone? He wasn't hurting them – he just wanted to go to sleep.

The kick in his side woke him up. The pain was the ache of a hard impact on an old bruise. It made him realise he hurt in other places too, his ribs, his head, his hands, his legs… Suddenly a thought bubbled up inside him… I have a Boy… and a daughter… Mo… Moor… And I have a wife! A beautiful wife…

The hand flicked his ear hard. It stung.

'What's your name? Tell me! What is your name?'

Through the jumble of pain, thirst, and confusion came a single, clear thought. He wanted to shout it aloud, but it came out as a hoarse croak.

'My name is Lachlan Ellis.'

There was a long pause. Exhausted by his effort, Lachlan let his head drop to his chest again.

A beautiful voice, deep and melodious, spoke from behind him.

'Start again. Walk him - do not let him sleep. Call for me when he no longer remembers.' There was a rustle of fine cloth and leather, and the soft pad of footsteps walking away.

Rough hands grasped him and hauled Lachlan to his feet,

yanking the manacles over his wrists and hands, making them dig painfully into his fingers. They half-carried, half-dragged him upright, and after putting a leather hood over his head, started to walk him up and down the seemingly endless stone corridors, over and over and over…

Chapter One

Through the tall window, the late afternoon sun glowered sullenly. A giant ball of dull red fire, it shone on Morag's pale face and made her unruly hair look even redder. Rag felt so angry - if the rooftops opposite, flamed golden-orange by the setting sun, could have exploded from her staring at them... they would have done. But nothing happened to the rooves, or chimneys, or the streets below.

Timson, Macleod and Macleod were the most recent generations of a very old law firm. They resided in dark wood-panelled offices on the upper floors of a grey stone building in an older part of Inverness; the high windows looked out over the wide grey-green river Ness as it flowed northwards to the sea. Their conference room was cold. The sunlight outside, now fading fast, barely made it past the window-sill.

Morag and her elder brother Boyd had been escorted to Scotland from England by Alice Sheldon from Social Services, but after being met at Inverness Airport by their new guardian, Wulfric Kennetson, they had been brought here and left to sit on a cushioned window seat out of the way -while *things* were discussed by the adults. More welcoming was the afternoon tea that had been served to them in antique porcelain cups; some very good beef sandwiches had arrived on matching plates.

Rag turned from the window to the mahogany side table, and sat heavily on the cushion. She was deciding whether a second chocolate éclair from the well-laden, triple-tiered cake-stand would be permitted when Boyd nudged her,

'What?' she mouthed silently with a frown.

Boyd nodded to the far side of the large room where they could see their newly designated uncle, Wulfric Kennetson, Alice Sheldon from Social Services, Mr Timson and Mr Timson's clerk facing each other across one end of an enormous, antique boardroom table. Mr Timson and his clerk were gathering up legal paperwork. Uncle Wulf had pushed back his chair and stood up. He was impressively tall.

Morag was fascinated by his pale blond hair; tied tightly back in a thick plait, it was much longer than her hair. It hung right down his back, a shimmery silver rope against the worn leather of his long, brown waistcoat. He looked, and dressed, a bit like the Huntsman out of that Snow White movie, she thought, but older. Though she couldn't tell how old because he didn't have many wrinkles, not like Mr Timpson, who reminded her of a tortoise at the zoo.

'I believe we are finished,' said Uncle Wulf. Morag could hear from his tone of voice that meant there'd be no more talking. Mum used to sound like that when she'd had enough of arguing with her over hair-brushing and teeth-cleaning.

'But Mr Kennetson, what about schools? There are still things to discuss...' said Alice Sheldon.

'They will be home-schooled. Anything else I shall see to in due course. Your papers are signed and witnessed. I have answered your questions. We have a long way to travel and I wish to start now.'

'But...' protested Alice, stubbornly remaining seated.

'Miss Sheldon,' Mr Timson spoke quietly. 'Mr Kennetson is now the children's legal guardian, any decisions he chooses to make regarding their welfare are his alone - the Social Services of England are no longer part of that process.'

'Yes, I know, but...'

'Miss Sheldon, my clerk will be very happy to drive you to your hotel, and arrange for transport back to the airport tomorrow if you wish. Donald...'

The smiling young clerk dressed in a dark suit stepped forward to take her chair.

'This way Miss Sheldon.'

'Of course,' said Alice after a moment. 'I'll just say goodbye.'

She looked a bit sour, and definitely put-out... like a bulldog sucking a wasp, her mother used to say, thought Morag.

Miss Sheldon stood up slowly, as Donald eased her chair out of the way. She picked up her shoulder bag, fishing out two business cards from a front pocket as she walked over to the seated children. She handed one to Boyd.

'I do hope you are happy up here with your Uncle Wulf, but if you need any help or you want to speak to someone, you can call my office any time, there's an answer-phone after office hours...'

'Goodbye, Miss Sheldon.' Boyd stood up and held his hand out formally – just like Uncle Wulf had done to Boyd when he'd first met them at the airport, thought Rag.

Miss Sheldon hesitated a moment, then took Boyd's hand and shook it politely, before turning to Morag.

'Goodbye, Morag, dear.'

Rag refused to stand up, she just stared up at her. ''Bye,' she said eventually and turned her attention back to the cakes. Miss Sheldon paused for a second, and seemed about to speak, but then just slid the other business card onto the table top.

Out of the corner of her eye Rag saw Miss Sheldon walk back to the waiting men. Wulf offered her his hand; he shook the woman's hand firmly once and released it. Morag strained to hear what Uncle Wulf said, still curious that he didn't sound at all Scottish, not like Mr Timson and Donald.

'Thank you for accompanying the children.'

'Yes. Well – we all want what's best for them in the end.'

'Miss Sheldon…?'Donald held her overnight bag in one hand and the door open with the other. She had no other option than to go with the attentive young man.

Wulf turned to the children, 'We will leave shortly - you may like to get ready.'

'Can we take the cakes with us?' said Rag.

'Certainly. I will have a box found for them, and some more sandwiches too.' Mr Timpson said, smiling. 'If that is acceptable, Wulfric Kennetson?'

Wulf nodded and smiled back warmly, Morag could see he liked this man.

'Your hospitality is welcome, Timson. We will leave in half an hour children…' Wulf turned to Timpson again, '…will your man do me the service of filling the car with petrol?'

'He will be very pleased to assist you. If I could just have a brief word on another matter before you leave…?'

Wulf spoke to the children, 'Morag, Boyd – please remain here. I shall only be a short while.'

Uncle Wulf and Timson left the room, leaving the children at the window-seat. There was so much to say that neither of them could think of where to begin, so they sat in silence for a few minutes.

Eventually Morag whispered fiercely to her brother. 'We could still go. We could catch her up at the airport and get her to buy us tickets home – Auntie Carol would pay her back.'

Boyd sighed and shook his head; he took out his music-player and pushed the white ear-buds firmly into his ears. Rag watched as he leaned forward so that his dark curls fell across his face – pulling the curtains her Mum had called it.

'Boyd - we can still go if we hurry! We could stay with Auntie Carol until Dad comes back – it won't be long.'

Boyd stretched his long legs out and sat nodding his head to the music, arms crossed firmly across his skinny chest. Morag leaned over and yanked the ear-buds out of his ears by the wire.

'Heh – don't do that!'

'Listen to me – we could still go home…'

'We don't have a home!' Boyd spoke sharply. 'Mum is dead. She is gone. She got cancer – and she died. Dad - could be anywhere. Mum wrote and emailed lots of times, he didn't reply. He hasn't come back – he might never come back. We don't know where he is, or what he does. Or… anything!'

Boyd stuffed the ear-buds back into his ears. Morag could feel the hot tears filling her eyes. Boyd looked at her; he pushed his hair back… and then pulled one ear-bud loose with a sigh.

'Rag… we have to stay with Uncle Wulf now. Ok, he looks a bit weird with that whole rock-star roadie sort of thing, but Mum and Dad lived with him when they were children. He has a castle, that'll be cool. They trust him, or Mum wouldn't have put it in her will for him to be our guardian. He will look after us, until… until…'

'Dad is going to come back.'

'He's been gone a long time this time…'

'But he wouldn't leave us! Not now Mum has… gone away.'

'She is dead, Rag. She got cancer and she died very quickly. Look, I don't much like being signed over, like we were parcels left for collection, but Mum's dead, and we're out of options.'

'Oh shut up! Shut up! You're only saying that because they told you not to bottle things up!'

Boyd pressed his lips together, retrieved his ear-bud and replaced it without speaking. He lowered his head, retreating behind his curtain of dark hair.

Rag knew she'd gone too far, but there was no way back… She turned quickly and knelt up on the window seat so she could stare out of the window - still nothing burst into flames or exploded. Neither Morag nor Boyd spoke, there was nothing left to say.

CHAPTER TWO

Tea in the solicitor's office seemed a long time ago now; it was dark outside the car, not just the 'city-dark' of night under the orange light of sodium street-lamps, but the genuine, wilderness darkness of no light at all except for the Moon… when it came out from behind the rapidly drifting clouds that is.

Rag had taken to staring straight ahead, at least there, there were the comforting beams of the big car's head-lamps to illuminate the world – beyond those wide cones of light was blackness. It was a bit scary – nothing but black hills against black skies… although she could see more stars than she'd ever seen in her life if she leaned her head against the car's wooden-framed windows.

Uncle Wulf had said the car was called a shooting-brake when she'd asked him about it in the airport car park. She'd never seen a car half made from varnished wood panels before, and it was huge. Uncle Wulf had just given that little smile and nodded as if it was perfectly normal to have an enormous wooden car.

There was very little noise outside the old-fashioned car, and virtually no traffic now they were so deep into the moors. Boyd had tucked one of the tartan blankets lying on the wide, leather back-seat around him and was fast asleep, his head bouncing occasionally when the car swayed around a bend in the road. The outside world slid swiftly by.

Morag had been half-asleep herself since it had gotten completely dark. Before that she'd watched the hills rise around the road that headed west out of the city towards the setting sun. Uncle Wulf didn't speak to them apart from telling them to wrap themselves up in the car-rugs if they got cold. Boyd still didn't want to talk to her and had closed his eyes – whether he was pretending to or not, soon he really had gone to sleep; Rag could hear him breathing slowly.

The stone and brick buildings had swiftly been left behind, the traffic thinning, changing from the shiny cars of commuters leaving work for home, to lorries or farm trucks, and a few mud-spattered 4x4's, some with anxious-eyed black and white sheep-dogs in the back, red tongues lolling as they bumped along inside their master's vehicles, eager to be outside, running on four feet again.

The main road ran alongside a river, then a narrow lake, then the valleys got narrower and the road twistier, and the river divided into broad streams that had tumbled down the hills and across the flood-plains. They had to criss-cross them via steep little stone bridges as the streams meandered. After a while they branched away from the tarmac road, up a rough track shrouded on both side with ranks of dark fir trees. This climbed slowly upwards in wide zig-zags, the road dark and narrow enough that Wulf had to drive much more slowly, changing gear frequently.

Sometimes the tree branches brushed against the polished panels of the big car, making a sound like sinister fingernails scraping along the wood. Now it felt secure being inside it

– when she'd first seen it at the airport car-park she'd laughed out loud. It looked like it should belong to *The Munsters*, it was so big and old-fashioned. Of course, Boyd had liked it at once because Uncle Wulf said he could learn to drive it – which she thought wasn't fair. Just because she didn't have long enough legs to reach the pedals… although Uncle Wulf had told her she could have lessons when she'd grown a bit…

Miss Sheldon had been cross – she said Boyd was still too young to drive 'he's still only fifteen', she'd said. Uncle Wulf had given her that cold little smile that didn't reach his eyes, and ignored Alice's protest. Anyway… Rag thought, it will be his sixteenth birthday in a few months' time, and not that long after I'll be fourteen – and I'll have grown too.

Morag didn't like this forest; the tall thin trunks of the trees were planted in straight lines that confused the eye - if you ever got lost in here, she thought, you'd never get out again. Every direction looked the same, empty and bleak. The dark branches blotted out any sense of space, and at every change of direction, the car's head-lights made harsh, flickering shapes leap away from the road into the thick darkness that lurked on both sides. Behind them, the night closed in, winding them ever more tightly into shadows and darkness.

Once, she'd turned to look back and been scared by how black and gloomy the forest was, just the dim red glow of the rear-lights briefly illuminating the lines of marching trees before they disappeared into murky shadows. She'd quickly turned back and wrapped her tartan rug around her, closing her eyes to keep out the night.

In some ways that made things worse - for what came to mind was swaying along in her parents' car as they drove down a tiny winding lane in Cornwall to get to the beach. Her parents were singing some silly song about 'going to see the sea', and Boyd had been rolling from side to side pretending to be sailing over the waves. He'd been laughing and whooping and kept falling on top of her and she'd shouted at him to get off – then they'd clashed heads and it made her cry… Mum had turned around, stretched out her hand and reached back to her…

But when Morag opened her eyes with a gasp - there was no concerned, smiling face, bright with sunlight, looking back at her, and in place of her father's dark hair was the back of Uncle Wulf's white-blonde head, his long plait lying across his wide shoulders. Morag gasped again with the ache of them not being there anymore.

Wulf half-turned his head, unable to take his eyes completely off the winding track ahead of them, he slowed the car.

'Are you hurting, little one?' he said.

Morag shook her head.

'Do you need to get out?'

'No!' she said quickly – no she didn't want to get out here!

'Is it far to go?' she said her voice cracking with the pain of memories.

'Not too far – as the crow flies it is about fifteen miles or so, but we must wend our way around the foot of the hills.'

Ahead of them the track left the forest and opened out to a shimmering expanse of water stretching to right and left, while across the lake dark woods strode up the hills before deciding the ground was too steep; they stopped abruptly, bunched together in a solid line, leaving the rounded hilltops above them bare under a moonlit sky. Wulf steered the car into a sharp turn, driving along a rough, pebble-paved track, banked above the shining waters.

Morag turned her head to watch the wind-driven ripples… ever-changing patterns of black and moon-bright silver – like the swirling taffeta skirt of her mother's favourite evening dress... Tears filled her eyes as she thought of her mother… I want my mummy…

She sniffed, wiped her nose on the back of her hand, then bit her lip so Uncle Wulf wouldn't hear her crying and think she was a baby.

'It is normal to grieve,' Wulf said without turning, as if voicing his thoughts aloud. 'Tears are not a thing to be ashamed of.'

Morag sniffed loudly, but said nothing.

Out of the corner of her eye, she thought she saw something moving. She stared out over the lake, at first she wasn't sure… but there it was again! A large black shadow above the lake, keeping pace with them, slowing when they slowed, speeding up when they did. Thin clouds drifted across the Moon, dulling its brightness. She blinked, rubbed her eyes, stared hard – no, it really was there, something blacker than black, like an empty hole in the darkness. Her mouth suddenly dried as her mind conjured memories of fairy tale monsters, ghosts and… and…

Morag swallowed hard and took a breath, she opened her mouth, but no words came. The large black shadow seemed to be running on all fours over the water, getting nearer and nearer to them - but there were no splashes, no white water spraying up beneath its feet.

The Moon broke through the drifting clouds and for a moment she saw it clearly, a huge black horse galloping across the head of the lake… now turning towards them, galloping closer and closer…. Morag could swear she saw its eyes flash an angry luminous red in the moonlight.

'Uncle Wulf!' she gasped, 'there's something on the water – it's following us!'

Wulf glanced quickly sideways, but the track abruptly turned away from the lake to follow a bluff high above a large stream; a stubby clump of Rowan trees shut out any sight of the water.

'Are you sure? Perhaps it was moonlight on the ripples, or maybe you were dreaming.'

'No, it was a big black horse – with red eyes, I saw it.'

'Ah…' said Wulf, relaxing back into his seat, 'don't worry about him.'

'But he's chasing us.'

Even now she thought she could hear distant hoof-beats pounding along behind them, muffled by the turf to a dull thudding, but - turning to peer backwards, she couldn't see a thing.

'What is it?'

'It is alright, there's nothing there to harm you – now, why not go to sleep. The night is dark, and it is time for sleeping… time for sleeping… sleeping… sleep…' His voice had taken on a soft, almost sing-song tone. Morag felt herself nodding, felt her eyelids droop… Struggle as she might, they felt heavier, and heavier, until they finally closed.

Wulf glanced up to the rear-view mirror. In the darkness behind them he could see the sleekly powerful black shape getting closer – he smiled, and drove faster.

Chapter Three

After the car had stopped, the lack of movement made Boyd begin to stir. He looked around; they were in a courtyard in front of a tall stone building, at the foot of which was a big pair of wooden doors above wide stone steps. The area was lit by large glass lanterns on either side of the doors. Boyd could see the shadowed outlines of surrounding buildings, some high, some low, which must be old stables and barns, but above them all loomed the great square tower of Wulf's castle. Lower wings leaned against the tower, obviously built at various times later; their grey stone walls held tall narrow windows glazed with small glass panes – a few showed lights were on inside, but most were dark. All the buildings had steep roofs of dark grey slates that blended into the darkness of the night skies. Between the brass-shaded outside lights, Boyd now saw the large wooden doors of the house stood open.

Boyd blinked – he glimpsed a flicker of movement, somebody's shadow disappearing through the open doors. He thought at first it was Rag – at least it was someone her size. He turned, and saw his sister half-awake and stretching beside him – couldn't have been her, maybe there was another child? Boyd yawned; Uncle Wulf opened the car door beside the boy.

'Come – your rooms are made ready. It is late. You should go up to bed and we will talk in the morning.'

Boyd was still sleepy.

'What about our bags…?' he mumbled.

'We will bring them in later – there are night clothes laid out on your beds.'

Boyd stumbled out of the car dragging his tartan rug with him. He shrugged it around his shoulders and stood looking around – grey stone walls and wooden barn doors, each tightly closed, faced on to the cobbled court yard – strange cobbles, Boyd thought, very small, and quite pale… funny patterns… He tried to follow the curves, but his eyes were too tired to concentrate on the intricate shapes that disappeared into darkness at the far side of the yard.

Wulf had gone to the other side of the car and scooped Morag up in his arms; she barely struggled before he shushed her back to sleep. Boyd followed Wulf into the house.

The floor of the lofty hallway was paved with large pale grey flagstones; on the high walls hung many faded woollen tapestries. Across one wall was a huge sideboard made out of dark wood, heavily carved with complicated designs of fruit and fantastical animals. Two large brass candelabra stood at each end of it, and a great brass bowl of dried rose petals and lavender was placed in the middle. Ahead of them was an enormous, polished staircase with great thick banisters and elaborately turned newel -posts; it rose towards the dimly lit upper floor, turning its way up and around, and up again, following the square of the hall's walls. Wulf was already walking up to the first landing, Boyd, bleary-eyed, followed.

Muted whispers caught his attention and he looked down

towards the far corner of the hall, but the door there quickly closed before he could see who was behind it. He followed Wulf wearily; up the great staircase, along a corridor and up another smaller, twisting staircase until they finally came to a corridor with several doors leading off it.

'These are your rooms – your bedrooms are here, the door there is your sitting room, your school room is the one beyond it – and your bathroom is at the far end.'

'Really… all these… for just us?'

Wulf nodded. 'The one thing we have no lack of is space.'

He opened Morag's bedroom door, stooping slightly to grasp the brass handle because he still cradled her in his arms. The main light was already on – a four-branched coloured glass chandelier, which hung from the middle of the heavily moulded, decorative plaster ceiling. Boyd saw a white-painted wooden four-poster double bed piled high with pillows; a long, white cotton nightdress lay across the patterned velvet quilt. Uncle Wulf laid Rag down on the bed and knelt to take off her trainers. He glanced across to see Boyd watching him from the doorway.

'Come and turn back the bed cover – she can sleep as she is.'

As Boyd did, Wulf unzipped Rag's jacket and slid it backwards from her arms, the girl woke up enough to mumble that she could do it herself. Uncle Wulf lifted her up to the pillows and let her pull the covers over her up to her chin and struggle out of her jeans beneath them.

'Your brother's room is just across the hall,' he said. Rag nodded, yawning widely, only half awake, she curled up against the pile of feather pillows, pulled the blankets around her neck, and went straight back to sleep. They left her room and Uncle

Wulf turned off the light behind him as he closed the door

Across the hall, Wulf opened the door to Boyd's room. His double bed was framed with dark, polished wood; the wide, panelled bed-head reached almost to the ceiling. The projecting wooden canopy was hung on either side with heavy curtains embroidered in wool with red lions and heraldic beasts; they matched the floor-length curtains drawn over the two tall, narrow windows. This bedroom was bigger than the entire living room at their old home.

'Would you like a hot drink, or would you prefer to go straight to sleep?'

Boyd realised his mouth was caked and dry; he nodded, realising how thirsty he felt.

'Tea? Hot milk? Chocolate?'

'Chocolate would be good – the bathroom is…?'

'At the end of the landing – I will have your drink brought up shortly.'

Wulf padded away, and Boyd noticed that their new guardian had changed his Doc Martins for short leather boots that gathered in soft folds around the ankle. We must have been here longer than I thought before I woke up… thought Boyd. He yawned and shuffled off to the bathroom, still hunched inside his tartan blanket.

The black and white tiled bathroom was equally enormous. The old-fashioned white porcelain fittings were large and sturdy, topped with big polished brass taps. A huge copper bath stood in the middle of the room raised on enormous lion's paw feet. The inside of it was enamelled white; placed over one end, with a voluminous white shower curtain bunched up behind it, was a tall contraption of curved copper pipes and brass nozzles that seemed to be designed to shoot jets of water at you from all angles if you stood under it. Scary… thought Boyd.

He finished relieving himself, mindful to put down the thickly varnished, wooden hinged-lid on the lavatory, and pulled the chain on the high flush; which thundered impressively before refilling with much gurgling of pipes. He washed his hands, drying them on one of the fluffy, pale towels hung over a rail of polished copper pipes, still slightly warm to the touch. Gathering up the tartan he'd dumped on the wicker chair in the corner by the big bronze radiator, he went to leave. As he paused to find the cord to switch off the light, he caught a glimpse of movement near the door of his room.

'Is that you Rag? The bathroom's down here…'

He heard small feet pattering away down the carpeted stairs.

'Rag…?'

He walked down the corridor – no one was in sight. He opened the door to Rag's room – she was still in bed, fast asleep.

He closed the door and went back into his own room – on a bedside-table was a tray with hot chocolate in its own silver pot, a white mug and a plate of home-made biscuits. He didn't feel particularly sleepy now, but he got undressed. There were some old-fashioned, striped pyjamas laid out ready on one pillow – they smelt faintly of lavender. He put them on, poured a mug of chocolate and got into bed.

As he sipped the rich milky drink, he looked across at the old-fashioned toys, books, and wooden boxes stacked on the shelves running all across the far wall, and realised with a shock… this must have been his father's room when he was a boy – and nothing had been changed!

There were two large globes on wooden stands at either end

of a huge old-fashioned desk under the shelves, one terrestrial, and the other celestial. Near a window was a sizable brass telescope on a tripod stand. Three old model aeroplanes hung from the ceiling on fishing line...The books on some of the shelves... many looked much older than his father's should have been... his father... his Dad....

Suddenly, Boyd started to sob very quietly. He tried not to, but uncontrollable tears rolled down his cheeks and his nose got wet. He used the linen napkin on the tray to wipe his face, before he found a crisply folded white handkerchief in the pyjama jacket breast-pocket. There was a plaited cord hanging beside the bed-head that turned the main light off. Boyd grabbed it and pulled, drawing a veil of darkness over his father's things.

He sat propped up among the pillows, his eyes slowly becoming accustomed to the darkness, alternately sipping the sweet chocolate, nibbling the biscuits, and wiping his nose until he had nothing left but a few sniffles. He put down his mug and listened to the wind humming softly as it danced across the tiled roofs outside. He heard a distant, soft rustling of many leaves coming from somewhere just beyond the castle's walls. As he drowsed he thought he heard a horse in the courtyard below him, but it wasn't the harsh clip-clop of iron-shod hooves... more a muffled, heavy regular tread, so perhaps he was mistaken... but he finally relaxed and went into a deep sleep.

Only to be suddenly half-woken up by a swishing noise as his door opened and brushed across the carpet. A small figure in a long white gown glided into his room, calling his name. His eyelids flickered open...

'Boyd… Boyd…'

He shot bolt upright with a yelp of fear as a pale figure approached silently through the gloom. It hovered at his bedside…

'Boyd… where's the bathroom? I need the loo.'

Boyd fell back into the pillows – it was his pesky little sister!

'Door at the bottom of the hall – and don't flush, you'll wake everybody up!'

'Oooookay…'

He heard bare-feet pad away as he turned over and dragged the blankets closer around his neck, drifting back to sleep. Moments later it seemed, he heard the door slide over the carpet again and after a short pause he felt the mattress rock as if something heavy had climbed on to the bottom of the bed. He seemed to hear a softly breathy voice.

'I comes in?'

Boyd grunted sleepily, 'Ok, if you must.' He hitched over to create a space… after a moment something chilly touched his back.

'Keep your cold feet to yourself Rag or you're out,' he growled into his pillow.

The coldness withdrew… and then the mattress rocked again and something heavy thudded softly to the floor.

His sister shook his pyjama sleeve. 'Can I come in with you?'

'Wha…? I said yes before didn't I?' Boyd mumbled.

'I didn't ask before.'

Boyd jerked awake and looked around, his eyes still had their night-vision - the heavy curtains made the room dim, but outside the moon must have been very bright. He could see his sister at the side of the bed, dressed in an old-fashioned, long-sleeved, white cotton night-dress that buttoned up the front.

'You were here a minute ago.'

'Yes, I wanted the bathroom.' Rag climbed up onto the double bed and tunnelled under the blankets.

'And then you asked to get into bed.'

'I just did, didn't I?'

'I mean before that.'

'I dunno what you mean...' Rag yawned. 'Go back to sleep, you were dreaming.'

It took a while before he went back to sleep - even after he pulled the blankets up nearly over his head. Surreptitiously, he leaned closer to the warm body of his sleeping, now gently snoring sister.

There are no such things as ghosts... He must have been dreaming... mustn't he? Yes, dreaming... because ghosts aren't real...ghosts aren't real...

CHAPTER FOUR

What woke them both was the hollow clank of wooden buckets banging together out in the courtyard and the low murmur of voices, too far away for the words to mean anything.

Boyd nudged his sister; Rag rolled over, curling up into the bedclothes. He nudged her again - harder.

'Stoppit!' she mumbled from deep within a pillow.

'Wake up, Rag – do you know where we are?'

'In bed. Asleep.'

'Besides that.'

Outside the window he heard the unmistakable noise of chickens clucking eagerly and a voice calling 'chuck, chuck, chuck'. The noise faded as someone led the hens away. Though now Boyd heard a muffled 'moo'…

'Uncle Wulf has a farm…' he muttered.

'E-i E-i Ooohhh… Now just go back to sleep!'

There was a sudden sharp *tap-tap* against the outside of the window. The two of them froze; they looked at each other, avoiding looking at the window. The insistent noise was repeated… *tap-tap, tap-tap-tap…*

'What. Is that?' whispered Rag.

'A tree branch.'

'Really?' she said.

'Must be,' said Boyd, but he didn't sound confident.

Tap-tap, tap-tap...

'Why don't you draw the curtains?' said Rag.

'Why me?'

'It's your room.'

'It's nothing. Anyway, why don't you go back to your own bed and leave me in peace.'

'I'm not going anywhere until you see what's out there!' she said.

Tap-tap-tap-tap...

'There's nothing out there!'

'Then open the curtains!'

'All right!'

Boyd jumped out of bed, but paused to straighten his shoulders before walking slowly towards the window. The tapping had stopped. He took a deep breath, and reached up to the curtain, pulling it open quickly.

On the window ledge outside a large black crow flinched, fluttering its wings before settling down. It stared up at Boyd. The bird tilted its head to one side, then the other, and then leaned forward to tap the glass sharply with its beak.

'Woooah! It's - a bird. Maybe a crow, I don't know...' Boyd relaxed after the initial surprise.

The bird wasn't at all flustered - it just regarded Boyd with a beady black eye.

'A crow? Really...? Let me see.'

Rag bounded out of bed and ran to the window. The crow was startled by her sudden appearance and flew off in a hasty flurry of black feathers. She watched it circle the nearby roofs before landing to stalk moodily along the ridge tiles of an outbuilding. It opened its beak repeatedly, but its harsh *caw-caws* were muffled by the glass.

In the yard below them was Uncle Wulf , dressed much as he had been the day before in long brown leather waistcoat and dark cargo trousers tucked into laced-up Doc Martin style boots; he'd come out of a barn and held up a wooden bowl. The crow flew to perch on his raised left arm, sidling along to dip its head to the corn in the bowl. Wulf dropped his arm, scattering the grain on the cobbles; the bird flew down to peck at it eagerly as the tall man turned and walked back inside the barn.

'He wanted his breakfast,' said Rag, '...I think I do too.'

She padded away, back to her bedroom, leaving Boyd at the window. He pulled the other curtain open and stared out. At a distance, beyond the slate roofs of the outbuildings, hills rose steeply into craggy tops of exposed granite. The castle was built in a valley with a flat floor. Boyd tried to remember his geography lessons about valleys and glaciers, but decided it didn't really matter; they were 'here', wherever here was... He just had to hang on until Dad got their messages and came back. But a small voice inside his head whispered - if he comes back...

He pulled the curtains at the other window open. Through that one he could just about see beyond the outbuildings to high-walled gardens - for vegetables maybe... and beyond that, a shelter-belt of oaks and pines, and a thicket of slender Silver Birch trees which shivered in the breeze. Over the furthest tree-tops he could see the open moorland that gradually rose into mountainous rocky outcrops. The castle sat at the valley's widest point, cupped between sheltering outcrops covered by heather, jumbled stones and sloping moorlands.

Miles from everywhere and everyone, thought Boyd glumly, what on earth are we going to do all day?

Back in her bedroom, Rag opened her one suitcase she'd been allowed to bring. Her tightly packed clothes were now wrinkled into jagged creases. She looked around the large room; the furniture was light, shimmery-grained wood, big and old-fashioned: a tall chest of drawers, matching dressing table with three mirrors, and a double wardrobe with a mirrored door. There were empty shelves above the white-painted cupboards built into the big alcoves on either side of the chimney breast, which held a proper fire-place for a real fire, now securely fenced off behind a brass mesh guard.

Shelves of books stood above a wide desk with more drawers… another door set into the wall probably held even more shelves… and all she had was in one suitcase and a rucksack. She wished she had her own stuff here. Looking at all the empty spaces reminded her of her little bedroom at home, and all her things that had to stay packed away under the bed or stacked in plastic boxes because she didn't have room to put them out... here she had loads of space and nothing to put in it.

She pulled her two favourite soft toys out of the rucksack, along with some of the bean-bag cats she wasn't supposed to have packed. She had a huge and much loved collection at home, colourful velour bean-bag animals of every sort. It had been a wrench to leave them behind. Miss Sheldon had said they had to leave everything for the moment, and they could come back later to get the rest of their things once they knew they were settled. Rag had decided to bring as many of the cats as she could get in her bag without being discovered.

Looking around she decided the little cats could sit on the dressing table with the silver-topped cut-glass jars and bottles – all of which were empty, apart from one perfume spray that smelt like roses - the liquid splashed up the dressing-table mirror when she gave the silky bulb an experimental squeeze. Rag hastily grabbed yesterday's tee-shirt to mop it up, then wrinkled her nose at the stale, un-washed body smell and dropped it on the floor.

She rooted through her clothes, leaving some spilling onto the rug, pulled out the wash-bag with her toothbrush in – should she clean them now or later? Better do it now, she thought. As she got up she noticed a thick, fleecy dressing gown hanging on a hook on the back of the bedroom door. It was pale grey and when she took it down she saw a complicated design of silk-embroidered intertwined letters on the chest - 'M M E'... Morag Mia Ellis. Uncle Wulf had it made especially for me... One part of her was pleased, but another part thought ...as if that is going to make me like it here! She pulled it on and stomped off to the bathroom at the end of the hall.

Boyd heard the door opposite slam and bare feet slap down the carpeted hallway, then the bathroom door slammed shut. She won't be long, he thought. His sister only washed as much as necessary, Mum was always telling her to clean her teeth properly and to wash every morning...

Boyd's grip tightened on the suitcase handle as he heaved it up onto the bed with more force than was needed. He stood for a moment, pressing his lips together hard to force the sigh away. Then he sniffed loudly before his nose got wet again.

Mum always told him not to tease Rag if she was smelly… now he'd have to be the one to nag her to wash properly. He tilted his head back, inhaled deeply then blew the breath out hard - determined to be in control of himself. He unzipped the case and took out a pile of his neatly folded clothes.

There was a big chest of drawers, taller than he was, against the wall opposite, and another shorter one with a framed mirror on top between the windows. He walked across to the larger chest and pulled out a drawer at waist height and dumped the clothes inside. He opened the drawer below; it held more pairs of striped pyjamas, and some crinkly plastic packets of white vests and Y-fronts – he sneered at those and closed the drawer.

Curious now, he investigated the rest; some drawers were empty, but others held soft, long-sleeved, checked flannel shirts in earthy colours, another had thick jumpers knitted in complex patterns of knots and cables, and in the very top drawer, which he had to stand on a chair to reach… he found a complete Highland outfit of heavy, pleated kilt, white linen shirt, and two short, wool jackets, one pale grey, one dark green, both decorated with multiple rows of silver buttons… though what impressed him was the short knife in its finely embossed leather sheath. The shaped handle was made of dense black wood, carved with finely beaded spirals, made so it would fit snugly against the palm… but the buckled strap attached to the sheath was far too short to go around the waist. Maybe it hung on something?

He heard the bathroom door close and Rag's feet pattered back to her room. Boyd put the knife back – he'd get it out and look properly later on. He climbed down, searched his wash-bag out of the suitcase and went to the bathroom.

Rag was dressed and sitting on his bed when he came back.

'Get out of my room!'

'I was only waiting for you.'

'Well wait in your own room.'

'All right', she slid off the bed sulkily. 'No need to throw a fit.'

'I'm not throwing a fit, but this is my room…' Boyd bit back his annoyance. 'Just… just wait in your room until I'm dressed and we'll go downstairs together.'

'I was only sitting, I didn't touch anything!' Rag left, slamming the door behind her.

Boyd looked around, some of the books had moved and a different country was now uppermost on the globe. Good job I left that knife out of sight, he thought.

He dressed in his own clothes, left his room and tapped on Rag's door. She opened it immediately.

'Sorry for shouting', he said.

'Sa'right. Can I look through your telescope later?'

'Ok – but ask before you do.'

'Yeah. Sorry. Which way do we go?'

'I guess we'd better go that way, I think that's where we came up,' said Boyd.

They walked down a small staircase, which they found led to a landing, before it carried on curving downwards and around in tight, looping spirals. Further along the hallway they could see the large, carved wooden newel posts of the big staircase they'd come up the night before, so they walked that way. Their rubber-soled trainers squeaked on the polished wood as they went down the wide staircase.

Obviously alerted by the noise, Uncle Wulf came out of one of the doors in the big hallway.

'Come this way,' he said and led them through the polished wooden door.

They were in a lofty corridor with doors off to one side. Uncle Wulf led them through the third door along and they entered a sunny room with a tall window. A table big enough for eight was laid with two place settings. On a large sideboard a number of lidded, silver chafing dishes sitting on silver frames were arranged in a row, each with a little candle-burner mounted under the dish to keep the contents hot.

'They did not know what you liked so they made a selection, you can tell me later what you prefer.'

Uncle Wulf went over to a large pair of polished wood cupboard doors set into the wall. At the side was a small brass funnel attached to a flexible pipe; a whistle was built into one side of the funnel. Wulf blew into it - after a few moments a muted voice, from wherever the other end of the pipe led, made a wordless questioning reply to the whistled summons.

'Will you have tea?' he said, turning towards them. Rag and Boyd nodded.

'Tea for two,' Uncle Wulf said loudly and clearly. The pipe mumbled assent. Wulf put the funnel back on its hook. He opened one of the gleaming cupboard doors to reveal a large square shaft built into the wall with thick ropes hanging down inside the dark space.

'They call this contraption a 'dumb-waiter'- they will send your tea up in it. I shall come back later to speak to you when you have eaten.'

He closed the hatch and went to leave them.

'Who's they?' asked Morag.

'My housekeepers – please, take what you want, but be careful, the dishes are hot.'

And with that, Uncle Wulf left them on their own.

Boyd sniffed hungrily, he smelt bacon. He lifted the lid of one dish - it was filled with scrambled egg. The next one held fishy-smelling, bright yellow rice. He put the lid back and tried the next – curling rashers of crisped bacon and golden cakes of fried potatoes. His mouth began to water and he realised how hungry he actually was. There were white china plates in a stack and a tray holding tongs and spoons, Boyd put the lid down on the tray and picked up a plate.

'Do you want me to put some out for you?'

'No, I can do my own. They haven't got any cereal though - I like cornflakes for breakfast.'

His sister lifted the lid over the next dish – sausages and grilled tomatoes, and finally, a large tureen stood on its own tray. Rag stood on tip-toe to reach the lid.

'Careful,' warned Boyd.

'I can do it!' She reached to tilt the lid open; the warm smell of cooked oats drifted out,

'Ugh - porridge!' The hinged lid slipped back into place with a clang. She came back to where Boyd was adding scrambled eggs to his plate of bacon.

'You can put some of them on my plate,' she said, 'and I want to try some of that rice stuff.'

'You sure?'

Something inside the hatch in the corner rattled and a distant whistle sounded from the pipe as somebody blew into it from the far end.

They looked at each other, then at the closed doors of the hatch. Boyd shrugged his shoulders, put his plate down and went over to open the doors. The rope pulley rattled and shook as a big, open wooden box came into view, inside which was a wooden tea-tray on which was a thickly padded fabric cylinder. Boyd lifted the tray out and put it on the table; he lifted the padding, underneath was a brightly coloured china teapot of steaming hot tea on a matching pottery stand.

Rag meanwhile helped herself to the yellow, fish-flavoured rice.... She tasted it and pulled a face.

'Mmmm... salty, but I quite like it... I think.'

She sat down with her plate and reached for the toast and butter set out on the table.

'There's more here than we can eat, do you think Uncle Wulf will want some?' she said.

Boyd shrugged, 'I think he must have eaten already, there's no place set.'

They settled down to eat a bigger breakfast than they'd ever had before.

Chapter Five

Boyd was finishing his second helping, a plate of sausage, tomatoes, and potato-cakes, while Rag was busy tasting each of the several small pots of jam arranged on a large revolving plate that turned on its base, when Uncle Wulf returned.

He nodded at the toast crumbs and empty plates. 'Good, you eat well, but it is considered polite to put the covers back on the dishes, should others wish to eat after you.'

Boyd half rose, but Wulf waved him back and replaced the lids over the cooling remainder of the food on the sideboard. He went to the hatch, whistled and said 'Coffee'. After his call had been answered by a chirp of acknowledgement, he sat down at the end of the table. Rag gave the jam pots one last spin and sat back, looking down at the toast crusts in her hand. She saw Boyd tidy his knife and fork side by side on his plate, so she put the crusts on her plate and waited.

After a short period of silence the hatch rattled and the muffled whistle announced the arrival of Wulf's coffee. He fetched the tray of coffee pot, jug of hot milk, and a wide china cup and saucer and re-took his seat at the table.

'This must all seem very strange to you both,' he said, pouring his coffee.

Rag glanced at her brother, then looked back at Uncle Wulf and nodded.

'You will get used to it,' he said.

He sipped his coffee, seeming to consider his words.

'First – I think you might like to explore. There are walled gardens – you can walk where you like, but always remember to latch the gates properly to keep the deer out. They will eat the cabbages down to the ground if they can get to them. Outside the walls are the birch wood, and the oaks beyond them; I do not want you to walk beyond the trees until I have time to guide you. The moors can be treacherous; there are bogs, loose rocks and sudden mists. I will show you the safe pathways soon. The road at the front of the house leads down towards the loch; there is a shore at this end where the water is shallow. You can go there and along the loch's banks, but again, do not go out of sight of the house, even if it is just around a bend in the road, until one of us can show you the safe paths.'

Boyd shrugged, and picked up a crust of toast to nibble. Rag opened her mouth to protest, thought about it and just ended up saying…

'Why?'

'Why you should stay safe? Or why you should listen to what I say and obey me?'

Rag frowned and folded her arms. 'Why were we sent here if it's so dangerous?'

Wulf inclined his head and gave that little wintry smile.

'Dangers are for the unwary and unschooled. When you have been shown the places where you need to take care, there will be no harm to come to you… unless…'

'Unless what?' said Rag.

'Unless you walk in places you have no business to be. There are a few places in the Keep that are not your concern, at least not yet. The kitchens for one – if you want food or drink, come to this room and use the whistle, ask for what you wish and it will be delivered. The glasshouses and boiler-room are also out of bounds until I take you in there myself. As are the animal houses.'

Boyd focused his attention on the silver salt and pepper pots and didn't appear to be listening. Rag continued to frown, ready to start questioning the boundaries – which seemed to be set very tight and narrow. Uncle Wulf continued:

'The other places you are not to visit are on the far side of the Keep. This stone tower…' He waved his coffee cup to take the whole building in. 'This castle is very old and some parts of it are not in good order, there are stones in the walls that are loose and can fall. In places that leaves unsafe stairs and unstable roofs… The rooms on your side of the grand staircase you can visit, but do not go into the old rooms on the far side.'

'So what are we to do if there are so many places we can't go?' said Rag sulkily.

'For now you may walk in the gardens, you may explore this side of the house, there are books in your rooms and play things, and eventually there will be lessons. I have tasks to finish today, but another day I will show you more places where you are allowed to go. I will see you this evening for supper. We will eat dinner early tonight, at 6 o'clock, a formal meal in your honour so we will dress accordingly. The Broon will sound the gong when the meal is ready. I will eat with you tonight and I will tell you more about the decisions I have made.'

Morag leaned forward in her chair, hands flat on the table either side of her plate.

'And why don't we get any say in it?' she demanded.

Uncle Wulf finished his coffee, put down the cup and gave her his full attention.

'I will listen. But - I expect you to be guided.'

He spoke mildly and didn't say 'by those who know best', but Morag and Boyd both heard the silent words. Eventually Boyd spoke.

'Ummm... Uncle Wulf – our mobile phones – will you be able to take out new contracts for us? The old ones... they finished when Mum died.'

'I am sorry, Boyd. There is no reception for cell phones here, we are too remote - so I am told.'

Both the youngsters looked horrified, but almost speechless.

'But... but...' was all Rag could manage.

'You will have more freedoms here than you ever had down there, but you must earn your right to them first. Show me that you may be trusted, and I will trust you. There are places here where you can learn to dive like salmon and soar like eagles... but first you must learn to walk without causing harm to yourself or others.'

Uncle Wulf looked from one to the other. They both look sulky. He pushed his chair back, stood up and left them staring blankly at his departing back.

'What was that about?' Rag said eventually, 'And why aren't there 'phones?'

'Look, but don't touch, and enjoy living in the back of beyond. I'm going to my room.' Boyd slouched out of the door leaving his sister alone.

Morag sat at the table by herself. She felt resentful and annoyed, last night Uncle Wulf had seemed kind, now he was making up all sorts of silly rules… and what was all that stuff about salmons and eagles? What did that even mean? Stupid place! Stupid man!

Rag pushed her plate away from her hard enough to make it skitter up the table. She stood up, wondering how hard she could slam the big heavy door as she left the room.

A whistle blew from somewhere deep below them. Rag looked across at the pipe, then went over, picked up the funnel and looked into it. The funnel gave another modulated whistle that sounded like a question.

'Hello?' said Rag.

The little voice at the far end of the tube sounded distant, and definitely seemed to be asking a question, though she didn't understand what was being said.

'Hello?' she said again.

The distant voice spoke again, sounding impatient, adding a demanding whistle for good measure.

Rag looked into the funnel and spoke slowly and clearly. 'I. Can. Not. Hear. You.'

From the funnel erupted a stream of annoyance - words she couldn't quite make out, but the tone was clear enough. The ropes and pulleys in the dumb-waiter began to rattle and shake ominously. It seemed as if far down below, something heavy climbed into it. The ropes began to move in small, swift jerks – something was rising….

Rag swallowed a squeak of alarm, dropped the funnel and ran from the room. She didn't bother closing the door behind her, let alone slamming it.

Chapter Six

Boyd had a face like thunder now he was on his own – how dare this 'uncle' who wasn't actually related to them at all, treat him like a baby – don't go out on the moor, don't go near the water… He knew that! He knew he had to find his way around before going too far! He wasn't stupid, or impulsive, not like Rag… He began to calm down a little; of course – Uncle Wulf had to say that to stop his little sister from running wild. She was bound to get herself into trouble and fall off something, or down something.

Having decided that the rules were only there for Rag and not really for him… Boyd felt a little better. He thought he'd go and get some boots and go outside, down to the lake; he was sure he'd seen some wellingtons in the built-in cupboard in his room. He leapt up the wide stairs two at a time, nearly falling over an extremely large cat sprawled in the sunlight on the landing where the stairs divided. The cat jumped up and shot up the other branch of the staircase, to the side where they weren't supposed to go.

It paused and sat at the top of the stairs facing Boyd, its huge furry tail swishing in annoyance at being disturbed. The cat half-closed its yellow eyes and turned its head away. It had very long, brindled grey fur, with furry tufts at the tips of its ears. Boyd had never seen a cat the size of this one, at least not outside a zoo, and that one had been a wild cat, a sort of lynx.

Boyd took a step towards it; the cat opened its eyes and glared at him. At his second step up the stairs, it stood up, arching its back, at the third step it hissed at him.

'All right kitty, I get the hint,' he muttered, and stepped back.

The cat sat on its haunches, honour satisfied, and proceeded to lick one of its paws, revealing impressively long claws in the process. Boyd liked cats, this one just needed to get used to him that was all... He turned and went up the staircase leading to 'their side' of the castle. The cat watched him go, then lay down and continued to groom its paws.

In his room, Boyd went to look through his window to decide where he was going to go first. Something moving on the hillside beyond the wind-tossed birch trees caught his eye – was it a deer? He swivelled the telescope around and turned the brass rings to bring it into focus. At first he couldn't find his target, but then he caught the movement again.

It was Uncle Wulf, striding over the moor – and he had two huge shaggy dogs with him... and strangely, their coats looked... dark green. Boyd leant back from the eye-piece and gave it a rub, then looked again - Uncle Wulf and the dogs were just disappearing beyond a rise in the ground. Must have been the distance, or the light... thought Boyd, they can't really be green.

Just then he heard pounding feet on the stairs and the door of his room was flung open. His sister appeared, wide-eyed and slightly breathless.

'Don't you ever knock?' snapped Boyd.

'It was coming to get me!' spluttered Rag.

Boyd sneered, 'What was? You're just imagining things again – like the monster that lived under your bed!'

'I didn't imagine that – it was a dream!' shouted Rag. 'And it was only once.'

'Three times – you bawled the house down.'

'They were different monsters!'

Boyd tutted. 'Go away Rag, I'm busy.'

'But – I spoke to the funnel and it whistled back, and then it got cross when I said I couldn't understand, and it shouted at me and then the waiter-thingie started to shake like something climbed into it...'

Boyd waited until she'd run out of breath. 'It's just the house-keeper; she's probably got a thick accent...'

'Didn't sound like a woman.'

'Ok – a man then, he's probably got a Scots accent and a short-temper – and that's why Uncle Wulf told us not to go into the kitchen. You're just imagining things – I don't know, maybe we're supposed to put the plates back in and he was cross because he had to come up and get them?'

'Well, he only had to ask...'

'Maybe he did and got cross because you were too thick to understand him.'

'I'm not thick!' Rag turned on her heel and stomped out of the room slamming the door behind her.

Boyd sighed; they were both on edge and getting on each other's nerves... It hadn't used to be like this... well... only sometimes... And then Mum had been there to sort things out...

He remembered how his mother would listen and nod at Rag's long, involved explanations, when they just made him impatient... How his mother could find reasons for them to do stuff with each other – and how they had made things together, and played board-games together, while their mother and father talked and laughed quietly, or joined in with them. His mum and dad would often be holding hands if they were walking in the park… or flying kites… or any of that other old-fashioned stuff that they insisted he and Morag did with them that was actually good fun once you got started…

It was up to him, he decided, he was the eldest, he had to show Rag that they'd be ok here. The gardens sounded boring. Yes – we can go to the lake… and, he decided, he wouldn't mention anything about feeling something get on his bed… otherwise he'd spook Rag and she'd be sleeping with him every night! He also decided he must have dreamed the whispering voice… maybe he'd dreamed the whole thing.

In the cupboard, he wasn't mistaken, there were some brand new, green wellies, and a pair of hiking boots, both in the right size; like his father, Boyd had big feet. His mother often joked about falling over his father's big boots… had joked…

He paused for a moment staring at the boots – looks like Uncle Wulf had thought of everything. Boyd looked over at the thin, hooded jacket he'd worn to travel in hanging over a chair, and went to the drawer and pulled out one of the thick knitted jumpers. He put the hoodie on first and topped it with the jumper, picked up the wellies in one hand and went to knock on Rag's door.

Rag had taken her temper out on her pillows – which were strewn around the room along with various bits of clothing.

It looked like her suitcase had exploded and a fountain of clothing had rained down. She was sitting in the middle of the bed, her eyes red and puffy. Boyd tapped on the door then opened it slowly; he looked around and decided to ignore the mess.

'I thought we could go down and look at the lake, loch… whatever…' he said. 'I found some new wellies in my cupboard – have you got some too?'

'I don't know.'

Boyd walked to her window. 'Look – you can see the edge of the water from here. We could go stone-skimming.'

'Yeah?' Rag's face brightened, 'I'll look for the wellies.'

On the floor of the large walk-in cupboard, a pair of green wellies and a pair of brand new hiking boots stood side by side, same as in Boyd's room. Rag grabbed them, then paused and turned to Boyd,

'I wonder how he knew our size?'

Boyd shrugged. 'Maybe he asked Alice?' he said.

'And what's that? I've not seen that before.' Rag pointed at his dark green, cable-knit sweater, the wool of which was flecked with tiny threads of blues and ambers.

'It was in my chest of drawers, sort of country dress, I suppose – I bet you've got some too. Have you looked?'

Boyd opened one of the drawers; inside were two ornately knitted woollen cardigans – with matching berets with bobbles on. He held one up.

'I am not wearing a hat like that!' declared Rag.

She pushed him aside and found some other daintier wool jumpers, knitted with complex horizontal stripes, patterned in pale blues, pinks, greens, mauves. Boyd opened the drawer below and found a heavy, solidly knitted jumper like his, but this one was dark blue.

'Here put this on, those thin ones are too pretty to get dirty, and it's windy outside, you'll be cold.' He dragged the jumper out of the drawer and pushed it into her hands.

Rag insisted on searching through the other drawers and the wardrobe before they left – there were more cotton night-dresses, some old-fashioned white vests and pants in crinkly packets, several soft flannel long-sleeved blouses in various colours, some pleated tweed skirts, and a selection of frilly white cotton petticoats of various lengths.

'Are these for dressing-up?' Rag said, holding one up – it was gathered and edged with tiny ruffles of lace. 'And why aren't there any jeans?'

In the wardrobe she found three old-style party dresses, one in a bright tartan taffeta, one in dark tartan and one in light green, plus she found a swatch of coloured fabric samples of the same heavy silk. She held one of the dresses up against her - it had a nearly ankle-length full skirt and short puffed sleeves.

'Do you think they're bridesmaid dresses?'

'I don't know – look, are we going or not?'

'Yes, just a minute.'

Rag was investigating the boxes on the wardrobe floor; they held shiny patent leather shoes, several wide silk sashes, and one held a thin belt with a knife in a narrow gilded leather scabbard attached to it. Rag grasped the golden wire-wrapped hilt and pulled the slender dagger free of its gilded leather sheath.

'Cool!'

'Yeah – I've got one of those as well,' said Boyd. 'Are we going – or shall I leave you to play dress up?'

Privately, he thought that it was a big mistake to give his little sister a sharp knife, and after all those warnings about safety too. Boyd shook his head.

Rag pushed the dagger back into the box regretfully, and closed the wardrobe door.

'Ok, ok – I'm coming.'

They trooped downstairs. The big, lynx-like cat was still lying at the top of the staircase, watching them through half closed eyes.

'Wow!' exclaimed Rag, 'is that a Wild Cat?' She went towards it; the cat stared at her, swishing its plume of a tail slowly from side to side.

'Leave her alone, Rag, she's nervous of strangers.'

'How do you know it's a she?'

'Because she's moody and crabby, and she hisses and yowls when she's mad.'

'Yeah, well I know somebody else can be like that too…' Rag muttered.

They squeaked downstairs in their rubber-soled shoes and out of the big front doors. They left their trainers on the front steps and put on the wellingtons, before walking down the rutted road that curved from the front of the castle courtyard down towards the loch.

High overhead, a very large bird with huge, black-feathered wings circled in the bright sky, spiralling upwards on the rising thermals from the valley floor. He saw the children walk away from the courtyard, saw which way they were heading and increased the width of the circles of his flight so as to watch them more closely. He lifted his wings, stretched out his huge black talons, seeing the children below... then curled the sharp claws tightly, as if he could pluck them up from the ground from where he flew.

Duffy, Uncle Wulf's pet crow, also watched the children. She hopped along the ridge-tiles on the roof of the barn to keep them in sight, before flying to perch in a stunted oak tree at the side of the road. She flitted from one tree to another as they passed beneath – hopeful one of them might have corn in their pockets. Then she paused, cocked her head; Duffy sensed the great bird circling above her. She hopped deeper into the foliage; she was wary of Him... but curious about the newcomers to her master's house.

Rag and Boyd remained oblivious; they didn't notice the pairs of eyes that watched them – from the castle, and from high above.

Chapter Seven

The loch almost filled the very bottom of the valley, stretching westwards to where, at the far end, dark fir-clad hills gathered close together leaving a narrow gap, before further misty blue hills marched away to the distant sea. To one side of the water, a band of trees snaked along the contours of the steep bank for some way; twisted by the wind, they bent sideways, only the tall Scot's pines kept their heads up. Beneath and between that line of trees and tough bushes was the rough road they'd been driven up the night before. It approached the castle having twisted through a gap in the hills half way along the narrow loch.

The head of the loch shelved so that the water was quite shallow for at least fifteen metres or so before it sloped steeply into deeper, darker water. The pebbly shore was almost like a shingle beach, plenty of stones here for skimming across the little wind-driven wavelets. In their wellingtons they could walk out a short way, though neither quite had the nerve to take them off and wade out knee-deep or beyond. Boyd told himself it was too cold for paddling and they hadn't brought towels… maybe some other time. Rag really didn't much like the look of the deeper dark water, blackened by the peat-rich soil washed down from the moors.

On the other side of the lake from the castle, they found a clear brook running down from the moors and rising hills beyond. It splashed down over smoothed water-worn rocks, before taking a winding course across the shingle. The rapidly flowing stream had washed away the silt and exposed plenty of larger pebbles for them to skim over the water. At first it was sunny, although the wind was brisk, but after a while clouds began to gather together into larger clumps and the sun remained hidden for longer and longer.

It was Boyd saw the great, black bird first, circling over them and the water. He'd looked up to the sky to see if it was going to rain soon, then he spotted the drifting speck spiralling down from above them. He called Rag to look up; as she did the bird flapped its huge wings and headed away from them down the loch.

'Is that an eagle?' asked Rag

'I don't know. It's too high to tell.' Boyd replied.

'Look – its turning round.'

The bird had wheeled, banking sharply, the full extent of its wingspan silhouetted against the gathering grey clouds – they looked enormous, it was almost like watching a pair of barn doors flying down the loch! The bird spiralled down, getting lower and lower, and began to fly towards them. The youngsters were transfixed by the vast lazy wing-beats. They were expecting it to veer away, but the bird kept to its path. Boyd took a step backwards, then another. The bird kept coming.

'Rag… come out of its way.'

'It won't hurt us.'

'Rag – I'm telling you...'

The black shape was still some way off, but they could begin to see just how big this bird was, and that it was stooping lower - its wings flapping harder in great sweeps, so that Boyd could swear he heard the air whooshing through the feathers. It opened its beak wide, and they both heard the high-pitched '*scree, scree*' of its cry.

Rag turned and ran back, the water splashing up the legs of her jeans staining them with mud and peaty water. Suddenly the bird drew its wings back tightly, shot its black-feathered feet forward and plunged towards the water. It rose moments later with a large shining fish wriggling between its huge curved talons; water showered down in a heavy silvery rain.

Splashed by the drops of icy water, Rag and Boyd ducked as the bird's momentum took it up and over them, and on and up towards the castle's tower. Just then, the sun suddenly appeared again and in the dazzle they couldn't quite make out where the bird landed, but it was suddenly gone from the sky.

'Wow!' exclaimed Boyd, 'did you see the size of those claws?'

'I almost thought he was coming for us.'

'Nah… of course not. But he was pretty scary. I don't think he was an eagle, though, eagles aren't black,' said Boyd.

'We could ask Uncle Wulf.'

'I suppose… I saw him this morning walking over the hill. He had two really big dogs with him, great shaggy things, sort of like Newfoundlands – funny thing was, looking through the telescope they were a dark greenish colour.'

'Yeah? Must have been because they were so far away – can I look through your telescope?'

'Yes,' said Boyd, 'but only when I'm there - and you're not to go into my room without asking!'

'All right! I only asked…'

Rag paused and stared at the loch behind her brother's shoulder – something was swimming up the water leaving a rippling wake behind it.

'Look!'

'What…?' Boyd turned to see what had startled his sister and saw the expanding wake of something, no… two things… he glimpsed open mouths and large, white teeth. The heads were low in the water and they were swimming fast.

'Um… why don't we go back to the castle?' he said.

'I want to see if they're seals,' said Rag.

'Those aren't seals!'

Boyd took his sister's arm and tried to drag her away. They heard a sudden shout from the road and saw a tall figure with familiar long white-blonde hair emerge from the scrubby bushes; he strode through the trees and down to the water's edge. Uncle Wulf gave a piercing double whistle and the two heads in the water turned and headed towards him. He jumped down the bank and suddenly two enormous dogs, their dark coats streaming with water bounded across the shallows, and out of the loch to greet him.

They barked in tones deep enough to make your toes curl at the vibration, and when they shook themselves it was like someone turning on a sprinkler. They danced around him energetically, until Uncle Wulf quietened them with a word, and then they lumbered after him, shaggy tails held high and wagging furiously as he walked towards the children.

Rag and Boyd were both caught with their mouths open – these dogs really were dark green; their thick shaggy coats had that sort of oily, iridescent sheen over their dark fur, like the rainbow colours on a starling's feathers.

Uncle Wulf approached them with a genuinely pleased smile. 'Good – I'm glad you have come out to see your world.'

'What are… those?'

Rag pointed at the two dogs; one was ankle deep, broad snout down, lapping up the water where the spring joined the loch. The other dog stood still, watching them with large green eyes, it was panting, its tongue lolling from a wide mouth – which they saw was a dark purple-black, as was its large, wet nose.

'These are Geri and Freki, they are brothers – Geri has the nock in his ear, you see?' Wulf pointed to the huge beast watching them intently. 'And Freki has the scar on his foot.'

The other dog turned at his name and lopped towards them from the spring. They could see as he came out of the water a narrow line of white fur above his paw, like a slim cuff. 'He got his foot caught in a trap,' explained Wulf, 'I was lucky to find him in time to free him.'

'What sort of trap?' asked Rag.

'What sort of dogs are they?' said Boyd.

'A wolf trap.' Wulf was already turning away towards the castle. 'I must finish my business in hand. Look around by all means, but do not go far, it is going to rain. I will see you this evening. Oh, and remember to keep your doors shut at night – these two will come to get on the beds if they can.'

The dogs rushed by, giving single deep 'woofs' as they cantered past Uncle Wulf, racing back towards the castle.

They reminded Boyd of small horses more than dogs – then a thought struck him.... so that was what came to him in the night… and he must have dreamt the voice. That it was only a dog made him feel much better. Then he had another thought…

'They haven't had wolves around here for centuries,' he said quietly to his sister.

Uncle Wulf paused and called back to them. 'As I said, we dine formally this evening; you have the proper clothes provided for you in your rooms, please wear them when you come to dinner.' He looked up at the sky. 'It is after noon, the rain will come in a short while. If you are hungry go to the breakfast room and ask The Broon for food.'

Then he strode away after his dogs. Suddenly with a clatter and a flurry of feathers, a black shape exploded out of a tree nearby and flapped urgently after him. They glimpsed the crow land on Uncle Wulf's shoulder just as he was hidden by Rowen trees outside the castle's out-buildings.

'Those were not Newfoundlands!' said Rag.

'More like their bigger, weirder cousins – they really were green, too'

'We didn't get to ask about the giant bird either,' said Rag, 'but I do feel hungry come to think of it.'

'Mmmmm… who do you think 'The Broon' is?'

'The cranky voice at the end of the funnel – you speak to it this time,' said Rag, 'He nearly bit my head off this morning.'

'Maybe he really can bite your head off…'

Boyd bared his teeth in a ferocious snarl and curled his fingers into claws while doing a stiff-legged 'zombie walk' towards Rag, his feet crunching the gravel with each step.

Morag yipped in mock fear, 'You've got to catch me first!'

She ran off towards the road, Boyd roared, and chased after her.

They thudded into the court yard of the castle, the rubber wellingtons dulling their steps. Morag did a circuit of the yard, running part way around the meandering white path laid in a pattern of complex twists and turns, set into the dark flattened stone cobbles that covered the rest of the courtyard. She stopped suddenly and looked down, examining the white 'pebbles' more closely. Boyd was sitting on the front steps heaving one of his boots off.

'What are these?' asked Rag kicking at the small, dull white 'stones' the intricate pattern was made from.

Boyd stood up - from the top step he had a better view of the overall design

'Cool! It's a maze. You can see the pattern properly from up here.'

He walked awkwardly down, one foot booted, one foot with only a wet sock on. He limped to the nearest edge of the white paths, to a place where the cobbles were slightly loose. He leaned down and pulled... one came out of the ground, a white double knob on a short shaft. He turned it over in his hand then dropped it quickly as if it had burned him...

'They're bones.'

'Bones...? Ueewwwwww!' Rag hopped over the pale pattern, running and jumping to avoid the white bits to get to the safety of the stone steps. 'What freak makes their driveway out of bones!?' she yelped.

Boyd was wiping his hands convulsively up and down his jeans. He blew out a breath and composed himself, and gingerly picked up the knuckle bone between finger and thumb and stuffed it back into the pattern where it had come from. He shook his hand out and stepped back.

'It's ok – It's - just a very old thing to do.'

He came over to her and sat down on the steps again, but lifted his feet up off the patterned courtyard that ran nearly all the way up to the stone steps. 'When I went to the Tower of London with the school, the beefeaters told us some of the paths there were made from sheep's knuckle bones – just like this. It sounds weird, but it's just... medieval – not wasting anything.'

Rag looked down doubtfully. 'I suppose...' Her eyes followed the complex curves of the circular maze laid out in white bones among the dark granite setts. 'But that's an awful lot of sheep!'

Boyd shrugged, 'It's an awfully old castle. I suppose they thought it was a good idea rather than chuck them out. Anyway – I am hungry now. I think we should leave the wellies outside as they're wet, Mum always made us do that...' his voice trailed away.

Morag nodded, kicking off her wellies. 'They must have a back door somewhere – there are no wet dog-prints on the steps.'

'True – we could look for it later. We can leave them here and come and get them after lunch.'

Food seemed a better idea than hunting for another door. They abandoned their wet socks with the wellies and shuffled barefoot into their trainers and went inside, leaving the wet boots dripping muddy water down the granite steps.

From the crenulations of the tall stone keep, the great black bird peered down. He'd watched the children running in the courtyard, seen them scurry inside. The salmon was now completely devoured; he lifted his head to the west wind, he could smell salt on the air as well as rain. He spread his wings, felt the swift air catch beneath them – and launched himself out, turning as the wind took him until he was soaring high above the castle and the crags that sheltered it. He flapped vigorously with powerful strokes - into the sky and down over the loch… then he folded his wings close to his body, and dived, vanishing completely beneath the dark water.

Duffy was now perched on the barn roof cleaning her beak on the tiles; she saw the splash as He entered the lake, a great arrow of sleek black feathers… but He didn't come up; there was just the wind rippling the surface as the rain began to patter down making tiny, fleeting pockmarks in the water… even those where only temporary and soon vanished as rapidly and completely as He had.

Chapter Eight

In the breakfast room, Boyd blew into the whistle, after a few moments a questioning voice mumbled back hollowly from a distance.

'I'd like beans on toast and poached eggs on toast, and some Coke and a Sprite.' Boyd spoke as clearly as he could.

There was a pause then a burbling question came back up the pipe.

Boyd repeated slowly, 'Beans on toast. Poached egg on toast. Coke. And a Sprite… oh any lemonade will do.'

The burble seemed satisfied; a dull clunk indicated the far end had been put down.

The table still had just two places laid. All the silver dishes had been cleared from the sideboard; the faint smell of polish was evidence that the shining wood had been thoroughly cleaned of toast crumbs and finger-marks.

They sat at their places in silence, both looking around the room while they waited. The wallpaper had a huge old-fashioned print of colourful exotic birds, perched among trellises of curling leaves and flowers, and hanging from the high ceiling was a brass chandelier on a long chain. The dark brown wood of the table was so highly polished you could see your face in it. Rag lent forward with her elbows on the table.

'You're not supposed to do that.'

'So what,' she replied, 'there's no one here to see.'

'Do what you want – but Mum didn't like it.'

Morag pouted, but sat up and put her hands in her lap. Just then the whistle blew and the ropes inside the dumb-waiter rattled as the box was pulled up. Boyd went over and opened it. There was a tray with a large glass of cloudy white liquid and a white plate with a white paper doily… with a small, neatly arranged pile of coal on it.

Boyd stared at the coal, then picked up the tray and took it to the table to show Rag.

'I don't think he quite got the message.'

'What…?'

'It's coal, you know for boilers and power stations and stuff – this small stuff, they also call it 'coke'.'

He picked up the glass, sniffed it, had a tiny sip and paused before taking a bigger mouthful. 'This isn't bad - must be home-made lemonade - try it …Perhaps they don't do the proper sort in bottles.'

Rag took a tiny sip and wrinkled her nose, 'It's sour!'

'Maybe I could ask for orange juice – I bet they won't know what a Fanta is.'

The box in the wall rattled downwards again before he could replace the tray. A few minutes later the whistle blew, heralding the dumb-waiter's return. There was a tray with two plates, each with a small, silver domed cover. Boyd brought them both to the table and lifted off the lids – one plate had two poached eggs sitting on two slices of toast, the other had a row of green beans neatly lined up on the toast, each one carefully cut to be exactly the same length as the next. They looked at the 'beans on toast', looked at each other and burst out laughing.

'Good job I didn't ask for hot-dogs,' said Rag.

'Or fish-fingers.'

'Or toad-in-the-hole.'

'Or Pigs-in-blankets!'

'What shall we do with it?' she said.

'Leave it and send it back later – I can ask for orange juice, what else do you want?'

'I'll have a cheese sandwich - that should be safe.'

Boyd blew down the funnel and they heard the distant whistle and a mumble that sounded like a different voice. Boyd gave his order slowly and clearly and the single syllable reply seemed to be a 'yes'. Shortly afterwards, the dumb-waiter rattled, and up came a glass of fresh orange juice, plus a plate of sliced brown bread, white crusty rolls, butter and a thick wedge of cheese, along with quartered tomatoes, two different chutneys, plus some little brown pickled onions, all arranged in small white bowls.

'That looks better – I'm starving – what shall we order for dessert?' said Rag.

After debating whether to order Spotted Dick, Jam Roly-Poly, Lady-fingers or Cup-cakes, they decided Apple Pie should be ok. It arrived after a short wait, fragrant and warm, its crust golden and crispy; served with a jug of custard and a bowl of thick cream. They ate all of it and then wondered if they hadn't over done it.

Outside the rain tapped at the window.

'I think I'm going up to my room to read for a bit - maybe you need to change your jeans,' said Boyd.

Rag stuck her foot out and looked down – her jeans were splattered with mud up to the damp and grubby knees… that matched her damp and grubby feet. 'Ok – I suppose so.' She stood up. 'I can have a look at what to wear tonight if we've got to dress up,' she said brightly.

Boyd sighed, thinking - does that mean I have to wear the skirt in the drawer? He hadn't told Rag about his outfit … maybe there was something there with trousers?

'Yeah… ok. But knock before you come into my room. Heh – aren't you going to help put the plates away?'

But Rag had skipped off out the door. 'I'll do tomorrows,' she called.

'Yeah, right…' her brother grumbled, piling plates on the tray before putting them back into the dumb-waiter.

Later, up in his room, Boyd unpacked the rest of his own clothes and put them away. He found hanging in the cupboard two pairs of soft cord trousers in khaki green and two pairs of formal trousers in a fine dark green woollen cloth. He held them up – sometimes it seemed like magic here… you want something and it appears. He changed into fresh jeans and warm socks then went to examine the bookshelves for something to read.

Meanwhile, Rag was opening all the drawers and cupboards in her room to see what was tucked away in there. She pulled out various jumpers, shirts, tartan skirts, long white socks, thick white tights… but was disappointed not to find any other weapons. The clothes she left over-flowing from the drawers and cupboards, while she sat on the bed to examine the slim dagger further.

It had a fine point, from the tip down the blade was sharpened, but only along one edge, almost to the hilt, the other edge was flattened and one side had a thin groove running all the way down the blade.

...bet it's really sharp, like Mum's carving knife that we're not supposed to touch, she thought.

Thinking of that made her hold it carefully, but she still wanted to see how sharp it actually was. She went to the bookshelves and found a jar with some pencils; she broke one in half then set about sharpening it. The blade slid through the wood as if it was soft butter. She looked at the dagger with new respect, and then caught sight of herself in the long mirror on the wardrobe door. The slender blade glinted in her hand. She glowered at her reflection, then snarled and half-crouched... before leaping upright... there was something missing!

Morag returned to the mirror, a sash tied around her forehead, with another around her waist, and she'd draped a plaid skirt from shoulder to hip as a cloak. She snarled at her reflection - 'who you be lookin' at, eh?' she said in her best pirate-y voice, pretending her knife was a sword.

She slashed, feinted and jabbed like they did in films. Whirling around to avoid her imaginary enemy, she got too close to the wardrobe and the tip of her blade gouged a long scratch across the polished wood. Rag froze in horror. The pale wood under the varnish was clearly visible... Ooooooo noooooo!

She backed away from the wardrobe, found the leather sheath, hastily shoving the dagger in, and then throwing the whole lot into the open box it came from. She quickly stripped off the silk sashes and tartan skirt, dropping them to the floor. She went back and ran a finger along the scratch; the groove was deep into the wood at first and then skidded through the varnish for more than the length of her hand. She licked a finger and rubbed it along the wound; the wood darkened – maybe she could colour it in?

Rummaging through the desk drawers she found a large tin of crayons. She picked out the nearest shade of light brown and began to cover the long scratch. When she stepped back she could still see it, but it wasn't quite so obvious. Her shoulders slumped - maybe she should tell Boyd what she'd done?

She knocked on his door. 'Boyd?'

'What?'

'Can I come in?'

'I'm reading.'

Rag opened the door; she saw Boyd sprawled on his bed with a book.

'Whatever it is the answer's 'no',' he said, barely glancing up.

'Can we go out?'

Boyd waved an arm in the direction of the window.

'It's not raining that hard,' pleaded Rag.

'I've already said no, why don't you read a book?'

'Don't want to.'

'Then go explore.'

'Will you come with me?'

'No! I'm reading.'

She waited at the door in silence, picking at the threads

of her jumper, hoping he'd change his mind. Eventually he glanced up and sighed.

'Ok, Ok...Come back in an hour and I'll come with you then.'

Rag murmured, 'Mmmmm – then I need to show you something.'

'Yeah, yeah, whatever... close the door behind you.' Boyd didn't look up from his book.

Chapter Nine

Outside Boyd's bedroom door, Rag looked from left to right; there wasn't a sound, except for the light patter of rain when the wind blew it against the window over the staircase. She felt thirsty and decided to see if she could ask for proper lemonade – there must be somebody in the kitchen who knew what it was.

She walked to where the little staircase leading down from their set of rooms kept on going downwards into a shadowy, narrow spiral. Looking over the banister, she thought she heard some muffled movements and clanking from far below. She looked along the corridor that led to the wide stairs they normally used, and then down the stairs…why not? she thought, I can always come back up this way and start again.

She started the downwards spiral, after a few turns, the wooden stairs led through an arch cut into the wall and joined a stone staircase that went up, past their rooms, she decided when she peered up the narrow spiral - maybe up to the battlements and the roof… and it also went downwards. The stone steps going down were worn very smooth by many years of people's feet walking over them. She carried on down, thinking the kitchens must be downstairs if they had to connect a dumbwaiter to send the food up.

It was dimmer down here, only narrow slits in the thick stone walls, now filled by little panes of thick greenish glass set in lead frames, allowed light inside. The stairs spiralled down tightly enough that she almost felt giddy. She came to a thick oak door, tried the handle, but it was locked from the other side so she carried on down.

Two more locked doors later she began to wonder if she ought to go back up, she was sure she should be at ground level by now, but then, the kitchens might be under the castle because the dumb-waiter went down a long way… She trailed her hand along the smooth stone wall, the plasterwork had stopped many spirals ago, now it was raw stone, and it was getting colder. To one side of the spiral staircase, a square space came into view. It had a stone-flagged floor broad enough so that the wide, oak-planked door in the far wall could open easily without overlapping the stairs. A single plank of smooth wood was set into the wall like a bench, or perhaps a wide shelf to put things on as you went in and out of the door.

Rag leaned out precariously to peer down the spiral stairs. They went on and on… there didn't appear to be any windows and it was much darker down there; the stone walls looked rough and unfinished. She decided – if this door didn't open, she was going back up again. Stepping off the stone stairs into the tiny room made her feet tingle and her knees felt a little wobbly, enough for her to plonk herself down on the bench. Having caught her breath she stood to face the door and turned the big round brass ring and pushed – nothing happened.

Of course not silly, she thought, the space to open it was on this side! She pulled hard – the door opened inward. Disappointingly, the space beyond was another windowless, dark square room, bigger than the first, with another wide wooden bench set into the side wall and above it was a small shelf with a brass candle-holder and a dusty, wooden box of candles; directly opposite was another large, heavy wooden door with the same overly large ring handle .

It looked too far to reach from one door to the other… and if the door from the stairs shut behind her, she'd be in the dark. Rag paused for a minute to consider. She tried to keep hold of one door and reach across to grasp the handle on the other. She couldn't stretch that far, but crossing the floor she suddenly felt the pressure change, like being inside an aircraft. She paused, yawned deliberately and held her nose, like her mother had showed her; she felt her ears pop and the pressure eased, though her legs felt a bit like she'd had pins and needles and was still recovering.

Looking at the door she was still holding on to, she considered – if she pulled it completely open then ran to the other door there should be just enough light… and if the other one was locked, she could feel her way back, it was only a few steps… She checked where the ring handle was on the inside of the first door, then looked at the old scrape-marks on the stone floor… yes, that one pulls open inward as well…

Rag pulled back the first door as wide as it would go and dashed into the little room. Behind her the heavy oak door swung silently closed, just as her fingers touched the ring handle of the other door.

The room was in complete darkness. She grabbed the ring and pulled hard, nothing happened. She gave a little whimper of panic, rattled the handle, turning it and felt the door give a little. She turned the handle hard and pulled with all her strength – the door flew open taking her backwards with it. Light from outside flooded in.

Morag blinked, it was sunny. She looked up; the blue sky was quite clear - from what she could see of it beyond the wooden porch roof above the doorway. She was outside the castle, which she hadn't expected. And the weather had changed, which she hadn't expected either. She took a step through the door and felt her feet tingle again all the way up to her knees.

She was in a small yard that seemed to be between the bases of two rounded towers that she didn't remember seeing before. To one side was a walled well with a wooden frame and tiled roof over it, like the wishing wells you see at theme-parks, but this one had a couple of wooden buckets at the side of it so it must be one that was actually used for getting water. Angled away from the well was a long stone trough; she'd seen something like it, but in metal, when she went to the city farm with the school – there must be animals near here.

As if to confirm this she heard some muffled shuffling and some heavy breathing; it came from beyond the wooden fence that bared the way into the courtyard. She looked behind her, the wooden door had swung tightly shut, but a large ring-handle was clearly visible. If the animal that was huffing was big and scary she could run back inside. She walked gingerly over to the fence; there were some bare branches above the bushes on the other side.

The branches suddenly moved, dipping down. Something pawed the ground; she could hear the scrape of hooves. The 'branches' tossed up again and Rag stepped back, realising they were the antlers of an enormous stag.

She heard him blow and paw the ground again …and

suddenly felt that she very much wanted some water! She licked her lips, looked at the well and wondered if she could get some water in a bucket. She heard another loud snort, which made her whip her head around. She saw a large, grey-brown head with short, shaggy fur and enormous brown eyes watching her over the bushes by the fence. The stag's antlers were very wide and many pointed; he looked straight at her, and her thirst got worse – she really wanted some water. She looked back at the well – the stag huffed approvingly. Rag looked at him and thought… yes, you want some too.

She went over to the well. There was a bucket attached to a rope wound around a wooden spindle, you let down the bucket and then wound it back up again – that was simple enough, and the water smelt cool and sweet…That thought made her catch herself – since when had water smelt cool and sweet? Without really thinking, she knew she needed to take the rope loop off the winding handle – after which the bucket clattered down the shaft.

Fortunately the well wasn't all that deep and it was only a moment later that she heard the splash as the bucket hit the water. Rag began to wind the handle to bring the bucket up, which was harder work than she expected. The nearer the bucket came to her the more she wanted to drink. When it was at the top she nearly lost her grip before she - unexpectedly remembered - you must secure the handle with the rope loop to stop the bucket falling back into the well.

The water smelled so good – she dipped her face into the bucket and drank. There was an urgent bark from the stag outside the fence. Suddenly, Rag realised what she was doing and pulled her face out of the bucket, wiping it dry on her sleeve. She stepped back from the well, and then looked across the yard; the huge stag was trying to get closer to the fence. It came as a revelation - I'm not thirsty – He is!

She poured the water into one of the loose buckets lying by the well wall and struggled across to the fence with it. A few steps further down there was a wide five-bar gate. Rag climbed up the slats of wood and hauled the bucket up and held it over the gate.

The stag approached her, showing no fear; he huffed approval and sank his muzzle into the water, slurping noisily as he drank. Morag was entranced, she'd never been so close to a deer before, perhaps he was Uncle Wulf's pet and that's why he wasn't frightened.

When the bucket got easy enough to hold with one hand she raised her other hand to pat the deer's forehead. He raised a wet muzzle, sniffed her, and went back to drinking. The bucket was more than half empty when he stopped, and Morag's shoulders hurt from holding it out. She struggled to lift it back over the gate, splashing quite a bit of the remaining water over herself as she hauled it up. 'Next time, open gate.' The thought came unbidden to her, but she agreed, it would have been easier.

The stag watched her with interest as she walked back to the well with the bucket. It was then she realised just how wet her clothes were.

I'll go back and change, and get Boyd to come down, she thought, he is not going to believe this!

Chapter Ten

Boyd heard his sister's muffled running steps in the hallway and heard her door slam. He stirred and looked out of the window – still raining. He stretched, looked at his watch, it had been over an hour – she'd be knocking at his door in a minute. It was a good book, if very old-fashioned, it was about a young pilot in World War One - one of a whole series by the look of it; there were lots more books with the character's name in the title. It wasn't long before Rag banged on his door; she burst in before he had time to say 'yes?'

'You'll never guess what I've found!' she announced.

'You are supposed to wait until I say you can come in.'

'Yeah, whatever – you weren't getting dressed or anything – and go on – guess!'

'I don't know – a suit of armour.'

Rag pulled a face – as if that was exciting!

'A secret passage?'

'Very nearly,' beamed Rag, 'I went down the little stairs, and they go on forever! At first they were made of wood and then they were stone, and really worn. But just as I was giving up, I found a door and it lead to another door and you have to be really quick or you're caught in the dark and...'

'Slow down a bit...'

'Ok,' Rag said, jumping on the bed, 'I went down those twisty spiral stairs and - I went outside into another yard at the back of the castle…'

'Really? But it's pouring with rain.'

'It wasn't then, the clouds must have cleared because it was sunny outside – anyway there's an old well, and I got some water up in a bucket, one you have to wind up on a rope, and outside the fence was the biggest stag you've ever seen - and I gave him the water 'cos he was thirsty.'

'A stag? And he didn't run away?'

Rag shook her head, bouncing with excitement.

'Are you making this up?'

'No, no, nonono – come and see.' Rag grabbed his arm and tried to pull her brother off the bed.

'Hang on – let me get my shoes on.'

Rag led her brother down and down the spiralling stairs. They heard noises behind two of the locked doors as they passed, but Rag assured Boyd that it was fine. Eventually they came to the big oak door set to one side of the worn stone steps. Boyd sat down heavily on the bench

'Give me a moment, my knees feel like jelly.'

Rag sat beside him. 'Yes mine did the first time, they're not so bad this time,' she said. 'It goes away quickly. Ok now?'

Boyd nodded, the tingle in the soles of his feet was subsiding; he stood up.

'Now, you hold this door open, and I'll get the other door.'

Just as Rag touched the ring handle of the outer door, Boyd felt the weight of the inner door swing in heavily behind him, forcing him forward as the door closed. Boyd felt the pressure build up in his ears. The darkness only lasted a moment; once the inner door had settled firmly into place, fully closed, Rag was able to pull the outer door open more easily, letting the light in. Boyd shook his head.

'Hold your nose and blow,' said Rag, 'like you do on a plane.'

Boyd popped his ears and blinked, outside it was a sunny day.

'That's funny - it was raining when we were upstairs...'

Rag skipped out into the yard ahead of him.

'...it must be the wind blowing it away... and then the next lot of cloud comes in after,' Boyd said, squinting up at the clear blue sky.

'What?' said Rag.

'I was just saying about the rain...'

'Oh it comes and goes – look here's the well, and there's the fence, and I thought his horns were branches they were so big...'

But there weren't any antlers there now.

'He was over here...'Rag was climbing up the gate, but there was no sign of the stag.

Beyond the gate was a broad cobbled path winding between fenced enclosures that reached back as far as the castle wall, and on the other side of it were some low thatch-roofed sheds backed by trees. But not an animal was in sight.

Suddenly they heard a hoarse cry, rather like the big bird over the loch had given, but deeper.

'What was that?' said Boyd.

His sister shook her head.

'I think it was over there...' said Boyd, climbing up the rails of the gate to get a better look into the nearby paddock. He caught a glimpse of a long white-tail swishing before its owner walked away.

'Uncle Wulf's got a horse, quite a big one I think.'

'Where?' Rag clambered up the gate beside him.

'He walked around base of the tower over there.' Boyd swung his leg over the gate and jumped down to the pathway on the other side.

'Wait, I'm coming too!' The gate rattled as Rag scrambled up and over, Boyd was already walking away.

The fenced enclosures each had a large wooden shed in one corner; some places had hedges of tall bushes growing along the fences, or trees that cast big pools of shade.

'He was in this one, I think,' said Boyd. 'There.' He pointed.

Inside the doorway of a shed they could see the back legs of a dappled grey horse, its long tail swishing from side to side.

'Here, boy!' Boyd climbed onto the bottom rung of the paddock fence.

They heard a hoarse cough from inside the shed.

'Here boy, c'mon,' called Boyd.

The animal manoeuvred itself to turn around inside the shadows of the shed and came forward…

'Bloody hell!' yelped Boyd, staggering backwards, nearly falling off the fence in his haste.

'What… is that!' Rag was backing away too. 'Let's go Boyd – please, now.'

'Bloody hell…' mumbled Boyd again softly. He stood stock-still, his mouth open in amazement at the sight of the animal walking slowly towards them.

Across the enclosure padded the strangest creature, its head and neck were feathered in grey and white, as were its large tufted ears, and its feathered front legs had bird's feet with huge, powerful claws. It had a great curved yellow beak, and fierce yellow eyes, but behind the bird-like neck and shoulders it was a grey horse, but with rufflets of feathers around its fetlocks… and it had wings folded across its back like an enormous swan. It shook its head and ruffled its wings before folding them down again as it walked forward.

'Boyd!' Rag grabbed her brother's arm and tried to pull him back, 'we have to go!'

She couldn't move him. He was transfixed, staring into the golden eyes of the creature. It opened its beak and made a harsh coughing sound, as if clearing its throat to speak.

'Boyd!' Rag shouted and tugged at her brother, who remained rooted to the spot.

The creature came closer - darting its head forward to sniff them, and then tilting it from side to side, seemingly as if trying to decide how they'd taste. It pawed the ground with one foot and gave a louder 'caw', clacking its beak together loudly.

'Shooo,' shouted Rag. She started punching Boyd's arm hard as she tried to drag him away. He blinked and shook himself loose from her grasp.

'Apples,' he mumbled.

'Come on – run!' shouted Rag.

Boyd shook his head. 'Oh no…'

The creature was nearly at the fence. Boyd was backing away; Rag had a firm hold of his jacket, pulling him after her. The creature blinked and shook its head like a horse, its ears turning in their direction, but it didn't try to jump the fence.

'Apples…' mumbled Boyd again, 'Oh bloody hell!

He seemed to come back to himself, shook himself free of

Rag's hand and ran alongside her, back over the gate, across the yard and through the big oak door, which slammed shut behind them. For a few seconds they were in complete darkness.

'Please, please, please...,' whimpered Rag, searching for the handle. The force of running in had taken her almost face first into the inner door

'Where's the door Rag? Quick!' whispered Boyd out of the blackness.

She fumbled in the darkness until her fingers found the brass ring-handle. She twisted it and pushed - and they were out of the dark and into the dim light of the alcove and the stone stairway beyond it.

Boyd pushed through after her; Rag let the door fall shut behind them. It swung closed swiftly with a dull thud and a long puff of escaping air. Rag felt her feet tingling, as if she'd been sitting with her legs folded under her for too long, and collapsed onto the bench. Boyd flopped down beside her.

'What...?' she whispered.

Boyd shook his head.

Both of them sat there for a few seconds breathing hard, as if they'd run for miles.

Morag started again, speaking normally now. 'What was that...'

'Dunno...' mumbled Boyd, 'but – it was freaky...'

'You're telling me!'

Boyd frowned, 'Yeah,' he said, 'the bird horse thing... but I really, really wanted an apple. I don't particularly like apples.'

Morag eyed her brother. 'Is that all you've got to say? We were nearly attacked by a freaking, weird... thing – and all you have to say is 'I don't like apples'!'

'He wasn't attacking us. He was just curious.'

'What...?' Rag paused, Boyd was right - the thing had approached them quite slowly. It could have galloped up if it wanted to... but that big, curved beak had looked very sharp. 'Ok – but what was it and how did it get here?' she asked.

'I don't know – maybe it's some sort of weird, genetic experiment?'

'You think Uncle Wulf is some sort of mad scientist?' Rag looked startled.

'I... No... Mum would have known about freaky stuff going on, and she'd never have sent us here if something bad was going to happen,' Boyd said slowly.

'I suppose...' agreed Rag.

'She and Dad lived here all through their childhood, she'd have known if something wasn't right about Uncle Wulf.'

Morag nodded silently. Boyd stood up and shook his legs out.

'What do we do now?' she said.

'We go back upstairs and get ready for supper – I'm starving.' Boyd started to climb the stone steps.

'Just like that...?'

'What else are you planning on doing?' Boyd said from around a turn of the spiral stairs.

Rag followed him. 'Do you think we should say something to Uncle Wulf - about what we've seen?' she asked.

'Maybe – but I'd like to come back and have another look. If we say where we've been he might say we can't, or lock the doors or something. I'm not going to say anything just yet.'

Behind him, Rag nodded, 'But next time, I'm bringing my knife with me,' she said firmly.

'I don't think you need that. You'd do better bringing apples,' said Boyd, from further up the winding stairs.

'Apples? What is it with you and apples?' Rag grumbled.

CHAPTER ELEVEN

Boyd stared out of his bedroom window, the rain had eased off, but the skies were still full of swollen grey clouds… and it was so sunny earlier in the paddocks. He'd dithered about having a shower; he wasn't sure how to work the contraption over the bathtub and had settled for a quick bath before changing into the dark wool trousers, a dark knitted sweater and a white shirt. Uncle Wulf had made supper sound important; his parents had dressed up when they had friends round, and his mother laid the dining room table with all the best china. Since Uncle Wulf had said this was formal – he should probably check to see what Rag was wearing… He went and knocked on her door.

'Just a minute…' she said from inside.

A few moments later the door opened. Rag was 'dressed for dinner' – but she had gone the whole way – shiny tartan dress, sash, layers of petticoats, hair ribbons, white tights, patent shoes… and the fluffiest, white Angora wool bolero. She looked like a Disney Scottish princess on the way to the ball. Boyd's mouth dropped open.

'What?' she said. 'Jealous?'

'Uummm…' was all he managed to say, noticing her hands were still grubby.

'Would it have been an idea to wash first?' he said.

'Oh that – well I tried everything on - and then it was too late to begin again.'

The distant sound of a gong resounded from the hall downstairs.

'But I could wear these. See?' Rag swished back into her room and picked up a pair of white lace gloves from the dressing table.

'No. I don't think you need those.'

Morag dropped them on the bed as she passed. Her room was a mess of unpacked clothes lying all around. She turned on her heel, her petticoats and dress rustling, and strode to the door.

'Don't you think you should tidy your room up a bit?'

Rag shut the door behind her. 'Laters,' she said sauntering down the hall, enfolded in the *frou-frou* of rustling silk taffeta, and outlined by a halo of white fluff.

Uncle Wulf was waiting for them in the hall. He looked splendid, like someone out of one of the old oil paintings that hung on the corridor walls. He wore a knee-length dark green, blue and purple kilt, long white woollen socks, a gathered white shirt, laced at the neck with silk cords, and a short, dark wool waistcoat and jacket with lots of silver buttons; a wide length of matching tartan was folded and artfully draped over his shoulder, pinned in place by a huge disc of carved silver. Boyd began to feel a bit under-dressed.

The corner of Wulf's mouth quirked into the ghost of a smile when he saw Morag prance down the stairs in all her finery, he nodded at Boyd, and indicated they should enter the open door beside him.

'The large dining room can be cold in the evenings Boyd; you might consider wearing one of the jackets when you come down on another occasion...

Boyd hung his head and went to follow his sister into the dining room.

'...the rest of the outfit I can give you a hand with and show you how it should be worn another time. I overlooked the fact you may not be familiar with them...' Uncle Wulf rested his hand lightly on Boyd's shoulder as they entered the room. 'My apologies, I should have thought to explain about them sooner. It must all seem quite strange to you. I do not normally trouble with all this...' He waved a hand at his own clothes, '...myself, but I thought we would eat formally in honour of your arrival... and the Broons, my helpers, like dressing the part when they have the opportunity. They enjoy the prestige of working for - The Laird,' Uncle Wulf smiled and whispered the last words in Boyd's ear confidentially.

Boyd managed a smile in reply.

'Anyway... Please take your places'

The walls of the dining room were painted a rich, dull red; the dark furnishings were of carved oak, everything seemed to be twice as large as necessary and very imposing. One wall was hung with old tapestries of fantasy hunting scenes: medieval looking men and women on horseback chasing unicorns. Elsewhere, decorative arrangements of long spears, battle-axes, swords and painted shields were fastened to the walls in precise sheaves. The room was lit with many fat yellow candles set inside brass holders with tall glass shades, both attached to the walls, and placed on the sideboard.

The long table, big enough for at least a dozen people, was

laid with three places at one end, and one setting at the far end, and down the middle were three silver candelabra, each holding seven candles in their branches. The candlelight flickered off the crystal glasses and bowls on the table,

'Is somebody else coming?' asked Rag.

'It is our custom to always set an extra place in case a guest arrives unexpectedly – though I do not believe we will be joined this evening,' said Uncle Wulf.

He tapped the thickened foot of a small glass goblet on the table in front of him; it rang out sharply like a pistol shot. A door in the corner of the room behind them opened immediately. They heard some muttered whispers from outside and turned in their seats to see a very small man dressed in a miniature version of Wulf's clothing, but all in shades of brown. He was pushing a wheeled, two-tier wooden trolley covered in a long white linen cloth; on top was an impressively large, china soup tureen. He stopped at Wulf's side and bowed.

'You may serve the lady first, Broonie.'

The little man muttered, gave a stiff half-bow and turned to the soup tureen trolley.

Rag and Boyd sat in stunned silence. The little man looked old, but his posture was as upright as a guardsman on sentry duty. He had a very bushy red-brown beard, here and there streaked with grey, and very bushy eyebrows, so that virtually all you could see of his face was a bulbous reddish nose and dark sparkling eyes. He wore a dark brown, floppy tam-o-shanter decorated with pheasant tail-feathers sticking straight up from the brim, secured there by a round, silver brooch glittering with crystals; his neat jacket was fastened with rows of small silver buttons.

He moved to her left side and put a wide-rimmed soup-plate down in front of Rag, who whispered 'thank you' so quietly she could barely be heard. In reply she got a short grumble that could have been anything, as he ladled soup from the tureen to her bowl.

'Broonie is The Broon – he is the chief of my household,' said Uncle Wulf.

Broonie was back at Wulf's side. '...you may serve our guests first tonight,' Uncle Wulf said mildly.

Broonie muttered a bit more and took the soup-plate he was about to put in front of Wulf around to Boyd's place.

Boyd couldn't take his eyes off the little man and managed an audible 'thank you' after he had filled the bowl with soup. Seated, he could look Broonie in the eye and only after dinner realised what was strange - he couldn't see any whites to the little man's eyes – they were completely brown with a black pupil, like a dog's eye, or a horse's.

Broonie served Wulf, spooning soup carefully from tureen to plate with a large silver ladle. Afterwards, he wheeled the trolley back into the shadows by the door and stood beside it.

'Please eat,' said Wulf, picking up a silver spoon.

The soup was beef broth and vegetables and tasted very good. After that, Broonie served them fish in pastry cases with a creamy herb sauce, followed by slices of beef with roasted vegetables and gravy, then a sweet made of meringue, cream and fruit - while offering Wulf a wooden board bearing several sorts of cheese instead of dessert. Between servings there were urgent whispers from whoever was the other side of the door passing food through to Broonie, who growled back hoarse mutterings.

Morag and Boyd didn't speak a great deal during the meal;

they were slightly awed by the number of bone-handled knives and silver forks lined up on either side of their plate. Boyd caught Rag's eye and nodded that she copy which ones Uncle Wulf picked up - so they staggered through the selection of cutlery with only the odd mistake.

Wulf made polite conversation; he asked them about their journey, about the social worker. He told them about the many fish in the loch and he could teach them to fish if they wished. They mumbled their replies, their eyes either on Broonie, on their food or darting around the room trying to take in their surroundings.

Along with the fish course, Broonie had poured water into a glass beside each plate and then poured white wine into another glass for Wulf.

'You may give the children a small glass of watered wine,' instructed Uncle Wulf.

'Yes, please!' said Rag delighted at being offered a grown-up treat.

Broonie poured each of them a small measure and topped it up with water from crystal jug. It tasted very slightly of apples and smelt a bit like fresh cut grass – which for Boyd brought his sudden desire for apples back to mind. He eyed the large bowl half-way down the table piled high with carefully arranged fruit and wondered if he could take some later.

Rag pulled a face when she sipped the wine – it didn't taste sweet enough for her liking. She decided to broach the subject of food and drink.

'Uncle Wulf - earlier on when we had lunch, I don't think they could hear us properly,' she paused. Uncle Wulf turned his full attention on her. Boyd gave her a frown, but she soldiered on.

'We asked for a coke and they gave us coal, and the beans on toast were green beans, when they should have been in tomato sauce… Um… maybe you could explain…'

She caught sight of Broonie glaring at her from the corner and her voice trailed off.

'I see,' said Wulf. 'The Broon is not always up to date. I will speak to him. Perhaps, if I get you a selection of magazines, you can cut out pictures of the things you want and make an album for the cooks to look at… or perhaps some more modern cookery books…?' he mused.

'Oh…Ok… we could do that,' said Rag 'but don't they see adverts on television?'

'We do not have television here.

'No telly,' yelped Rag.

'No,' Wulf smiled, 'I remember how much that annoyed your parents when they were teenagers…' He nodded to himself, and then looked up at the youngsters. 'But - we do now have access to the Internet – I believe you can watch television on that.'

'Cool,' said Boyd, 'but, aren't we too far away to get a good signal? For the Internet - I mean, if there aren't mobile phones…'

'Broonie has made arrangements with some technical gremlins for cables to be laid – he and the others very much enjoy playing a game called, I believe… *World of Warcraft*? They sometimes even forget their duties…'

This was answered by a loud snort from Broonie, still standing in the shadows, now preparing to serve the main course of roast beef and all the trimmings.

'…I believe you can watch films on the Internet as well – and access 'social media'… so they told me. They have put a device in your sitting room upstairs.'

'Really? I haven't been in there yet.' Morag brightened visibly; she had some favourites she wanted to catch up with.

'You did say 'the others' – are there many more… people who work here?' Boyd asked.

Broonie was busying himself with covered dishes, and a cut-crystal carafe of red wine - which when eventually brought to the table was not offered to the youngsters.

'Of course, Broonie can work very hard, but the castle and its grounds are far too big for him alone. You will meet them over the next few days I expect. Thank you Broonie,' …which seemed to be the signal for Broonie to clear the fish dishes away and serve the main course.

At the end of the meal, Uncle Wulf announced they would take coffee in the Drawing Room. He got up and walked to the far end of the room, opening one of the double doors there. Rag could see into a big room with a large fire blazing in the huge, open hearth. Old-fashioned electric lamps with multi- coloured glass shades stood on the many small tables placed between the padded armchairs and large comfy sofas – it was a room that could have held twenty people comfortably. As she walked in she could see there were board games with wooden pieces on some of the tables, chess and backgammon amongst them, and some she didn't recognise.

Chapter Twelve

Uncle Wulf invited them to sit down, while he went to stand before the fire with his back to the hearth. Rag sat down in a padded armchair, her petticoats and skirt bunched up around her in great folds of shimmering fabric, and stared around her. There were landscape painting on the walls in ornate gilded frames; some looked like they were fantasies the artist had dreamed up. Boyd wandered around the room. After several minutes there was the sound of scratching on the door…

'Come!' said Wulf.

A different very small man came in to the drawing room pushing another trolley. This little man had the same potato nose, a dark yellowy-brown beard and curly hair nearly to his shoulders; he too was dressed formally in shades of brown, but lighter than The Broon's. They got the impression he was younger than Broonie.

'This is Gam – he is another of my helpers.'

Gam bowed to each of them, his face crinkling into smiles under his beard and bushy eyebrows.

'Pleased… Pleased,' he said to each of them as he bowed.

'Thank you Gam, I will serve myself,' said Uncle Wulf.

Gam bowed again and left. Padding away silently in the

thick felt slippers he wore on his rather large feet, Rag noticed. When the door had firmly shut behind him, Rag stood up and walked over to Uncle Wulf's side as he prepared to pour coffee.

'Erm…' she began, 'are all of them so… short… I mean, they are very small people…'

'Broonie and his kind have lived in these parts for many many years,' said Uncle Wulf vaguely. 'Would you like some tea? Or perhaps hot chocolate?' Wulf leaned over the trolley and set out some delicate porcelain cups and saucers.

There were three variously sized silver pots on the trolley. Rag guessed they held coffee, tea and hot chocolate… just to make sure everybody had a choice. …It's just like being in one of those films about olden times on TV, she thought. 'Can I have some tea please?' said Rag. But she was also wondering how soon she could leave the room to investigate the internet connection.

Boyd was still prowling the room looking at the games; he stood by one of the small tables, 'I know this one,' said Boyd, 'it's Nine-Men's-Morris.' He picked up a smooth stone counter from the board.

'Yes, that is one of its names - would you like to play?' Wulf poured himself coffee and went over to stand by Boyd. Morag went and sat back in the armchair and sipped her tea.

'Yeah – though I'm not really sure how,' said Boyd.

'I can teach you.'

'Can I go upstairs then?' said Rag.

Uncle Wulf paused for a moment in thought. 'There are still many things we need to speak of… but it need not be today. Yes, you can go upstairs. I suppose you want to watch your screen. At 9.30 please shut down the internet and get ready for bed.'

'Nine...?'

'I think that is late enough at present, you can read in bed until 10. Goodnight Morag.'

Rag put her half-full cup on the saucer, and took two biscuits from the tray on her way out.

'Ok... but that is well early.'

'Don't try to be Street, Rag, Mum didn't like it...'

She turned and saw Boyd was concentrating on lining up the counters beside the board. 'You're not my mother!' Rag flounced out of the double doors and back into the dining room.

Uncle Wulf said nothing; he watched her leave while slowly stirring his coffee.

Most of the candles had been put out and the dining room was filled with shadows. Rag paused for a moment as the double doors of the drawing room closed behind her, and then plodded slowly down the length of the table. Tears filled her eyes as she ran her hand down the polished oak surface; it felt silky under her fingers. ...Mum would have loved the painted china, she thought, maybe she ate off it when she and Dad lived here?

She halted at the tall carved chair that stood where the table was still laid for the uninvited guest. A fat tear rolled down her face, partly because she missed her mother, and partly because she realised she'd hardly thought about her all day. ...And Dad... where was Dad...? Why didn't he come back for them? Morag sniffed loudly.

Then she noticed that the place setting was incomplete - some of it had been used. There was still red wine in the glass, and the linen napkin was crumpled – nobody had said they'd been someone else here.

How long had they been in the other room? Not more than 15 minutes… The Broon must have served the visitor's food straight away… So he must have known somebody else was coming. But did Uncle Wulf know? Of course he did! He seemed to know everything that went on… So why didn't Uncle Wulf say anything…?

She froze – something rustled in the shadows in the far corner. It was moving towards her. Rag opened her mouth to shout… and then she saw a short figure dressed in brown, but this wasn't one of the men, it was a small woman in a long brown dress with a white apron tied around her waist. She glided quietly and very slowly towards Morag, as if she didn't want to startle the girl. As she came closer, Rag could see the woman wasn't even as tall as she was; her face was round and rosy, and full of tiny wrinkles, like an old winter apple, but her hair was as shiny-brown as a conker; arranged in lots of small plaits pinned to her head in a complicated pattern.

Rag blinked back her tears, wiping her face with her hand. The little woman came nearer, making soft tutting noises as if she was trying to calm a frightened animal. Eventually she was close enough to hold out a white handkerchief edged in fine lace, still neatly folded. She smiled and nodded for Rag to take it. Rag reached out cautiously; the woman smiled even more, nodding harder than ever as Rag took it.

Just then a loud questioning mumble came from the other side of the far door, followed by some squeaks and bumps. The little woman patted Morag's hand and picked up the half-empty wine glass and the unused cutlery from the table and scuttled away. In the shadows at the back of the room, she took hold of a trolley of used plates already cleared from the table and pushed it ahead of her out the door.

Rag wiped her eyes, the hanky smelt sweet and herby – she couldn't remember which one though… Mum would know… that thought bought a few more tears. She wiped them away. Leaving the dining room, she walked slowly back upstairs. Who cared if there were strangers in the house – the whole place was strange. But she also thought about checking to see if there was a lock on her bedroom door.

By the time she'd reached the landing where their rooms were she was still feeling sad, but the tears had stopped. She didn't feel like being dressed up anymore, she wanted her old comfortable clothes. When she opened her bedroom door and switched the light on she was amazed – all the clothes she'd left lying on the floor had been picked up and tidied away.

'Wow…!' she said aloud.

She looked around; her bed was made, a nightdress was laid out, and slippers by the bed and the dressing gown… everything was neat and tidy and in its place – it looked… weird! She came in and took her sash off, but did put it over a chair rather than just dropping it on the floor, followed by her dress and petticoats, making a big heap of fabrics that almost hid the chair.

I wonder if they'll do this all the time? she thought. She dug out a comfortable hoodie and some leggings and went to look for their sitting room. If they had the Internet, there were things she wanted to check out.

Chapter Thirteen

Uncle Wulf stood beside the fireplace sipping his coffee. Boyd was also impressed by just how tall he was… seeing him outlined by the light of the fire he looked even bigger, a real northern warrior – and Boyd noted the gleaming wire-wrapped hilts of the short knives Wulf wore tucked inside one of his knee-high white socks. …So that was why the leather strap was so short… you fastened it on your leg.

'Shall we play the game then? said Wulf.

He and Boyd moved to sit either side of the games table with the Nine-Men's Morris. Boyd has lined up the smoothly polished stone discs, nine black, nine white, on the table beside the varnished wooden board.

'Here, you take white. We start by taking turns placing our counters on the board one at a time, you go first,' said Wulf.

'Anywhere?'

'On any of the inked dots of the pattern – your aim is to place three in a row. This makes what's called a mill; when you have made one, you can take one of your opponent's pieces from the board. When any piece is gone from the game, it's gone forever.'

Boyd took his turns and laid out three pieces, taking one counter from Uncle Wulf, and feeling pleased with himself.

Wulf meanwhile added more counters when his turns came, occupying the inner intersections of the squares lining the board. As they played he moved his counters back and forth each time making a mill and each time taking one of Boyd's counters from the board.

'You have to look for advantageous positions and defend them,' said Uncle Wulf.

Boyd stared at the board trying to calculate his moves; very quickly he was down to three pieces.

'Now you are permitted to fly to anywhere on the board, but you still have to try and obstruct my progress,' Uncle Wulf explained, but Boyd couldn't stop Wulf forming another mill.

'You are down to two pieces, which means you have lost, because with only two you can't make a mill. Do you see the importance of strategy? Come let's play another – you will soon see how to position your troops.'

'I thought they were called counters?' said Boyd.

Wulf smiled. 'Any such game as this is a little battle - you win or lose, just like in war.'

'I didn't think it was that serious.' Boyd frowned a little, he hadn't expected this.

'It is practise. You learn how to think things through, how to manoeuvre. If you and your opponent are equally matched this game can be solved. With perfect play, it will always become a draw.'

'No winners or losers?'

'Simply the pleasure of pitting your mind against theirs.'

'I don't think I'm very good at it,' said Boyd doubtfully.

'You get better with practise. Come, let's play again.'

Uncle Wulf encouraged him and they played twice more;

Boyd lost each time, but in the final game Wulf took longer to beat him.

Boyd yawned. Uncle Wulf stood up from his armchair.

'I will have another coffee now. Do you want to play again?'

Boyd shook his head. He felt full, the meal, though nicely portioned, had been more than he was used to, and everything that had happened today left him full of questions he didn't want to ask – not yet anyway. The warmth from the crackling fire made the room feel comfortable, if a little airless; he was beginning to feel sleepy. He leaned back into the feather-filled cushions of his armchair, relaxing with a sigh.

Uncle Wulf re-filled his cup and sat down again opposite Boyd.

'Your father enjoyed this game, and Backgammon. Another evening I will teach you how to play Backgammon. I think you'll enjoy it too. Both your parent's played well.

'What were they like when they were here?' Boyd said shifting his position in the armchair to stay awake.

Uncle Wulf smiled, paused to sip his coffee. 'They were at home here. They were much, much younger than you when they arrived. This…' he waved his cup, 'was all they knew.

'So why did they come to you anyway.'

Wulf put his cup and saucer down on the table, picked up one of the smooth, flat counters from the board and flipped it through his fingers… under and over, under and over. Boyd watched… fascinated as the counter flickered in and out of view.

Wulf considered his words before he spoke. 'They were both orphans, very young, and I was able to help. They learnt how things grow and where to find them. Your mother, she liked flowers and plants – her botanical drawings were beautiful…'

Boyd remembered the framed watercolours of flowers in the hallway at home… what had been his home! He shifted in his seat, the thought was an uncomfortable memory - and now there was this… Boyd was going to ask if there was more of their family somewhere… why had Wulf become their guardian, but Uncle Wulf carried on speaking.

'Your father was always very good with animals – when they were older, they both helped me collect unusual specimens. They often had to travel, but when first you, then your sister came, we talked, and decided it was best if they only went away one at a time.'

'Were they still living here when we were born?'

'You were born here; your sister was born after they left. Perhaps you remember your father having a broken leg… About the time Morag was born?

'Not really. They talked and laughed about it later on, him only being able to stand on one leg and having to hop around… Mum used to say he'd done it on purpose so he didn't have to change her nappies – they said she was a stinky baby.'

Uncle Wulf smiled at the thought.

'And do you remember then that sometimes they would go away and return… hurt, or injured?'

'We used to go and stay for a few days with Mum's friend, Auntie Carol sometimes. Mum said Dad needed to rest after he'd been travelling. I know there were times they would argue about him going away – at least I know now they were arguing. I think Mum was worried about us - I don't know, maybe catching something from them, or ...something happening to us?' Boyd shook his head.

Wulf put down the counter and steepled his fingers in front of him, resting his elbows on the arms of the chair.

'Sometimes the places they needed to go to were not always... hospitable.'

'You mean like malaria and stuff?' Boyd yawned, remembering to cover his mouth with his hand.

'Something like that. Aurelia was fearful sometimes for your safety, which is why they moved away when you were a baby. What had not frightened her before, became different once she was a mother'

'So why did she send us back if this place is dangerous?' Boyd replied, frowning.

'You will not be in danger here. I am here to protect you.'

Wulf smiled and nodded, more at his own thoughts than at Boyd.

From what? thought Boyd. He didn't say anything, though he was thinking of the weird animal being kept secretly outside the castle walls – with all those paddocks, it probably wasn't the only one. He stifled another yawn, trying to pay attention to what Wulf was saying.

'... but perhaps it is time you went to bed. I have some other things to do before I go up. We should talk more another time. Tomorrow we will have supper in the small dining room where you eat breakfast; that will be our norm. All this...' he spread out his hand, 'is just for high days and holidays; I wanted to make you welcome, and the Broons insisted they provide a traditional display of hospitality. When there is another such formal occasion, I will get young Gam to come and help you dress in the proper Highland manner.'

Boyd nodded sleepily.

Wulf stood and brushed an unseen crumb from his perfectly pleated tartan with a slightly rueful smile.

'They like to see me dressed as their chieftain - believe me, they would have me wear even more silver and weaponry if they had their way.'

He walked over to the bell pull beside the fire-place. At a distance, Boyd could just about hear a tiny bell ring – he'd heard about servant's bells when they went on a visit to a stately home once. He hadn't realised his parents had spent their childhood in one.

Wulf turned to face him. 'You do realise you can come to me at any time? I will listen to whatever you wish to question. Or anything you want to tell me. This world is different from the town you have known - we live differently here, but at heart we have you and your sister's welfare and happiness in mind. You will become used to us. Things may seem strange to begin with… but…'

He paused, it seemed Uncle Wulf wanted to say more, but was not sure how to begin.

Just then there was a scratch at the door and Gam came in; he bowed to Uncle Wulf, and to Boyd, and came forward to collect the cups.

The little man spoke quietly to Wulf, 'Lord – he is here.' Wulf nodded.

Boyd overheard, and wondered who was here, but it seemed rude to ask. Instead he heaved himself up out of the armchair to say goodnight. Uncle Wulf patted him on the shoulder in a friendly manner.

'We have plenty of time, Boyd. I will let you both settle

in for a couple of days and then we will see about beginning your lessons.'

Oh great – home-schooling, thought Boyd; he smiled and nodded politely. How that was going to work he had no idea. He knew things were going on that he didn't know fully understand, but he felt helpless to do anything about them. A flash of anger went through him - we shouldn't be here. This stranger wants us to be good and quiet and nice, but we shouldn't be here! Mum and Dad should be here!

He found himself gripping the back of an armchair so tightly his knuckles hurt – then he realised Wulf was looking at his hand too... Boyd consciously released his grip and smothered the fabric, stroking the wrinkles out.

'I'm going to bed then,' Boyd announced, a touch louder than he meant to.

Gam looked up sharply, Uncle Wulf remained impassive.

'Goodnight Boyd. We will talk more another time – and perhaps you will permit me to show you how to play backgammon.'

Boyd shoved his hands deep into his trousers pockets. He nodded noncommittally, looked at his feet and deliberately slouched away - because that's how you annoyed the teachers at school.

He wants to be nice, but I don't need that! Boyd thought as he opened the double door into the dining room. The candles in the wall lights were still lit, but the table was completely cleared; only the fruit bowl remained. Boyd took a couple of apples in passing, and without thinking, bit into one with a satisfying crunch. He was suddenly very tired – he needed to sleep, and he needed to think things through, and he needed to keep an eye on Rag to stop her doing anything daft…

The room was shadowy, the hall and stairs beyond were lit by dim bulbs, more like night-lights. It struck him as he went upstairs that they were a long way off any power-lines. Uncle Wulf had said they couldn't go to the boiler-room – maybe they generated their own electricity? It was weird, it was all strange and a bit scary and… just weird!

By this time he was upstairs and at his bed-room door, it was well after nine. He couldn't see any light coming from under the sitting room door down the corridor – maybe Rag had gone to bed like she'd been told to? Fat chance! But he was too tired to investigate – if she gets into trouble that's her fault.

There were so many thoughts and unanswered questions turning over in his mind he thought he would take ages to get to sleep, but he closed his eyes almost as soon as his head touched the pillow.

He was fast asleep when his door opened slowly, the small figure at the door looked in to see him, and satisfied the boy was sleeping soundly, left silently and padded away.

CHAPTER FOURTEEN

The next morning, Rag got up and was going to get dressed quickly – then she thought, Boyd will only moan at me... So she went to the bathroom and splashed water over her face, used soap on her hands, and cleaned her teeth properly, before running back to her bedroom. As she was getting dressed she heard Boyd's door open, then the bathroom door close.

She sighed, he'd be ages yet. Much to Rag's puzzlement, Boyd liked showering and having baths... She took her hairbrush and decided to make a good job of her unruly hair – if she brushed it hard enough she could get it to crackle and stand up on end. Before she'd got that far, she heard Boyd go back to his bedroom.

Good! She had something to tell him. Shortly afterwards there was a brief knock at her door.

'Rag? I'm going down for breakfast, are you coming?'

She rushed to the door to pull the chair from under the handle – she could already hear her brother's footsteps on the stairs.

'Wait for me!' she shouted.

He was already at the top of the big stairs when she caught up with him.

'Wait, I want to show you something.'

'Later. I'm hungry.'

'Bo-yd!'

'I'm hungry.' He ran down the stairs. Morag stomped down the staircase after him. *Boys!*

When she got to the breakfast room, their places were laid with cutlery, glasses and teacups. Boyd already had the lid off one of the dishes on the sideboard and the smell of bacon made her realise she was hungry too. The whistle sounded by the dumb waiter and the ropes inside rattled. Boyd, still with a mouthful of toast went to see what was being sent up – a tray with the padded tea-pot cover, and a jug of orange juice sat inside the box. Boyd lifted out the tray, putting it on the table before he went over to blow the whistle; a chirp sounded from far below.

'I'd like a bowl of apples.' Boyd said clearly.

There was some distant muttering and after a moment the box started to rattle slowly downward.

'You want apples for breakfast? You're weird.'

Boyd just shrugged, sat down and went back to eating his breakfast.

'I found a picture of something,' whispered Rag loudly.

'So?' He poured out some tea.

'It's of whatever we saw yesterday…'

'About that…I don't know that you ought to go down there again,' said Boyd.

'What?'

'It might be dangerous,'

'But I know what it is!' Rag had given up the loud stage-whispering and was almost bouncing in her chair.

'How do you know?'

'I Googled 'horse and bird' and at first it said 'griffin', but when I looked it up a griffin was part lion and part eagle, then I saw it said griffins eat horses, but sometimes, and it's unusual, they can mate and then the…I dunno… chicks, foals… are half eagle and half horse and they're called Hippogriffs and that was what was downstairs…'

Rag ran out of breath, the words tumbling over one another.

Boyd ate his toast in silence.

'Well?' demanded Rag, 'Isn't that amazing? Don't you want to know how it got here?'

Boyd swallowed the last of his toast.

'I think…'He said after a pause, but he was interrupted by the whistle of the dumb-waiter; the ropes inside it rattled.

'You are not going to tell me I can't go down and see it! I found the door. I found the way out there!' Rag was prepared to furiously defend her right to go.

'I was going to say, I think… we should be careful. I know full well if I tell you not to, you'll go anyway, but I want you to promise you won't go down there without me.'

Rag stuck her bottom lip out and folded her arms across her chest. She watched Boyd open the dumb waiter. He took out a large blue and white china bowl piled high with apples, all of them polished, and arranged in a neat pyramid.

'Promise me, Rag – or I'll tell Uncle Wulf where we've been and I bet he'll lock the doors and nobody will be able to go.' Boyd put the big bowl down on the table.

'Alright,' Rag thought for a second. 'But Uncle Wulf must know that they're there…'

'He started to say things last night, sort of hints… about how old the castle was and how strange some things might seem to us, and how our parents had had to get used to unusual things as well…'

'And?'

Boyd picked up the topmost apple and turned it over and over in his hands

'It was all a bit hazy, and I started to get tired – he just said that some of the animals, like the dogs for instance, were very old breeds that weren't found anywhere else… and how Dad and Mum helped him do research and collect things…'

'What things?'

'He was a bit vague – 'unusual specimens' was what he said.'

'That's it – he's a mad scientist doing crazy experiments!'

'Don't be stupid – does he look like a mad scientist? He's more like one of those eco-warriors, a wild man of the woods, or an old hippy or something…'

Morag didn't have any answer – all the scientists she'd seen on TV had suits and ties or white coats; Uncle Wulf definitely didn't look like any of them.

'I still think we should have another look, just to make sure he's there or not.'

'He?' asked Boyd.

'The bird-thingie, the hippogriff – anyway, He didn't look like a girl.'

'How do you know what a 'girl' hippogriff would look like?' said Boyd.

'I would, cos I'm a girl.'

Boyd had no answer that wouldn't involve a row. He sighed, stood up and started cramming all of his pockets with apples. Rag went to the door.

'I thought it was your turn to clear the table?' he said.

Rag looked back, opening her mouth to argue, but Boyd stared at her hard and she gave in, quickly putting their plates and cups onto the tray inside the dumb waiter.

'See?' said Boyd, 'It's not that hard to be tidy is it?'

Rag stuck her tongue out at him.

Uncle Wulf was nowhere to be seen as they walked through the house, neither where any of the Broons, only the big, long-haired cat, lying in its usual spot, in the sunlight at the top of the stairs. The cat watched them through half-closed eyes as they turned and disappeared down the back-stairs.

Morag and Boyd descended the winding staircase to the outer door, the strange feeling came over them again as they arrived. Their knees seemed to go weak, but knowing it would soon pass made it feel less alarming. They found the alcove, went through the first door into what Rag could only think of as 'the air-lock', and out into the yard.

The sunlight seemed brighter and the air crisper somehow… but Rag put that down to the contrast between the dark, enclosed space of the twisting stairs and the light reflecting brightly off the grey stonework around the yard. Boyd walked on ahead of her, while Rag breathed in a big lungful of fresh air and felt… happy. She'd already begun to like it out here – it felt… right for her somehow.

They found their way to the pen where the hippogriff lived, the paddock was empty. Boyd climbed up onto the bottom rung of the wooden fence for a better look.

'How do you think we should call to him – what do you call

one anyway?' said Rag clambering up beside him.

'You not have shouts,' rasped a voice from inside the nearby stable. 'I hears you.'

Startled, they both scrambled backwards off the fence.

'Waaaaaa…?' gasped Rag.

The Hippogriff stalked slowly from his stable, this time they could see he favoured one back leg, and walked with a slight limp.

'Apples?' he said, 'apples you have?'

Boyd stood frozen to the spot a metre from the fence, his jaw still wide-open with surprise.

'That… just spoke…' hissed Rag, peering out from behind her brother.

Boyd nodded, 'I heard him,' he gasped.

'Animals do not… say things!' Morag shuffled forward to her brother's side.

'Apples… …now - please?' said the Hippogriff, standing close to the fence, shifting his clawed feet impatiently.

'Well this one can!'

'Ask it something… go on!' said Rag. She took a half-step forward.

Boyd cleared his throat, eventually he managed to squeak…

'You can talk!'

'Yes. Little. Thinking pictures is best, but Two-legs like words.'

'Why didn't you say anything yesterday?' asked Rag, getting over her shock she took another step.

'No Rag – not too near!' Boyd put his arm out to stop his sister.

The Hippogriff gave a sort of raspy snort and shook its head so the quills of the long feathers around its neck rattled together.

'Not bite. Apples – I like apples.'

'Go one, Boyd, give him an apple.'

Boyd took one out of his pocket and slowly held it out. He had to take a step closer and the apple rocked on his open palm and almost fell off. The Hippogriff hissed.

'Let me. I'll do it,' said Rag.

'No – I'll do it.' Boyd squared his shoulders and took a couple more steps, stretching his arm between the rungs of the fence, the apple balanced on the flat on his outstretched hand. The hippogriff sniffed delicately then took the apple in the tip of its beak, before tossing it into the air, catching it and chomping on it with a loud crunch.

He gobbled it quickly. 'Apple?' he said again, eyeing Boyd expectantly.

Boyd got another apple out of his pocket and offered it – this was eaten equally quickly.

'Let me give him one,' said Rag.

'Careful. Put it on the flat of your hand like you're feeding a horse.'

'I know how to do it.' Notwithstanding, her hand shook a little as she thrust it under the hippogriff's beak.

He backed off half a step, looked down and took the apple gently before crunching it up loudly, allowing some small pieces to fall to the ground.

'Good apples – more?'

A flurry of movement caught Rag's eye and a blur of green and gold raced in, snatched up an apple fragment near her foot and disappeared back under the bushes. The Hippogriff stamped its foot in annoyance and snorted.

'What... what was that?' said Rag.

'Pukis!' snorted the Hippogriff.

'Careful, Rag!'

'Pukis is little thieves – but not biters. More apple?'

'Are you sure they don't bite?' said Boyd.

Hippogriff shook his head until the quills rattled. 'Not bite... scratch maybe... steal things, to keep.'

'He's over there,' said Rag, pointing under a nearby bush. She could just see a face that looked like a small cat, with big green eyes, bat-like ears and sharp teeth in a short muzzle, gnawing at the piece of apple held between its front paws... that looked scaly rather than furry.

'He wants some apple too, have you got another one?'

'My apples!' huffed the Hippogriff, rattling his neck-feathers.

'You have to learn to share!' Morag announced solemnly. She turned to the bush and rolled a piece of apple along the ground. The Pukis squeaked and disappeared back into hiding in the bush.

'My apples...' The Hippogriff sounded like a sulky child who had been told off.

'Here you are then,' said Boyd offering another apple.

The Hippogriff ate it quickly, moving away from the bush, so anything that fell was beyond the reach of the pukis.

'Don't they feed you?' laughed Boyd as the apple vanished with much loud crunching.

Hippogriff clacked his beak together. 'Not enough apples,' he said, 'Little two-legs come with food. Sometimes apples. The Liosalfar comes with medicine – for leg.'

He turned slightly and they could see the long ragged cut across his back and down his hind leg. The wound was shiny and pink were it had been stitched together. In his head Boyd suddenly had a flash of what the hippogriff saw – a very tall man with long, pale hair, his outline shining slightly at the edges, who smeared something cold on the raw pain of his injured leg. In surprise, Boyd clutched his own thigh, which felt like ice-cold ointment had been wiped over it.

'It's Uncle Wulf!' he gasped.

'What?'

Rag was still watching the small cat-like creature reach out to grab the apple fragments and scuttle back to shelter. She could see it had little green bat-wings to go with the bat ears. She looked over at Boyd.

'Uncle Wulf looks after the animals – there are lots more of them. He showed me – up here.' Boyd put a finger to his forehead.

'So he's not a mad scientist doing experiments?' Rag almost felt a bit disappointed.

'No… he's more like a… guardian, or a … zoo-keeper. He looks after them when they come for help, or if they get lost – he comes to find them.'

'Don't be silly! How would they get lost! They'd be in all the newspapers if they were outside the castle.'

Boyd stood very still, his eyes unfocused; his face looked blank, lost in thought.

'Boyd…? Boyd? You're scaring me!' Rag shook her brother's arm.

'No… stop that…' Boyd mumbled. His voice sounded slurred as if speaking was a great effort.

'Boyd!' Morag shook his arm harder, 'Boyd, Boyd come back!'

After a moment he snapped out of his trance, staggering a little. He leaned against the fence and then slid down to the ground. Rag crouched beside him.

'What is it? Are you sick?'

Boyd shook his head.

'Boyd – talk to me!'

'He knew Dad,' Boyd's voice was just a whisper.

'What!!' Rag shot to her feet. 'That's not funny, Boyd!'

Boyd scrambled slowly to his feet, shaking his head, like a swimmer trying to clear water from his ears. Across the far paddocks came the sound of wooden buckets thudding together.

'Little two-legs – food!' The Hippogriff trotted away.

'We have to go Boyd, before they see us,' said Rag, 'Can you walk?'

'I'm fine – I want to go back. Inside the castle… I need… I need to sit down.'

They hurried towards the door in the corner of the castle yard. They were so intent on getting back to safety, they didn't notice the little green and gold pukis who flew after them and whisked inside the door behind them just before it closed. In the darkness of the inner room, Rag and Boyd didn't see the little creature. They didn't look back down the shadowy stairs so they didn't see him following them; they were too intent on climbing the steep steps.

Rag was leading the way; she called back to her brother.

'Boyd – are you ok?'

'Yes – I think so. I'll tell you when we get upstairs – not here.'

Once inside the castle, they rushed to their rooms. Both of them were panting by the time they'd got back to the safety of their familiar corridor. Before Rag could blurt out her pent-up questions, Boyd gasped, 'I'm going to the bathroom. Just wait for me. I'll knock on your door when I'm ready.' Boyd was a bit unsteady as he walked away from her down the corridor.

'Boyd? Are you sure you're all right?' Rag called after him.

He waved, but didn't look around before he closed the bathroom door behind him and locked it.

Rag stood at her open bedroom door; she crossed to Boyd's door, opened it, thought better of going inside and stood in the doorway hopping from one foot to the other with impatience. Her back was to her own door and she didn't see the little pukis creep along the edge of the hallway in the shadows, then dash inside her room and scuttle under the bed.

Shortly afterwards, the lock slid open on the bathroom door. Boyd came out. He looked a bit pale and shaky, and his hair was wet from splashing his face with cold water. He walked slowly towards Morag.

'Well?' she squealed, 'Well? What's going on?'

'Hush! Quiet down – we need to talk!'

He pushed his sister into his bedroom and closed the door behind them.

CHAPTER FIFTEEN

Once inside, Boyd flopped down on the bed. Rag was dancing up and down with frustration,

'What happened, why won't you tell me?' she demanded.

'Sit down and I will.' Boyd took a deep breath, paused, and then took another… 'Ok, ok – don't explode Rag, I just don't quite know where to begin.

'The Hippogriff put a picture in my mind, but it wasn't just one picture, it was a jumble of images, all one on top of the other so that sometimes they moved so fast they got mixed up. He showed me Uncle Wulf looking after his wound, and how Uncle Wulf looks after lots of different animals – but none of them looked real. There were funny combinations, like half lion and half goat, and things with scales and wings and… all sorts...' He paused for a moment, 'And there were unicorns. I saw a unicorn… and they nest and lay eggs!'

Boyd waved his sister's questions away. '…but most, most important - I saw Dad. He was here… or rather there…'There' is a different place to here. I don't know how to describe it, because the Hippogriff didn't know how it worked, but 'there' where the fabulous sort of animals live, is different. And it's not just a little 'there' where the yard is… it's a whole world!

'There is not a whole world on the other side of that door!'

'No, not all of it… but that's it – it is a door to another world!'

Morag looked astounded, then she frowned. 'You're making this up!'

'Rag, think about it - how else could we have a hippogriff on our doorstep?'

'For real?'

Boyd nodded.

'Wow…!'

Rag sat down on the floor. They both sat in silence for a minute, taking this tremendous idea in.

'But… what about Dad… how did he get there? And are you sure it was him?'

Boyd nodded. 'I recognised him straight away. He was dressed funny, a bit like Uncle Wulf. They were standing talking, then they hugged each other and… and Dad rode away… Bloody hell!' Boyd's eyes widened as the remembered scene in his head became clearer. 'He was riding a giant deer! The Hippogriff said he'd gone hunting… and he had a bow and arrows on his back, and a big rucksack was behind him on the saddle - and he was riding a huge stag!'

Neither of them spoke and the silence between them lengthened…

'Like the one I saw when I first went there…?'Rag said quietly.

She got up from sitting on the floor and went to the window. 'But if he's out there somewhere… we need to get him back.' She turned around, 'we need to talk to the Hippogriff again. And we need to talk to Uncle Wulf.'

'And what do we say? We went where you told us not to and

we found your 'unusual specimens'... your zoo full of fabulous animals? No – it's not really a zoo, it's an animal sanctuary. Whatever - we still need to find out more about what's going on. Did Mum know about all this? Of course she did! Did she know where Dad had gone? Is that why she made sure we came here to Uncle Wulf, because she knew Dad would come back here too? But she knew there were dangers too... Oh there's too much to think about... you'll have to give me some time on my own,' said Boyd.

'What - now? We need to do something.'

'We need to have a plan, a strategy – you can't just rush into heaven knows what... I'm going to have a bath and think about it.'

'Aaargh!!!'growled Rag in exasperation. 'Why do you DO that?'

'I don't care. I think better in the bath. Go wait for me, or go look up more animals on the Internet... Come to think of it, I think there's a book of mythical beasts on the shelves...'

He got up from the bed to search for the book. 'Here... go read that – but first promise me, cross your heart and hope to die, that you will not do anything without me. Promise? Promise!'

Rag snatched the book from his hand, 'Ok...I promise! But don't be all day in that bath.' She stamped off back to her own bedroom.

Rag tossed all the cushions from her bed onto the floor and then threw herself down on top of them. She could almost feel the heat of her anger radiating from her skin; though she soon calmed down and everything cooled to normal. Rag turned the book's pages slowly, absorbed in the coloured illustrations of strange, fabulous creatures of all shapes and sizes; some she'd vaguely heard of, but many she hadn't, and some she was absolutely sure were impossible... but then again...

The pukis wanted to know what she had got that fascinated her so much – he liked things of value, he liked to collect them and have them around him... He shuffled silently around the edge of the room, hiding himself in the shadows under the furniture until he could get close enough to see for himself. He knew about some of the animals in the pictures... even if the colours weren't right, but he soon got bored and crept off to find things that he thought were more interesting.

The bathroom was steamy from the hot water that almost filled the bath. Boyd was nearly submerged; the water was up to his jawline. As it lapped in his ears, the noise of the bathwater became magnified into sloshing bubbly noises that echoed every time he moved; the outside world faded as he closed his eyes to concentrate on the images in his head...

Boyd felt he was looking through the eyes of the Hippogriff - he was the Hippogriff, seeing... feeling... hearing...

...Lachlan Ellis - it was the two-leg friend of the Liosalfar... He looks into our eyes - pats our head, scratches between our ears. He walks around us - we are laid down because our leg hurts. He stops to look at the wound on our leg- then he wants us to stand up. He looks all over of us, running his hands over us and lifting our feet.

Here are three of the little Polewiki standing near – they found us; we think they sent for help. Funny little two-legs, not like the Liosalfar and his house of Broons; these ones dress in black and white- their hair is made of green grass.

They talk to the big two-legs, but we can't hear what they say. They point at us, then over to the lake...we hear them say – Fuath... and we are afraid. The Polewiki want to go. Two-legs wants them to stay with us, but they keep saying 'Svartalfar will come'. They will not stay.

We want to run away, but the Two-legs Friend catches us and talks noises to make us be calm. He searches his bag and has apple for us. He puts a rope around our neck and leads us. Tall Broon steps out of the air...

We look back – something bubbles up and sits on the water... black and swirly, and filled with red, glowing eyes, and fangs, and claws... It makes us feared. It grows bigger and creeps across the lake...

Boyd woke up with a start and pushed himself to sit upright. The water surged up and splashed over the tiled floor. He grabbed both sides of the bath-tub, panting with alarm, not sure if he had dreamed that he was the Hippogriff... or simply remembered more of what the Hippogriff had shown him.

As the warm bathwater subsided from tsunami-sized down to little waves, so did his panic; calmer, he took a deep breath and slide slowly under the water... listening to the metallic splunks and ripples, thinking what to do next... When he needed air he pushed himself up slowly until his nose and mouth were above the water and he could take a breath; some of his hair lay plastered across his face, the rest floated freely, like kelp in the ocean. He'd have to explain as much of this...

dream… vision… as he could to Rag. She'd self-combust if he didn't turn up soon…

He emerged from the water, his pale skin glistening with tiny, silver-white droplets that clung to every one of fine dark hairs on his legs and body. He flicked his wet hair back, reached up to squeeze as much water as he could out of it, and then stepped out of bathtub and reached for one of the big towels to dry himself down.

Chapter Sixteen

It didn't take long to get dressed; he rough dried his dripping hair with the towel and ran his fingers through the shaggy curls to clear them from his face. Looking into the mirror he could suddenly see some of his father in his face… his long straight nose, heavy eyebrows and long eyelashes - Mum always said she envied him and Dad for their eyelashes…, but was that partly remembering what the Hippogriff saw? He frowned at the thought – things weren't really straight in his head yet, but his sister wouldn't let him rest until he'd spoken to her.

He left the bathroom and knocked on her door; he heard her shout through the solid wood.

'About time!' Rag flung the door open. 'Well?'

His hair was still damp, and he shivered a little after the steamy heat of the bathroom. He would like to have gone to get another jumper from his room, but he knew she couldn't wait. Boyd went in and shut the door behind him.

'Well?' Rag was almost bursting with impatience. Boyd put his hands deep in his pockets and pushed his shoulders up around his ears as he walked slowly around her room.

'I think I know some of what happened. It's really difficult to explain – some of it seems impossible… I can see it, but I know it didn't happen to me, even if I sort of dreamt that it did… What was that?'

'What? Tell me Boyd – it's not fair!'

Suddenly distracted, Boyd pushed past her and walked towards her four-poster bed. 'I saw something move – it went under the bed.'

'What – there's nothing there, you're just stalling!'

Boyd stood beside the bed, 'No – I saw something. It was too fast to get a good look… is that cat in here?'

'No. Nothing's there. What are you doing?'

Boyd knelt down and very gingerly lifted the white valance that reached almost to the floor. Rag crouched down beside him and went to grab the bed-cover and pull it back down.

'Stop stalling! I can look for myself – and there's nothing under there anyway!'

'Wait!' said Boyd.

He looked around, and reached for one of Rag's wellingtons lying in front of her walk-in cupboard; putting his hand inside right down to the foot, he cautiously lifted the edge of the bed cover. They both leaned down to peer underneath.

Peering back at them was the green-gold scaly face of the pukis. He was sitting on top of a small pile of Rag's clothes, shoes, and cat toys, including one of the shoes she'd kicked off earlier. He hissed at them. Boyd dropped the cover and sat back.

'There is something!' he said.

'It's the little cat dragon thingie I fed apple to.'

'What did you bring it back here for?'

'I didn't! I swear. It must have followed us.'

'Well how are we going to get it out?'

'I don't know,' said Rag, 'doesn't that voice-thing in your head tell you anything?'

'It's not like that,' Boyd said.

'Well I don't know, do I?'

Boyd lifted the edge of the cover again with the wellington still on his hand and they both peered underneath the bed. The pukis had huddled lower into the pile of stolen goods, with just his eyes and pointed ears clearly visible. Boyd dropped the cover.

'He liked apples,' said Rag, 'you got any left?'

'Might have.'

Boyd quickly went back to his room and retrieved the left-over apple he'd taken from the dining room the night before, and grabbed a thick woollen jumper while he was there. He came back, pulling the jumper over his head while he bit into the apple. He placed a small chunk of apple on the floor, pushing it under the cover with the sole of the wellington-boot.

They both listened. A few moments later they heard some sniffing and then a few crunches. Boyd bit off some more flakes of apple and placed the bits just under the bedcover's edge. They heard more crunching, it obviously liked apple.

'Let me,' whispered Rag. Her brother handed her the apple and she bit more pieces off, laying a trail out from under the bed.

'Get a hoodie or something thick to catch it in,' whispered Boyd.

The cat-like little pukis must have been hungry; it followed the bits of fruit eagerly... Rag pounced and dropped her hoodie over it. Boyd grabbed it and scooped the pukis into a bundle, rolling it tightly inside. The pukis mewed and squealed in fear as Boyd wrapped it tighter.

'Don't hurt it,' cried Rag.

'What if it hurts me?!'

Boyd put the quivering bundle on the floor and sat back, examining his hands for scratches – there were none. The quivering bundle continued to give tiny mews. Rag very carefully rolled back a corner…the pukis froze - shivering with fear.

'Oooooo…There…there…' Boyd kept quiet when Rag offered it another bit of apple. The pukis paused, sniffed… grabbed the fruit and burrowed back into the folds of the hoodie to nibble at it. Rag reached out very slowly until she could just stroke its head with her fingertips.

'Be careful…' said Boyd.

The pukis chirruped at her touch and stiffened at first, then relaxed and carried on nibbling the apple as she scratched behind its ear.

'See? It's fine.'

Boyd slowly stretched out his hand; the pukis unfurled his little bat-wings and gave a small hiss, along with a tiny puff of flame. Boyd snatched his hand back.

Rag laughed. 'No, you don't like the big bully do you?'

The pukis purred in response to her.

Rag handed Boyd the remaining apple-core, 'Try offering that.'

Boyd held the fruit between finger and thumbnail and offered it. The puckis arched its back, but smelling food, he settled and gently took the apple-core to nibble.

'What are we going to do with it?' said Boyd.

'Keep it,' replied Rag.

'We can't just kidnap it.'

'It came after us on its own – it can live in the empty cupboard by the fireplace. I can find it a box or a basket or something and put some old clothes in it.'

'What about letting it out? It's not going to be house-trained.'

'I'll find some old newspaper to put down, and I can carry it outside in my back-pack to let it have a run around.'

Boyd stood up. 'We have to tell Uncle Wulf.'

'No, not yet,' pleaded Rag, 'I might be able to train him - to do tricks and stuff.'

'I'm not sure it's clever enough for that,' said Boyd

The pukis gave a little belch... emitting a tiny puff of smoke, before spreading his wings and flying up onto the bed. He turned in circles like a cat before curling up on the quilt.

'See?' said Rag, 'He likes it here.'

'He?'

'I think so,' said Rag. She got up and sat on the bed and stroked the pukis who purred with satisfaction. 'Anyway – what's more important... what about Dad? You haven't told me what happened yet.'

Boyd went to sit on the chair by her desk. He dragged his hands through his curls – they were nearly dry now, springing up tightly because he hadn't had time to brush them smooth. He sighed, rubbed his face with one hand and tried to order his thoughts and make some sense of the images in his head.

'Dad... was, is ...some sort of guardian, or animal ranger maybe. He helps Uncle Wulf, but it's confusing because I only know what the Hippogriff showed me and he only knows what he's seen. Dad and Uncle Wulf help wounded animals. They also come to find them when they get lost, and take them back to where they should be – there is some sort of barrier between these worlds that in places is thin and it tears open; that lets the animals wander through.

Uncle Wulf is… I don't quite understand… the Lord… Master… of this place? But what is more important - the Hippogriff knows that he and Dad are not quite the same… they look different to him – and we do. …Rag – I don't think Uncle Wulf is… you know… human – and there's something a bit different about Dad as well.'

Rag stared at him, and then frowned. 'You mean – Uncle Wulf's like… an alien?'

'No, not from out of space… At least…I don't think so… No, definitely not that sort!' Boyd sighed, 'I know,' he said, '…it's weird, but the Hippogriff knows they, we, aren't all the same thing… the same sort of person... It's like if you went to the park - there would be lots of dogs running around and being walked, right? And you would look at them and know they were all dogs, but you'd also know that one was a poodle, another was a German Shepherd, or a corgi, or a mix like a cockapoo… Well to him we're all 'two-legs', but different kinds.

He had a word for Uncle Wulf, but I'm not sure how to translate it… the nearest I think it comes to is - Elf.'

'You mean like… fairies sitting on toadstools?' said Rag with a puzzled frown.

'No! Not the fluttery, dragonfly-winged sort… more like the Elves in those movies, you know, very old and powerful – and there are other sorts too, not just ones like Uncle Wulf. Yes, I know, I know, it sounds crazy.

Rag looked down at the drowsy pukis, its eyes closed, enjoying having its ears scratched.

'Yeah... but this is crazy too. I've never ever seen anything like this – and here it is.'

Just then they heard the sonorous sound of the bronze dinner gong being struck downstairs in the big hall.

'Is it that time already? We need to go for lunch. You'd better tidy up,' said Boyd.

'Do I have to change?'

Boyd shook his head, 'No, I think, from what Uncle Wulf said last night, we're back to what's going to be our new normal. We have lunch in the same room as we have breakfast, and Uncle Wulf will eat with us when he's around.'

'Is that going to be every day?'

Boyd shrugged.

'What are you going to say to him?' said Rag

'I don't know. I think I want to see what he has to say to us first.'

'We could try and ask about the animals – without letting him know that we've already found out about some of the weird stuff,' said Rag. 'And we need to ask some more about Dad.'

'Do you think he's going to tell us everything straight out?' Boyd scoffed, 'Are you sure about that?'

'Well, he's got to say something, sometime.'

'You think?' said Boyd, '...our parents never did.'

He stood up. 'You better put that... whatever it is, into the cupboard before you come down. Put it in your suitcase for now, just unzip it and leave the lid back.'

Rag looked up from stroking the little creature with a dreamy expression on her face.

'He's a pukis.'

'What?' said Boyd.

'He's a pukis; he told me so.'

'How?'

Rag shrugged, 'Like you and the Hippogriff I suppose - it just came into my head.'

Boyd paused at the door; he looked back at his sister sitting on the bed, stroking what from where he stood looked like a bright green cat... with scales.

'This is so weird,' he muttered as he left the room.

CHAPTER SEVENTEEN

In the breakfast room, Uncle Wulf, Rag and Boyd sat at the table finishing their lunch. Rag kept glancing at Boyd, who frowned at her 'not yet'. Uncle Wulf put down his knife and fork and sat back.

'You are both very quiet – are you tired?'

'No, we're fine,' said Boyd quickly before Rag could speak.

'Good,' Wulf nodded to himself. He ignoring the slight movement as Rag attempted to kick Boyd under the table and continued: 'We should talk about what interests you, and what lessons you would like to have.'

'We get a choice?' said Rag, suddenly sitting up - this had got her attention.

'Yes. There are many choices you can make. You can learn as fast as you wish, so if the subject interests you, you can take it further than your school would. You must have been taught the basics already – now you can see what you can do with them. And if there are things that are not yet clear, they can be practised. Some I may do with you, for most lessons there will be tutors.'

'What choices did our parents make?' asked Boyd.

Wulf pushed his plate away and leant with his forearms on the table, considering how to answer.

'They were much younger than you are when they came here. Besides the regular scholar's lessons from books, they learnt animal husbandry from the Broons, and how to cook and clean and mend things. I taught them to swim – your father was always a keen swimmer – and how to ride, that's important out here, there are many places a horse can go where the usual vehicles can't. They learnt archery and weaponry, how to stalk and hunt; they knew more about this world than they did of the outside… Their choices were different to what yours might be.'

'When you say… 'this world', said Boyd.

'The Highlands. It is quite different from living in a town.'

'Yes,' said Rag, 'we were going to ask you…'

Boyd quickly interrupted her, 'About what life's like here. What sort of things we can do.'

Rag glowered, but kept quiet.

'We have many things, more than meets the eye. If you wish, we can leave the table, and come back later for dessert. Would you like to meet some of the animals? They will still be outside - later they will be penned up for the night - you might decide you wish to help look after them.'

Rag shot out of her seat, 'Oh yes, I'd like to do that!'

'Boyd?' Wulf looked at him, smiled and raised an eyebrow as he stood up, 'do you wish to join us?'

'Yeah, why not?' said Boyd.

They followed Uncle Wulf out of the room.

From a rear door of the Keep they went across another courtyard, and entered a large barn and walked through it between sacks of grain and racks of farming tools: hay-forks, sickles, saws, sieves and things the children had no idea what they were for... all hung neatly, all the wooden handles gleaming, polished from use by many hands. Behind the barn was a big shed with a run attached for the chickens.

One thing Boyd did notice was the wire mesh was made of copper, the majority was covered in greenish verdigris, but the metal glinted brightly here and there where it had been repaired. He looked more closely at things around the yard after that and realised, they used steel for tools, that had wooden handles, but water troughs were made of lead or bronze, and hinges, latches, handles and chains were all bronze, brass and copper; everything else was wood. The thought struck him then that many of the things they had at home, their old home, were made of wood, or brass and copper, and stuff like that.

Wulf was pointing things out: 'We have chickens - we have a few cows for milk - the dairy is over there. We keep some pigs beyond the wall on the other side of the yard. We have some ponies and a horse in the stables – Can you ride at all? No? You would like to learn? Good.' Wulf nodded to himself. 'You've met my two dogs. There is Frithjof the cat, you may have seen him? He likes to sun himself at the top of the stairs. His name means 'peace-thief' he can be very mischievous...'

'See?' said Rag, nudging her brother's arm. 'It's not a girl - he's a he!'

Uncle Wulf raised a quizzical eyebrow, but Boyd just rolled his eyes and dismissed it. A large crow flew down from a nearby hawthorn tree and landed on the chicken-coop roof; pausing to inspect them with a beady eye before slowly walking down the wooden slats towards them.

'Here is Duffy,' Wulf stooped to collect a handful of feed from one of the nearby sacks; he threw it up on the roof. 'She had a damaged wing as a fledgling, now she likes to think of me as her family. She'll come to be fed when she's used to you – she prizes corn above aloofness.'

'What about the… other animals?' Boyd said.

'Others?'

'Deer… and things…' said Rag.

'Yes, there are deer on the moors – have you seen them from your window? Sometimes they come close to the house - if they can, they would get into the gardens and eat the young shoots.'

Wulf picked up another handful of corn and scattered it in front of an expectant, gaudily feathered hen who'd come into the run to see who the visitors were. The grain attracted the attention of a few more and soon a group of colourful clucking birds were busy pecking the stone flags for nuggets of grain. Wulf watched them. None of the Broons were in sight.

'These hens are descended from Eastern jungle fowl that were brought back here years ago. The Broons crossbred them to improve the local strain. You will have noticed their eggs are a darker brown compared to the usual sort of eggs,' said Uncle Wulf.

'Um… I don't think I've had a boiled egg yet - I hadn't noticed,' mumbled Rag.

Boyd decided to try again. 'Yesterday, we saw a big black bird fly over the loch, then up to the tower.'

'Ah, him…' said Wulf, 'he is a rarity even here.'

Uncle Wulf picked up a small brass bowl, scooped up some feed and handed it to Rag. 'If you hold it out in your left hand, Duffy may come down and land on your arm to feed. Always you hold your left arm up for a bird to land – so if needed, you can adjust the hackles with your right hand.'

'Is that like... for hawking?' asked Boyd.

'Yes, I have none at present, but we have had falcons here in the past.'

'But the black bird... He wasn't an eagle...?' said Boyd.

'No.'

Rag trickled a little stream of corn in a trail, one of the unusual hens followed her. There was a squawk from the crow, she hopped down the roof to get closer to Rag. 'I'd like to see a hawk – and what about owls? Can you train an owl?' said Rag

Wulf watched the crow, which seemed to be deciding if the promise of food overcame fear...'Owls are more difficult to train. We have several rare breeds around here, although none are used for hunting - many of the hens are old breeds. If you like birds, I shall find you a book about them...'

There was a soft cough from the shadows in the doorway to the barn behind them. Wulf looked over their heads; Broonie was waiting in the half-light inside the building to speak to him.

'I think there's a book of rare breeds in my room... magical ones...' said Boyd.

'A moment.' Wulf walked over to the little man. He and Broonie spoke quietly for a few moments, then the Brown withdrew and Wulf walked back to the children.

'I am called away. I may not be back for supper, but please go ahead, and eat without me; use the board games in the drawing room if you wish, they will be on the tables. I may not be back until after you have gone to bed, so I will see you in the morning.'

'But... we have more questions... about stuff,' said Boyd.

Wulf strode down the yard towards the stable block, passing another broon coming from an out-building carrying fishing rods and wicker baskets.

'Good,' Wulf said.He paused and turned to Morag and Boyd, 'This is Buff. He is going fishing and has rods for you – to see if you enjoy it.' Then he disappeared into the stable buildings - much to Boyd's frustration.

CHAPTER EIGHTEEN

Rag and Boyd didn't quite know what to do – it seemed rude just to walk away from the little smiling man approaching them with arms full of fishing tackle. He had wiry brownish-blonde hair, lighter than Gam's, his clothes were a lighter brown too. He was about Gam's height and had the same potato nose, rosy wrinkles and all-brown eyes without whites. He was wearing all-in-one rubber waders that reached right up to his armpits over his old-fashioned button-up overalls, and a tweed hat with lots of feathered hooks stuck into the wool. He bowed to them and carefully placed the rods on the floor at his feet.

'You need boots.' He pointed to their feet. 'Coats too. I wait here.'

'I… er…' began Boyd.

'Yes. I wait here.' Buff smiled and bobbed his head. 'Yes.'

Reluctantly, they turned away, back towards the house.

'I don't think we can get out of this,' whispered Rag.

'No, but we can stay for an hour then leave – I'm going to grab a book and bring it along in case we're stuck out there.'

Fishing was not something either of them had considered before. 'But you never know, maybe this new one will let something slip if we ask carefully,' said Rag

Boyd nodded glumly, 'I'm taking my music player as well.' He went up the stairs ahead of her.

Rag took an apple from the big fruit-bowl, now on the sideboard in the hall, with her up to her room. She found the pukis asleep in the cupboard, with both of her wellingtons, an assortment of shoes and other things. She removed her velour cat toys from the nest he'd made, and put them safely back on the dressing table. He rumbled sleepily, curled up again and settled down. She got her little dagger from the wardrobe, took it from its gilded sheath and sliced the apple up for the pukis.

This left the blade sticky with juice, and as much as she didn't usually bother with cleaning things… she thought she'd better look after this. She went to the bathroom and ran the hot-water tap over the dagger. At first she thought the water had made the patterns that shimmered over the blade, but decided it must only be reflections on the shiny metal, because water can't turn into rainbows…. She heard her brother call from the corridor.

'Rag – are you ready?'

'Coming!'

She quickly dried her hands and the knife, and ran back to her room.

'What are you doing with that?'

'I cut an apple up for Pookie.'

'I'm not sure that's what it's for.'

'It's just a knife – wow, what are you wearing?'

Boyd had on a waxed outdoors coat lined with quilted tartan; he also had on long green wellingtons that reached up to his thighs.

‘Fishing stuff. It was in the walk-in cupboard. Go and look for yours. I’m going downstairs. I’ll wait in the big hall.’

A similar coat was hanging on the rail in the big cupboard in her room, as if by magic, along with thigh-high green wellingtons.

She felt pretty stupid when she came downstairs. ‘I don’t really fancy this. I feel like a moon-walker in these boots,’ said Rag

‘I know. But it would be rude to refuse, especially after they’ve provided all the gear. We’ll just go for an hour. I’m sure this guy Buff will let us come back here.’

‘I’d rather stay and play with Pookie,’ Rag grumbled. ‘And we still haven’t found out where Dad might have gone.’

‘I know. I’d rather read a book or go online,’ said Boyd, ‘but it does give us a chance to try and find out more of what’s going on.’

They trudged outside. Buff was waiting patiently. He handed them each a lidded wicker basket on a shoulder strap and a small folding stool of wood and canvas. The fishing rods he carried himself as he led them away towards the loch.

They walked past the shallow head of the loch, along the road above the dark muddy bank. As they turned a bend they saw two young men further up the hill; they had their trousers rolled up as they waded in a wide stream that fell in a series of small rocky pools, which eventually feed into the loch.

They looked up as Buff passed them; their nodded greetings were returned by his grumpy, ‘Hah’. As Buff stumped ahead, the two men smiled at Rag and Boyd and touched their floppy tam-o-shanters briefly in salute.

Rag and Boyd smiled back and nodded; Buff called back to them, 'Come.'

'Do they work for Uncle Wulf as well?' Rag asked, curious about the two men.

Buff nodded, but his loud sniff showed he didn't think much of them. 'They are *fad* – long brothers.'

Rag looked back at the two brothers, who had stood up to watch them go by. They were at least as tall as Boyd, whereas the other Broons were more her height. Mmm… yes, even I can see they're different, thought Rag.

They were both very good-looking, with light, unmarked skin, not rosy and wrinkly as the Broons all seemed to be; their longish dark hair was tucked beneath their wide, Scottish berets. They had straight noses, not lumpy like the usual large, round noses of the Broons, and they had very dark eyebrows above deep-set eyes, and high cheek-bones.

They looked similar enough to be brothers, or at least, closely related, maybe in their late teens or early twenties. They both wore cargo trousers like Uncle Wulf's, but in mottled dark browns and greens, currently rolled up to their knees and stained with water. Their heavy woollen sweaters were dark brown, knitted in complicated patterns; the sleeves were rolled up, showing their forearms, muscled from hard-work, and at the moment, dripping wet.

As she continued to watch them, one pulled off his brown beret and made a little bow. The sun glinted red on the dark brown hair that fell loose over his face. His brother nudged him and the first man laughed, screwed his long wavy hair up on the back of his head with both hands, and pulled his bonnet on firmly to keep it in place. Rag turned and blushed - he was making fun of her for staring… but… he was rather nice looking…

Rag stumbled over a tussock of grass, which made her embarrassed and cross that she looked like she was clumsy. She sneaked a look back, but both of them were heads-down doing whatever it was in the stream; so neither of them saw her.

Though Boyd did… he didn't say anything; he thought he'd save it for teasing her later - if she got annoying again. Especially as he was pretty sure that all these men were some sort of *fae* – at least the Hippogriff thought so, so it must be true.

Buff eventually had them follow him down the sloping turf bank to where a narrow spit of shingle slid under the water, backed by a series of rocks and large boulders that had tumbled down the mountain side millennia ago; they now formed a natural pier reaching into the loch. The sun shone between the many high-piled fair-weather clouds moving in from the west, but the wind remained quite chilly.

They were now face to face with their first fishing lesson. Buff picked up a cane rod, fitted a little feathered hook to the line and turned to face them.

'You – watch me,' he said. He walked out into the loch to above his knees. He flicked the rod back and forth a couple of times then gave a hard flick forward that sent the hook and line out onto the water. He turned to see that they were watching, then did it again, before wading back to them.

'Now – your turn,' he said.

Rag and Boyd looked at each other.

'You go first, 'said Rag.

'Ladies first,' said Boyd.

'I'm not a lady, and this is a 'boy' thing,' said Rag.

'That's an excuse. And you never say that!'

'Ok – you're the oldest, how about that.'

'Please. Come,' Buff said, holding out the rod.

Boyd sighed and stepped forward, scrambling over the rocks and into the water. Buff put Boyd's hands into the right places on the wooden cane, and showed him again how to flick the rod. The first time Boyd accidentally let go and the whole lot went into the water. Buff tutted, shook his head and retrieved the fishing rod. He got Boyd to do it again, and again …and again. Eventually, Boyd could just about get the fly to skim down the water, but not that far.

Buff turned to beckon Rag forward for her turn. She heaved a great sigh and stumped down the pebbles. Buff smiled encouragingly, bobbing his head to emphasise that 'yes, you can do this' as he fitted her hands to the rod. After the first few tries… it became clear Rag was a natural. The fly whizzed across the water on the end of its line and settled where it could drift. Buff was very pleased with her. He smiled and nodded so much Rag wondered if he was going to hurt his neck. The little man turned and beckoned to Boyd, who had retreated up the bank. He'd left them to get on with it since his sister was doing so well; he shook his head and held up the book he'd bought with him and waved.

'I'm fine,' said Boyd, smiling, nodding, giving a thumb's up just to emphasis he was all good when it came to the outdoor life.

Buff shrugged, collected another fishing rod and took Rag down towards the far end of the tumbled rocks to cast from there.

Boyd retreated further up the bank to where the grass was thicker and softer and sat down. He took his basket with him as a head rest; he opened it out of curiosity and found a paper-wrapped slice of apple pie, a knob of cheese, another apple, and a small paper bag filled with chunks of sugary fudge, along with a cylindrical leather case containing a glass bottle filled with water. Ok, he thought …not so bad.

He put his earbuds in, music on and settled down with the apple pie and his book. At one point, over his music, he heard cries of delight; he looked up. Rag had caught a fish; it flip-flopped in the air as Buff guided a net underneath it.

'Look, Boyd! Look!'

Rag was dancing about and so excited, Buff had to grip her arm to stop her sliding off the smooth boulder into the loch. Boyd smiled, waved, gave her a big thumb's up… and went back to his book. There was another brief bout of enthusiasm a bit later; it turned out Buff had caught a brown trout this time.

After nearly two albums on his music player, and several chapters of his book, Boyd was finding the ground hard and uncomfortable. He shifted, stood up stiffly and strolled down to the water's edge. Buff and Rag were concentrating on the water and the fish.

'I think I'm ready to go now,' he said.

Neither of them appeared to have heard him. He walked along the rocks to get a bit nearer.

'I said, I think I'll go now.'

They both turned at his voice. 'Ssshush,' said Rag. 'What is it?'

'I'm going back to the house – are you coming?'

'Just a bit longer – you go ahead and I'll see you later.' Rag suddenly had a thought. 'You won't go anywhere without me will you?' she said.

'No,' said Boyd. 'I'll probably go online for a bit. I'll be upstairs anyway.'

'Yeah, that's great. I'll find you.' Rag returned to casting, the line flew in a fluid sweep across the surface.

'Good, good,' said Buff. He waved one hand, seeming to be looking for the right word, '...wrist, yes...wrist.' He said the word with a long rolled 'r' sound. He cast his own line further and higher than Rag's, but then he'd been doing it for years.

Chapter Nineteen

Boyd gathered up his basket and stool and started back up to the track; he wondered if he'd see the 'long brothers' on his way back. There was nobody else around here – no noise of cars, nothing but the wind, and a few birds.

The brothers weren't at the first stream, but as he got nearer the castle he saw they'd moved to the other side of the loch, further up the stream where he and Rag had been skimming stones their first day.

Boyd stopped, thought about it, and decided to go and introduce himself. They seemed to be part of the place, and it looked like he and Rag were going to be here… he didn't want to think - forever - and pushed that thought aside. …And they might know something useful.

One was wading knee-deep in a stream and the other stood on the bank with a pair of wooden buckets at his feet. They were both barefoot with their sleeves and trousers rolled up; even more dark, wet stains marked the fabric.

Boyd had been mentally preparing an introduction, but when he saw their wet legs and feet and the rushing icy water, he blurted out the first thing that came to mind.

'Aren't you cold without boots?'

The one in the stream turned to the other and grinned, before replying.

'We manage – you can keep a better footing without boots.'

'But aren't the rocks sharp?' said Boyd.

'Not in an old burn like this, the stones are rubbed smooth. It's the craws that will get your toes.'

'Craws? What are they?'

'Show him, Peat.'

The one on the bank held up a bucket half-filled with water, it was crawling with lots of small black, ugly lobster-looking creatures. Boyd pulled a face.

'They taste good,' Peat assured him. 'And this sort are not supposed to be here, we catch 'em to keep them from the mussels. Look way along the stream, further up there - you see?'

Boyd took a few steps up the bank; some way along he could see a long clump of oval dark shells, close together, half buried in the coarse sandy gravel and rocks on the bottom of the crystal-clear stream.

'Those are freshwater pearl mussels, very rare these days.'

'Yeah? Do they make real pearls?' Boyd said.

'Yes, sometimes - that's what makes them valuable. A mussel might be fifty, sixty, seventy years old before it makes a good pearl.'

'Wow.'

The one in the water lifted up a long wicker trap and said, 'Here Peat – I'm coming out.'

He handed over the trap and climbed up onto a large boulder sitting half out of the water; he grinned cheerfully, before wiping his hands on his trousers and reaching out to shake Boyd's hand.

'I am Russet, call me Russ. That is my brother, Peat,'

'I'm Boyd.' He noticed that the brothers' eyes had whites to them, like ordinary eyes, and they both looked cheerful and friendly, and… normal.

'Yes… you are Lach's son,' said Peat, the darker-haired brother, shaking out the trap; another couple of signal crayfish fell into the bucket. 'You have his look.'

'You know my dad?'

'Yes, we know him.'

'Did you see him when he was last here?'

'We did,' said Russ. He put his hand out for his brother to give him a heave-up to a firm footing on the bank and out of the stream.

'Do you know where he is now?'

The brothers still had a firm hold of each other's arm, wrist to wrist; they looked at each other and their smiles faded, the pause was long enough to make Boyd suspicious.

'You do!'

'No,' said Russ quietly. 'We don't. We wish we did.'

Peat let go of his brother's hand and slapped him lightly on the back in a comradely way. 'No time for talk like that now. We have to put the traps back. You have some fine waders Boyd - why don't you help us,' said Peat, changing the subject.

'Not yet,' said Boyd, beginning to feel annoyed. 'You need to tell me what you know.'

'We don't know anything. We would like to tell you something, but we can't,' said Russ, wiping his still wet arms on his trousers.

'I don't believe you!'

Peat sighed, 'Boyd, it is not about believing. It is about knowing and we do not know where your father is – we would be more than happy to have the answer to that. We have to be going now.'

The two picked up their leather boots that were lying on the grass, and took the trap and the wooden buckets. Russ winced after he bent and lifted one of the buckets with his right hand. Peat nudged him aside, gave him the wicker craw trap to carry, and took both the heavy buckets himself.

'I can do it,' said Russ.

'Yes, and so can I,' said Peat. They walked away up the stream bank; Peat limped slightly, favouring one leg.

'Wait. I'm sorry,' Boyd called after them. 'I could… I can help.'

The brothers paused again and looked at each other, Russ nodded; Peat turned back to Boyd,

'Yes, you can come, but understand - we cannot answer your questions – not about your father.'

'Ok, I understand. Where are you going?' Boyd felt frustrated, but if they weren't going to talk… he could still maybe discover a few hints about what was going on.

'Upstream to check the traps, then back for evening chores. Here – you can take a bucket.'

Boyd tucked his fishing basket behind him and took one of the buckets; it was surprisingly heavy, no wonder Russ had winced when he went to lift it.

They walked up stream for about ten minutes in silence. Boyd was full of questions, but he didn't want to be sent away so he kept quiet and tried to think things over.

‘Here, this a good place, ‘said Peat. He dropped his boots on the grass, pulled his trouser-legs up again and slide down the steep bank into the clear water. As he did, Boyd saw the pink, newly healing scar that ran down his calf muscle from knee almost to ankle; it reminded him of the wound on the Hippogriff's leg.

‘Er… you hurt your leg - it looks nasty,’ said Boyd.

Both of them carefully avoided looking at Boyd.

‘Yes. An accident. It's getting better now,’ said Peat wading into the cold water, which was deep enough to hide the wound running down his leg. He bent over to take a look at the muddy bank.

‘Yes, there are holes. Pass me the trap.’

Russ stepped forward; he winced as he bent low to hand down the trap and put a hand to his ribs.

Peat looked up. ‘Have a seat, brother, rest a minute. I'll be done shortly.’

Russ smiled, ‘Can't let Broonie catch me sitting down.’

‘I figure we are far enough away from even his eagle eye – keep Boyd company for a bit, eh?’

Boyd was sitting on a nearby hummock of grass. He remembered the packet of fudge in his basket and took it out.

‘Sweet?’ he offered the paper bag to Russ.

Russ sat down next to Boyd with one hand pressed against his ribs; he gave a grateful sigh and eased his shoulder, then leaned over to peek into the bag, ‘Ah, Hazel gave you some of her tablet. Oh, this is good!’

He took a square of the sugary sweet and nibbled a corner at a time to make it last longer.

‘You save some for me you greedy beggars,’ called Peat.

'Don't worry, I will,' said Boyd. He looked around him, they were well above the loch and he could see quite a bit of it. He could even make out the tumble of rocks leading out from the bank where Buff and Rag were, though it was too far to see them clearly. 'Are they related, Buff… and I saw Gam last night, and Broonie?'

Peat had climbed out of the water, hanging on to tussocks of coarse sedge that grew from the bank. Boyd held the paper bag out to him. He took a piece and put the whole lump in his mouth and chewed slowly – which also meant he couldn't speak. He sat chewing slowly, his legs sprawled in front of him, gazing around the landscape, occasionally looking up at the sky.

Boyd waited a few moments before trying again.

'I just wondered…' began Boyd, but didn't know where to go with the rest of the question.

A few moments passed in silence, except for the wind in the grass.

'Any more tablet?' asked Russ.

'Sure – here.'

Russ picked another square and bit into it. 'They are related. And so are we…'

'Really? You don't look like them,' said Boyd, and instantly realised he had put his foot in it again.

Peat rolled down his trouser legs; he took a strip of dark green towelling from one of his many pockets and dried his feet off, then he took his socks out of his boots, and put them on. Russ took out his own cloth and did the same, drying his feet, and appearing to concentrate hard on tightening his boot laces.

'Sorry,' mumbled Boyd.

Peat turned around once his boots were firmly tied. 'No.

You'll hear the stories soon enough, best we say something now for ourselves.' He looked at Russ, who nodded agreement.

'We... there are three of us brothers... Our mother is a Broon, but not from these parts, she's a different lineage. She was took. Our father was not... one of us. That's why we're 'long', as they say, you'll notice we're taller, paler-skinned, and darker-haired, we don't see so well in the dark as other Broons, and we speak different.'

Boyd nodded,

'Our mother found her way out, she brought us with her, but she came through in a different place, somewhere she didn't know, down south near the city. We boys were all very, very young; we learnt the sound of the Angles' words early and lived there awhile. Wulfric Kennetson heard about us; he came to find us and bought us all here, and his Broons accepted us... well, mostly.'

Boyd wasn't sure what to say, he'd clearly stumbled on something that was difficult for them to talk about. He had lots of questions – through from where? Was it where the animals came from? What are the Broons? What does 'took' mean? Eventually he asked. 'Is your mother at the house as well?'

'No, said Russ. 'She found a place in the Islands with the Laird's help. She's comfortable there. We go and see her now and again.'

'You didn't want to go with her?'

Peat shook his head. 'We like it here. And we can be useful – nobody looks twice at us when we drive down to the village for supplies, or to the post office. 'Cept for him...' Peat leaned over with a broad grin and ruffled his brother's hair, '...all the girls have an eye for him!'

'Don't!' protested Russ, whether at the hair scrubbing or mentioning the girls, Boyd wasn't sure – yeah, he is pretty good looking - they both are I suppose. And, he thought, I can definitely tease Rag about him now.

Peat looked at the sky; the sun was lower in the west. 'Time we were going.'

'Can I come out with you again?'

The two brothers had already stood up. Peat looked at Russ, then Boyd, 'It can't hurt. Sometimes anyway – we could teach you how to tickle trout – could we not, Russ?' said Peat.

'What's that mean?' said Boyd.

'It's the old way, no hooks - you reach into the water so slowly the fish doesn't notice, and you stroke him gently… then you catch him up!' grinned Peat.

Russ nodded, 'We reckon you'll be better at that than flinging a line through the air – you're more a waterman.'

'I don't know – I didn't do that well at fishing.'

'Aye – we saw you,' Peat said, pretending to thrash the air furiously with a rod.

Even Boyd had to smile ruefully as they laughed.

'We're not always here…but you can come with us. Russ here - the Laird has him down to teach you archery anyway, when his shoulder has healed, and I'm to help teach you to ride. I'm sure Wulfric Kennetson will have something in mind for Van too – he's our older brother. He's not here just at the moment.'

'Archery – that's cool!'

'And your wee sister as well,' added Russ.

'Really? She can be a bit… annoying, you know?'

Peat handed Boyd one of the buckets of crawling crayfish.

'I can carry it!' Russ said.

'He's young - and your shoulder and ribs need a wee bit more time,' said Peat.

'How did you hurt them?' said Boyd.

'It was an accident,' said Peat and started to walk away, still limping slightly

Boyd took the heavy bucket and they started down the hill - he obviously wasn't getting any further answers, but if they were around he could try again tomorrow… and hope to find out more. They clearly knew things they weren't telling him.

As they got to the head of the loch Boyd saw Rag and Buff walking up to the house.

'Boyd, Boyd, I caught two fish!' Then she realised who he was with… 'Ooh…'

'This is my sister, Morag, we call her Rag… this is Peat… and Russ…'

They both took off their wide tam-o-shanter berets, and gave a touch of a bow. Buff hurrumphed and spoke to them in a language Boyd and Rag didn't understand, and walked away.

'He wants us to take the creels and rods back with us, and you are to go and get ready before supper,' said Peat, pulling his beret back on.

'But what did he say it in?' said Rag.

'Scottish Gaelic. That's the native tongue. They mostly understand the English, but they don't all speak it well,' said Russ.

'You do though… why's tha…' said Rag.

Boyd thrust his bucket under her nose. 'Look what we've got!'

Rag squealed and jumped back. 'Urrgh! What are those?!'

Boyd kept pushing the bucket towards her. 'Crayfish – you can eat them.'

'Yerch, no, go away. They look like creepy black spiders – you know I hate spiders!'

'We have to go,' said Peat. He put out his hand for the bucket. Russ collected the creels and rods.

'I could help you,' said Boyd quickly.

Russ shook his head; with his hair loose he had to toss his head to flick it clear from his face. 'No, these are light enough,' he said, 'Good evening to you. Miss Morag…' He gave a nod in Rag's direction and walked after his brother.

Rag's mouth gaped open… he called me 'Miss Morag', like in one of those old films…

Boyd playfully pushed her, 'With your mouth open like that, you look like one of your fish.'

'Oh Boyd, don't be horrible!'

She stomped off ahead of him towards the house. From a nearby tree, Duffy the crow watched with interest.

CHAPTER TWENTY

Uncle Wulf didn't come for supper, so they ate alone. After she'd finished her meal, Rag stood up and started to scrape the leftovers into one of the vegetable dishes.

'What's that for?'

'It's for Pookie,' said Rag

'How do you know what he's called?'

Rag was already on her way out of the room; she paused to check the corridor was empty before replying. 'I already said - he told me.'

'Wait – how did he tell you?' Boyd finished his last mouthful and quickly stacked the used plates and dishes into the dumb-waiter, then followed his sister upstairs.

'How did he tell you – was it words or pictures?'

'I don't know really, it just popped into my head,' said Rag

'That's what the Hippogriff did. I need to go back there tomorrow and speak to him again,' said Boyd.

'*WE* need to go back. Do you think he'd talk to me like that as well?'

Rag pushed her bedroom door open and headed straight for the small, alcove cupboard. The pukis was awake and wiggled with pleasure – whether at seeing her, or at the smell of the food, it was hard to say.

Boyd shrugged, 'Dunno. I'm going to use the computer. Are you ok - with him – with Pookie?'

Rag sat down on the floor and put the vegetable tureen down beside her. The pukis was almost instantly nose deep in the dish; Rag scratched him behind the ears.

'We're going to be fine, aren't we Pookie-woo?'

Boyd snorted, 'Pookie-woo!' He left them to it.

Rag sat back to watch her new pet gobble down the vegetables.

'He's just jealous - isn't he Pookie-wookie?

After a while Morag began to feel sleepy, the little clock on her bedside-table read 9 o'clock; she felt about ready for bed. The pukis had finished his dinner, and after she'd watched him drag some more of her shoes and things into the cupboard to add to his pile, she began to yawn and realised just how tired she was. She left the curtains partly open and the window ajar. She didn't know what to do about taking the pukis out to do his 'business', but there was a wide ledge outside the window so she hoped he might do it out there. He seemed happy here with her, so she didn't think he'd run away. As she climbed into bed she heard Boyd walk back to his room, and his door shut. She curled up and it wasn't long before she fell fast asleep.

It was after midnight. In Rag's bedroom, little snuffly snores came from the cupboard, and the occasional tiny wisp of smoke. Something scratched at her bedroom door. The scratching became more persistent - loud enough to wake Rag up. She opened bleary eyes, at first she thought it was the pukis, then she realised it was from outside the door. She rubbed her eyes, pushed back the covers, and stumbled over to the door and opened it. Frithjof the cat ran in, straight past Rag; he ran across the room, sniffing and mewing, and then made for the slightly open cupboard door.

'Whaaaa… No, no – go away cat!'

Rag tried to catch him, but Frithjof had clawed the door open. A pile of clothes and shoes fell out, along with the sleepy pukis.

The cat yowled and pounced. The pukis hissed in alarm and struggled free from the cat's claws, which scraped down his scales like fingernails on a blackboard. Hissing and giving tiny belches of flame, the pukis flew around the room and then up onto the curtain. Pookie clung there mewing and hissing flames… which singed the fabric. The big cat lunged and jumped after him, but the pukis was out of reach.

Rag frantically tried to get the cat out of the room; she grabbed pillows and threw them at him; he dodged out of the way easily, still intent on catching the flappy flying creature overhead.

'Shoo, shoo – don't hurt him!'

The cat ignored her – not taking his eyes off the pukis, he growled and jumped up at the curtains. The pukis mewed harder, and gave a proper little gout of flame, which made the curtains smoulder more… to the point of bursting into flames.

The cat jumped up the curtain again, wailing and hissing; he swiped with his claws at the pukis, making the little creature screech in alarm and spit more flame, before launching itself from the scorched curtain onto the chandelier. The coloured glass drops rattled and shook as the pukis flapped its wings, hissing in fear.

'Nooooo…' cried Rag.

The cat growled louder - leaping down from the curtain to dance and jump up and down – trying hard to reach the chandelier above him. Rag looked around helplessly. She spotted the spray perfume bottle on her dressing table and squirted some at the cat, who ignored her. Then she realised the curtains had flames flickering up them. All she could think of was 'put out the fire' – so she squirted the perfume bottle at the flames.

There was a *whoosh* as the alcohol in the perfume fed the blaze. Rag screamed. The cat howled at the pukis, who was chattering with rage from the safety of the swinging chandelier.

Boyd comes to the door in his pyjamas.

'What the…'He grabbed a jumper of Rag's and beat at the flames now spreading rapidly up the curtain.

'Go and get help!'

'How?'

'Run downstairs - shout fire!'

Rag ran outside shouting *Fire! Fire!* at the top of her lungs.

The cat kept howling. The pukis belched fire in its direction. Boyd picked up a shoe and threw it at the cat. 'Stop that!'

Suddenly Uncle Wulf appeared at the door, his hair loose, just an unbuttoned shirt over his trousers, and barefoot; close behind him was Gam carrying a leather bucket. Wulf switched the lights on, the sudden brightness made the pukis wail louder. He strode into the room and picked Boyd up under his armpits and swung him off his feet and safely out of the way.

Gam trotted over to the window and threw the contents of the bucket up the curtains. A great spray of white flakes, like thick snow settled over the blaze, damping it down, before the remains drifted to the floor and melted into a puddle. Broonie was close behind with another bucket; he flung flakes over the remaining flames - which died out completely, leaving a great blackened patch of ragged, singed cloth. He flicked the last few flakes at the cat, which ran out the door, pushing past Rag's legs. Rag stood in the doorway and stared at the chaos in front of her, at a complete loss for words.

Wulf put Boyd down now he was out of any danger, and stepping forward, held his left arm up towards the chandelier, making crooning noises to soothe the chittering pukis. The little creature settled its scales and calmed, before flying down to perch on Wulf's forearm. He stroked its head between the ears and the pukis mewed pitifully.

Rag crept slowly back into her wrecked bedroom. Wulf pushed his hair back from his face and looked at her in silence.

'Erm… Can I keep him?'

Wulfric Kennetson looked from her to the pukis, which dropped its head, looking the picture of guilt and remorse.

'Gam, Broonie – see that the fire is completely out. We will clear everything up tomorrow. Leave the window open to clear the smoke. Morag – are you hurt?'

She shook her head.

'Then we will speak tomorrow. Boyd are you hurt? Then go back to your room, back to bed.'

The Broons checked the curtains, collected their buckets and left.

'But…' said Boyd.

'Now is not the time. Go back to sleep both of you. Are you happy to remain in this room? Then into bed, Morag.'

Wulf stood in the middle of the room with the pukis riding

his forearm, waiting until Rag had climbed back into bed and pulled her covers up.

'Good.' Wulf guided Boyd out of the room. 'I will see you both at breakfast.'

Rag opened her mouth to say something.

'Goodnight Morag – you will sleep!' He moved his free hand in a tight gesture. No sooner had her head touched the pillow than Rag fell fast asleep. Wulf switched the light out and left, following Boyd into his room.

'I'm sorry,' mumbled Boyd. 'I… we didn't know it could do that.'

Uncle Wulf watched him climb back into his bed.

'No,' said Uncle Wulf, 'you did not. Go to sleep Boyd.' He made the same gesture with his fingers and paused for a moment to see that the boy's eyes were closed and his breathing slowing before he put the light off and left the room.

The pukis perched on his arm cheeped pathetically. 'Yes…' said Uncle Wulf. 'I know you are.'

CHAPTER TWENTY-ONE

The following morning, the youngsters got up and dressed quickly and quietly and went downstairs. All was as usual in the breakfast room, but Uncle Wulf was nowhere to be seen. Breakfast for Rag and Boyd was a matter of buttering toast and eating bacon and poached eggs quietly and trying hard not to guess what might happen to them.

'What do you think he'll do?' Rag said when she couldn't bear the silence any longer.

Boyd shrugged, his mouth was full of toast. Rag, rarely at a loss for words, didn't know what else to say. They carried on eating and waited.

Uncle Wulf arrived just as they were finishing, he came into the room, the pukis riding on his shoulder; it now had a little leather collar on. Wulf was carrying a wide basket, which he put on the floor in the corner. He pointed to it and the pukis meekly flew down and curled up inside. Uncle Wulf sat down at the table in silence. The three of them looked at each other. Eventually Wulf spoke first.

'You will have questions.'

Rag and Boyd nearly fell over each other trying to get their questions heard first.

'Who... What are they?'

‘Why are the animals here… what’s out there?’

‘What do you do…?’

‘Where is ‘there’… why is it different?’

Uncle Wulf raised a hand to stem the torrent of questions.

‘Where is our father?’ said Boyd.

At that Wulf paused, and with a sigh said, ‘I can honestly say – I do not know.’

‘Why not?’ said Rag.

‘Where’s he gone – Why’s he gone!’ said Boyd.

Wulf raised his hand to calm them down before he spoke.

‘You have found some things out for yourselves. This was not the ideal way for you to discover the nature of this place … so I will show you properly, and explain what I can. I will answer as many of your questions as I am able to while doing so.’

‘When?’ demanded Rag.

‘If you have finished breakfast we can go now.’ He stood up.

Both Rag and Boyd were on their feet straight away.

Uncle Wulf led them through unfamiliar corridors towards the back of the house, past what, by the resounding clash of pots and pans, was the kitchen and pantry; other small folk dressed in shades of brown peeked around corners to watch them as they went by. They walked past some half glazed doors that gave a glimpse into a very large glass-house full of plants, and even some small trees, and another heavy-looking door that muffled the dull rhythmic whine of a large engine, until they emerged through a very small door that Uncle Wulf had to duck his head down to get through, into an inner, covered courtyard.

The place was as big as a hay-barn, flagged with large, heavy stones worn smooth by years and years of feet walking over them. At both ends were almost full-height doors, large and wide, both sets had heavy bronze hinges and large ring handles, as well as an intricate engraved lock. Daylight shone down dimly through narrow, glazed panels in the roof.

Wulf led them towards the doors at one end of the barn. He placed his palm on the lockplate and muttered something. They heard the flick and glide as the mechanism inside released the tumblers, and the heavy bolt slide back. The doors opened, revealing another large, stone-floored room, now in darkness, and another set of huge heavy doors at the far end; these had two great beams of bronze barring them. Uncle Wulf went inside and beckoned the children to follow him.

As soon as they stepped over the threshold they felt the now familiar sensation, as if they were going down in a speeding lift; it felt for a moment like they'd left their stomachs behind and their legs had turned to jelly. Silently, the great doors swung shut behind them, closing with a solid thud and a whisper of air, leaving them in complete darkness.

'*Lios!*' called Wulf loudly.

The globes of the wall-mounted torches on either side ignited into glowing light. Wulf walked forward and palmed a second lock set into the wall beside the doors; he muttered and the great bronze bars slide smoothly back into recesses carved deep into the stone walls to either side of the door frame. He lent onto the huge doors with both hands and pushed hard, putting all his strength into moving them; slowly, they ponderously eased open, revealing... a stunning view of a whole new world.

They were high up, before them was a panoramic view across

rolling, vivid green grassland and trees, to wide brown moorlands sweeping up into rounded foothills, and beyond them, steep grey crags and white-topped mountains. A distant silvery river winked in the sunlight, before tumbling down a cascade running towards a long lake reflecting blue skies. The river ran onwards out of the far end of the strip of water, disappearing out of sight as it entered a sprawling forest of tall trees that marched up and over a series of hills. It was like their world, but not their world; this place seemed brighter, and the colours somehow clearer, more intense.

To their left, a wide paved road led away from the castle down the slope of the hill towards outbuildings, pens and animal enclosures. Boyd looked behind him, the castle loomed upwards; the towers and crenulations that had looked ruined before, now appeared whole, and more extensive, forming an altogether larger building.

'We had to go down a long way, down lots of stairs… to get to our door,' said Rag.

'There are half-forgotten doors here, both high and low – it is the nature of the Veil and the way it can tear. We seldom need to use this entrance, this is the largest portal, built for armies, but I wanted you to see from up here just how vast this land is. It is not just another place, it is another world, older perhaps than yours, certainly it is different – different inhabitants, and different rules are at work here.'

'But… what do you do? What did… does our father do?' said Boyd.

'Come this way and I will show you.' Uncle Wulf walked ahead of them, down towards the pens and stables.

At the bottom of the hill they meet Peat and Russ walking

back with empty feed buckets. They nodded their heads and touched their bonnets to Uncle Wulf. He nodded to them in return.

'How is your shoulder, Russ?'

'Aye Lord, it's healing nicely.'

'This is Morag and Boyd, they are my wards.'

'Yes, Master Kennetson, we met them yesterday when they were down by the loch,' said Peat. He favoured his injury as he stood, putting his weight on his other leg.

'Good. You will see more of them when they're ready to begin their lessons – we will not keep you.'

Uncle Wulf walked on, Rag and Boyd followed. The brothers smiled and nodded to Boyd as they went by. Russ winked at Rag as he passed her; she blushed and walked quickly after Uncle Wulf and Boyd.

Peat gave his brother a deliberate nudge in his injured ribs, which made Russ gasp, but he still gave a chuckle... which made Peat roll his eyes and shake his head. 'You know I don't mean anything by it, she's only a wee lass,' said Russ.

Rag turned her head to watch the brothers walk back towards the base of the castle and through a pair of open barn doors, nowhere near as massive as the ones she and Boyd had just walked through. It looked like that was the domestic route for the keepers, leading to store rooms and work rooms – she turned and quickened her step to catch up with Uncle Wulf and her brother.

Broonie came to the out-building door and stood, his hands on his hips, watching Wulf lead the children towards the pens. He shook his head, and then turned to Peat and Russ to give them gruff orders before stalking away. The brothers put away the buckets and started loading sacks of feed onto a low cart.

'They are very young,' said Russ.

'So were we once,' said Peat. 'We will soon see what they make of it.'

Chapter Twenty-Two

Wulf's two huge dogs, Geri and Freki, careered through the barn, and bounded out of the doors past the brothers. They cantered ponderously down the road, giving deep 'woofs' in greeting, their dark green, curly tails held high, and long shaggy ears flapping as they ran towards their master.

Down by the pens, Uncle Wulf stopped by several wicker baskets of windfall apples on a stone bench.

'Here, take some, most of the animals like apples,' he said.

Boyd nodded and took several. The dogs caught up with them, milling around them, their long, purple tongues lolling out of open mouths of sharp white teeth.

Rag rubbed Freki's head and ears; the big, dark green dog leant against her legs with pleasure at being fussed and nearly pushed her off balance.

'I mean… these aren't ordinary dogs are they?'

'They are *Cu Sith*,' said Uncle Wulf. 'It translates as Fairy Dog, but they aren't the bringers of doom and death that the local legends say. Likely that comes from the grain of truth behind most of those old tales – one of them probably came through a tear between the worlds and howled because he couldn't find his way back again. The locals will have chased him, and then suddenly, he found the hole, jumped through, and vanished. So they became howling demons that foretold bad luck and death.

Rag had stopped petting Freki at this point.

'Morrrrrrrrrrre…' rumbled Freki.

'Leave her Freki, you have had plenty of fuss,' said Uncle Wulf.

'Bissssssssscuit….?' whined Freki.

'Go and ask Gam… politely,' said Wulf.

Freki and Geri snuffled and trotted away.

'They talk!'

Uncle Wulf nodded, 'Not all animals can. Some have a few words, but their tongues do not always wrap around language easily – oh, as I said, given the chance, those two will sneak upstairs at night to get on the beds. Be sure to send them away, they know they are not supposed to sleep there.'

'Oh so it was really one of them who spoke to me!' said Boyd.

Uncle Wulf raised an eyebrow.

'Nothing – our first night, something got on the bed… Doesn't matter. So… is it we can understand their language? Or do they understand ours?' asked Boyd.

'A little of each. It is a phenomenon of this world, that unlike yours, although there are obscure tongues, and the language of rituals, everything here can communicate in the same speech.'

'So you don't have to learn, I don't know… something like you would French, or Spanish…' said Boyd.

'You could, but you do not need to – having said that, most races keep some secret words they only want their own kind to know. Some call the universal language Commonspeech, but it is really a case that you will always be understood if you want to be understood.'

'I don't get it,' said Rag.

Uncle Wulf smiled, 'It means that whatever is spoken aloud will be understood by the listener.'

'Do the animals know they are speaking Commonspeech or do they think they are just talking 'dog', or whatever they are,' asked Boyd, still trying to work this out.

'Some creatures are able to talk freely; some only have a few words. Some can briefly touch your mind with their thoughts. Some – do not communicate well - their minds are full of darkness, anger and panic; those we often cannot reason with or persuade, we have to catch them with nets and ropes and bring them back to where they belong.'

'That's here,' said Rag.

'To this side of the Veil, yes,' said Uncle Wulf.

'All those legends… about monsters and weird animals and stuff…' said Boyd, thinking about the pictures in the old books in his room.

'Many are true, some are very much exaggerated.' Wulf stopped by a pen and clicked his tongue. A dainty white horse with an exceptionally long mane and tail raised its head from a cropping the grass and looked at him warily; it had a narrow spiralling horn growing from its forehead.

'That's a…' gasped Rag.

'Yes,' said Uncle Wulf, 'They are very pretty beasts, but not really the brightest of creatures.'

The unicorn blinked long eyelashes at them and walked slowly towards them; avoiding Wulf, it made its way towards Rag. She noticed it had the neat, cloven hooves of a stag, rather than horses' hooves.

'They do love to be adored. I think that's why they seem to

deliberately look for places to push through the barrier between the worlds; they love being petted and admired. Unfortunately, they are the only animal that can make its own tear – the horn can piece the Veil, so we must keep a close eye on them, especially when a female looks likely to lay her egg.'

'They lay eggs…really?' said Rag.

'Yes - often in the nests of other creatures, or they just abandon them in hollows - parenting is not one of their skills.'

Out of reach of Wulf, the unicorn had headed for Rag, until it realised Boyd had apples in his hands. It immediately changed direction, put its head over the fence and whinnied softly, trying to nudge Boyd's arm. He gave it an apple. It nickered, and crunched the apple before staring at Boyd, blinking winsomely. Boyd saw it had a gilded leather collar around its neck, attached to a length of metal chain that glittered in the sunlight.

'Most, but not all, the creatures of legends and myths in your world are real in this one. For one reason or another they will have stumbled through and found themselves in your world, and having been seen, they were chased away or hunted – and became fabulous creatures of legend. Some of them are very frightening to look at, but are not necessarily dangerous, unless cornered. Some look benign, but will not give a second thought about eating you, or trying to. We find them and bring them back here where they belong.'

'And this is a… zoo?' asked Boyd.

The boy patted the unicorn's neck and the creature nudged his arm for another apple. Finding no more forthcoming, it transferred its attention to Rag. It nudged her hand resting on the fence and gazed into her eyes when she looked at it.

'More like a sanctuary... perhaps a rescue centre,' said Uncle Wulf, 'I am the Guardian; this portal is the largest in the North on this side of the ocean. And because I have to stay reasonably near to make sure the portal remains stable, I recruit helpers for the longer journeys that take time. They pass between the worlds, mainly helping find lost and injured creatures.'

'And you bring them all here,' said Rag, stroking the unicorn's head.

'The ones from this part of the world - in other places there are other Keeps and other Guardians. There are 'normal' animals as well here, cats, dogs, birds, horses and cattle which are owned and farmed by alfar – and others, and by humankind, just as your animals are. The other, more exotic, creatures... there are many different kinds - they used to be more prolific, but now, even here, they are what you would term endangered species. I help look after them.'

'How long have you been doing this?' asked Rag. The unicorn nickered to get her attention and Rag scratched its ears.

Uncle Wulf gave a small smile, 'A very long time.'

'And Dad helped you? And he never told us!' Boyd said, suddenly annoyed. The unicorn shied away from his raised voice. 'He left us - to help you! He left our mum!'

'He made his choice to join me – he and your mother. They both helped with our tasks.'

'Did they really have a choice – you bought them up,' said Boyd, 'they couldn't refuse you.'

'Oh yes they could – we all, all of us still have choices. That is a facility that never leaves you.'

'But what happened to him?' said Rag, 'Why isn't he here?'

The unicorn blew down its nostrils and nudged her for more fuss.

'Truthfully – I do not know,' said Wulf.

'Why can't you find out,' said Rag.

'I have tried.'

'What about the animals,' said Boyd suddenly, 'can't they tell you?'

'There have been rumours…'

'Then go - follow them, find him!' said Rag. The unicorn stepped away from her, shaking its head.

'It is not that easy,' said Uncle Wulf patiently.

'But…' shouted Rag, 'Why…? Why not!'

'Little one – if I knew where he was, I would go this instant and fetch him.'

Rag folded her arms in a sulk. The unicorn dropped its head, huffed in disapproval and shuffled backwards, before turning away.

'Are you even looking?' said Boyd bitterly.

Wulf stared at him in silence. Boyd lowered his gaze.

'Listen to me both of you – your father was well-trained. He had made many such journeys, sometimes for weeks at a time.'

'But why did he have to leave now,' Boyd was becoming angry again.

'Boyd, when your father left… He did not know that your mother was ill. Her message arrived a few days after he'd gone. I sent word, but they couldn't find him. I have searched, the Broons have searched, but we have not been able to find him…'

'But it has been months!' Rag interrupted. 'Why isn't he back?' She'd forgotten her previous fascination with the unicorn, now all her attention was on Uncle Wulf. The unicorn looked reproachful and wandered away, stopping to nibble at a juicy tussock of grass.

'I wish I knew. As soon as the Brothers have recovered, they will ride out again. Their other brother, Vandyke, has gone to the far south, he is due back soon.'

'Is that were Dad went? South?' said Rag.

'We had heard rumours, but... there is no positive news.'

'That's not good,' Boyd frowned. 'And the brothers - they got hurt?'

'To hear nothing is neither good, nor bad,' said Wulf, ignoring Boyd's question.

'They got hurt – so Dad could be hurt?' Boyd persisted.

'He may have... difficulties, but we will find him.'

Gam came down the road towards the pens. 'Here is Gam,' said Uncle Wulf, 'he will show you the other animals that are here. I have to go now. Morag – keep the pukis in check, be firm, he knows he has to answer to you.'

Wulf turned to walk away.

'Is that it?' said Boyd, raising his voice.

'For now, yes.'

Wulf paused and turned back to face the youngsters, 'I do not take Lachlan's disappearance lightly, but you can see,' he indicated the panorama of hills leading to the distant mountains. 'This is a whole world. In places the Veil folds in on itself, if he has stumbled through such a fold he could be thousands of miles away. He may not even realise we are looking for him.'

'But is he alright?' whispered Rag.

Uncle Wulf paused, 'I do believe so, yes,' he said, 'I would know if he was no longer here.'

'You mean if he was dead!' growled Boyd.

Wulf simply looked at him for several seconds. 'No. He is not dead.'

He turned and strode away, 'We will speak again and I will tell you what I can.'

Then he had gone, up the path and through the lower set of barn doors.

Chapter Twenty-Three

Boyd kicked out at an old wooden bucket that had been left near the fence. It broke apart and the remaining rainwater that had collected inside sprayed everywhere with the impact. He turned his back on the Keep and stared into the distance, fists shoved deep into his pockets.

Rag was seething inside, finally releasing her annoyance by yelling after Uncle Wulf had gone… 'You better had tell us when you know!'

Gam stood patiently nearby with a bucket of feed in one hand and a basket in the other. He beckoned to the youngsters, then handed Rag another shallow basket of windfall apples and patted her shoulder, tutting sympathetically.

…at least he understands how I feel, she thought, still annoyed with Uncle Wulf.

'Come. Come. I show, please.'

The unicorn perked up at the smell of fruit and came to Rag when she picked out a large apple and held it out through the fence. The unicorn gazed into her eyes again and fluttered its eyelashes as it delicately took the apple in its teeth. The girl stood very still and stared into the creature's eyes, feeling herself growing calmer as her anger somehow swiftly drifted away.

'Come now. Others are over here,' said Gam.

Rag tore herself away from the unicorn reluctantly; she and Boyd walked with Gam down towards the lower pens. She saw Boyd hadn't yet recovered his temper because of the way he kicked out at offending tussocks of grass along the way. The sky had begun to cloud over a little as if there might be rain.

They walked with Gam as he showed them different strange animals in pens, and eventually they were both distracted enough, and more in the mood to pay attention to the sights around them. Gam pointed out something that looked like a large buffalo, but it had two sets of widely curved horns at the side of its head, and a fifth horn curving upwards from the middle of its forehead. It looked cross and miserable, so they didn't get too near.

Gam rubbed his stomach and pointed to the buffalo, 'Bad guts – he eat too many water-lily roots. Not good for him. But he likes them.'

The miserable buffalo gave a mournful bellow and belched… and a stream of dirty liquid shot out from under its tail with considerable force.

'Eeuuww' said Rag, wrinkling her nose.

Gam nodded agreement and they walked on. The next paddock had a huge black boar in it, its bristles were so long and coarse they were almost like huge porcupine quills. There were two big bald patches though, one over its shoulder, and one the other side of its body over its ribs; in the middle of each patch was a jagged cut that was healing. The boar sniffed and turned towards them and they could see one of its eyes was filmed over grey-blue. It swayed its head trying to gauge where they were by scent. Gam threw an apple in its direction. It snuffled about and found it.

'Here - you throw to him.' Gam offered Boyd the basket of windfalls.

Boyd picked up an apple and launched it, nearly hitting the boar on the nose. The creature huffed in surprise, then gobbled it down, 'What happened to him?' said Boyd.

'Fighting,' said Gam. Rag wondered if she could ask, 'fighting what – or who' as there wasn't any further explanation. She threw a couple of apples in front of the boar's front feet; he snuffled and found them quickly.

Gam led them onward. The two brothers appeared pulling a flat cart with bags of grain on it, as they passed, Peat called out, 'Gamboge… they can come along with us and fill the hoppers - if you like?'

Gam looked up to the sky where the sun was veiled behind a grey cloud. He shrugged nodded, then pointed after the brothers: 'Go – they show. Yes, you go.'

Gam collected the basket from Rag and shooed them off, before returning to the keep.

Rag and Boyd followed the brothers who had turned off the main path towards a row of small sheds, each with a long run in front of it fenced off with copper wire mesh stretched between wooden posts. Behind the shelters were lidded half barrels raised on stone blocks, one to each shed.

'If you want to help – you can put out their feed,' said Peat. 'Here - four scoops in each – see, the grain falls through the chute inside the barrel. I'll leave you this sack and we will go to the next row.'

He hauled the half-empty sack off the cart and put it on the ground and handed Boyd a large painted tin scoop. 'You don't have to worry about spilling it; the birds will finish up what you drop.' Rag saw that in the nearby bushes was a very attentive flock of brown and bright blue sparrows, cheeping and fidgeting in anticipation.

'We will fill the rest and come back for you, we won't be long,' said Russ. The brothers turned the little flat cart and took the other sacks across the main pathway to another set of sheds from where the 'baaaa' of sheep could be heard.

'Can I scoop?' said Rag.

Boyd handed it over. 'I'll hold the sack open for you.'

Rag shoved the scoop in and a big trickle of grain fell off as she took it out of the sack. There was a very excited round of cheeping from the sparrows.

'Wait your turn,' said Boyd.

Rag needed both hands to hold the over-filled scoop, so Boyd lifted the hinged lid of the barrel to let her empty it inside. They could hear bleating from the shed.

'Sounds like goats,' said Rag.

Boyd just grunted, 'Remember to count the scoops as you go,' he said.

They had nearly finished all the barrels when the brothers came back with an empty cart. The sparrows flew down to raid the dropped grain as soon as they walked away from each barrel. Boyd and Rag saw a number of the smallish goats inside each run as they worked – there didn't seem to be anything strange about them… just goats.

Peat took up the empty sack from Boyd and dumped it in the cart along with the scoop Rag gave him back. 'What's special about these?' she said.

'Nothing,' said Peat.

'Then why are they here?' asked Boyd.

Peat was pulling the cart away; it was much lighter and didn't need the two of them to move it now. 'Ah…' he said, 'Over here, we'll show you.'

The path wound through a stand of tall trees, away from the grassed paddocks that curved around the base of the castle wall. On the other side of the trees, the pens were larger and had much higher fences; some of which were very substantial and completely enclosed the pens in thick mesh, top and sides. They were screened from each other by clumps of dense bushes and small trees.

Boyd recognised this sort of enclosure from normal zoos. 'This is for the dangerous animals, isn't it?'

Peat nodded. He parked the cart against a fence.

'This is why we keep goats…' said Russ.

'Oh you don't kill them,' burst out Rag, shocked.

'These are meat-eaters, lass. They will not survive on grass and grain,' he said, walking ahead.

Peat gave Rag a pat on the shoulder, 'Come, follow Russ… and you can have a wee look…'

Russ led them between the trees separating the large enclosures. Peat walked a half-step behind, with his hands lightly placed on both the youngsters' shoulders.

In the first enclosure was something muscular and very hairy. He looked like something between a shaggy bear and a gorilla, until he stood up from four legs onto two, then he looked like a man with a bear's head, with huge canine teeth that jutted outside its top and bottom lips. He saw them, bared his teeth and snarled.

'Calm, yerself, calm yerself…' said Ross soothingly. He hummed a little melody, almost like a lullaby and the Ogre went from snarling to grumbling.

'I will be back in a minute,' he said, and crossed to a large stone-walled shed off to one side, and came out with a large wicker basket piled high with big loaves of crusty bread, and bunches of luscious looking grapes.

'He has been fed this morning, and will be this evening – these are a midday snack to keep him sweet.' He winked at Rag - who was getting over being embarrassed by his jovial attention. Russ went to the head of the enclosure where there was a cave-like shelter built of stone. There was a barred door to one side. Russ palmed the lock and went into a small inner area where he opened the low hatch to put two loaves and some of the grapes inside the cage.

'The Ogres, ones like these, live in remote caves, in the far mountains,' said Peat, 'this one had fallen through and was staggering around in… you would say Iceland. The people there had shot and wounded it. We had to go and fetch it.'

'Is that how you got hurt?' said Boyd. Peat just shrugged his shoulders. 'So how will you take it back?' Boyd asked.

Russ returned to them. 'With difficulty… as they say,' he grinned.

'Some of these animals are really dangerous then – there really are monsters out there who will eat you?' asked Boyd.

'Some will,' agreed Russ. Rag was impressed that somebody could be so brave, she just stared at him.

'Not all the monstrous looking ones actually eat people – though admittedly he might,' Russ said nodding towards the ogre, '…some take your life force, your energy - they can drain it without killing you. Or they might just take all they can - then you'll die if you cannot get help.' Russ told them as they walked away.

'Like a vampire in the films,' said Rag with a shiver.

Peat smiled, 'Something like that,' he said, 'but they don't suck your blood – or talk in that strange accent! They normally eat ordinary animals as food – like we eat farmed animals: cattle, sheep, goats, chickens, or fish. The same as many of your wild animals eat other animals – it's just the way of things.'

They were approaching a high, fenced enclose that had canvas blinds pulled down around the inside. From inside Rag could hear a musical crooning from something with a deep pleasant voice.

'I mean some of the oldest, you might say the most primitive forms, like the Ogre over there, will kill you for food, but they are not usually the sentient ones. Those sorts are the creatures that are cognisant: 'they have the ability to think and communicate complex non-literal ideas and concepts' - that's what the Laird says. And they can do it because they have speech, or they can successfully transfer their coherent thoughts and ideas into your mind,' said Peat.

They stood still a short way from the curtained enclosure.

'But even if they think, they can still be prey to another animal – a lion, or tiger… a shark doesn't ask you if you can think clearly before he takes a bite!' added Russ. 'There's this giant bird in Arabia called a Roc - he's not one of your animals, so to speak, but he will eat you given the chance, whether you are sentient or not,' he said.

'Thoughts… that's telepathy,' said Boyd.

'I believe that's the right word. Some are better at it than others,' said Peat. 'And then there are the others, the different peoples who are like us - more than creatures… that includes humankind.'

Boyd frowned and was going to ask a question, but Russ saw it coming.

'In your world, you've generally forgotten about the other races, except in folktales and old books. Your own kind - that is generally all that most humans can see. But over here, there are many folks; some were born in your world, some choose to live in both worlds, or pass from one to the other regularly, but over there, on your side, we all know not to let humans know… well, not everything,' said Russ.

'So, you live… in our world, but you're not like us, not really - human?' said Rag.

'Yes, that's true, but we like it there, we are used to it,' Russ smiled, 'and since Wulfric Kennetson found us, we have a proper place, both here and there. Now - let's see if we can introduce you to somebody very special – wait here.'

'Are you sure about this Russ?' Peat said quietly.

Russ just grinned at him and winked, then walked towards the covered enclosure and scratched on the canvas; he paused, then tried again a little louder.

'Whhhooooomm?' boomed a deep voice from inside.

'Russet of the Broons, your eminence. I and my brother have guests who would very much like to meet you, if you would allow it…'

'Visitors…? You may advance so I can see them.'

Russ beckoned them forward. Peat whispered to them, 'Best behaviour, he can be a bit touchy.'

Chapter Twenty-Four

They could hear something large and heavy shifting and rustling behind the hanging cloths, and then something sniffed the air, trying to get their scent.

'Will he eat us?' Rag whispered to Peat, who shook his head, 'I doubt it.' A phrase which Rag didn't find particularly comforting!

'Advance and be recognised,' rumbled the voice, and a section of the blinds rolled up, revealing the huge, knobbly, steel-blue scaled head of an ancient dragon.

He stared at them for a moment in silence. Russ and Peat made deep bows from the waist. Rag and Boyd stood open-mouthed and staring.

'Bow!' hissed Peat. Belatedly they did so. The Dragon blinked, the inner eyelid flickering swiftly across his great golden eyes before the scaled outer lid sank slowly, then rose; he flicked out a narrow forked-tongue, like a snake's, tasting their scent on the air.

'Russet of the Broons, you may introduce my guests…' the dragon boomed.

'This is…' Russ began, 'What are you full given names, quickly now!'

'Boyd Osvald Norman Ellis.' Boyd whispered. Russ repeated the name.

'Morag Mia Ellis,'

'Thank you,' said the Dragon before Russ could repeat her name. 'You have brought me a gift of fruit.'

'I have, your eminence.'

'Let the youngest, the Morag, bring it to me.'

Russ hesitated, 'These are the wards of Wulfric Kennetson...'

'Fool!' rumbled the Dragon, so deeply the ground vibrated under him. 'Do you think I would break the laws of hospitality, especially in His Hall?' The enclosure rattled as the dragon stirred.

'No, no – your grace.' Russ said hurriedly. He turned to Rag, 'You can leave if you want, lass. We can calm him... probably,' he whispered, looking unsure.

Peat had Boyd by the arm and dragged him back a step, before Boyd tried to pull away.

Rag shook her head, swallowing hard, 'I... I... just give him the basket, right?'

Russ nodded to her. 'Your eminence, I must come forward to open the gate for the maid.'

'Granted.' The dragon had settled again so its scaly head was resting on its two front feet... which had truly enormous, gleaming claws.

'You will be fine, lass – He has invoked the law of hospitality, it means he can't harm you,' whispered Russ. They walked the few paces forward and Rag slipped her hand into Russ's hand for comfort. He squeezed it and whispered, 'You're very brave, just be polite and speak when you're spoken to...' He unlatched a gate meant for someone of a broon's height.

'You may step back Russet of the Broons, I would have a moment.'

Russ squeezed her hand and gave her the basket of fruit and bread, 'I'm just here,' he whispered, then took three steps backwards.

Peat had a firm hold of Boyd. 'Do. Not. Do a thing!' he hissed in Boyd's ear, 'She will be fine.'

The dragon raised its head, rumbled at the back of its throat then put its muzzle down lower to get a clearer look at Rag; his tongue flicked out.

'I smell one of my distant cousins on you…'

Rag nodded furiously, shaking in her shoes.

'The pukis likes you…'

'I think so… sir,' Rag stuttered.

There was more deep rumbling from the dragon's throat… which Rag suddenly realised was laughter. Peat relaxed his grip on Boyd's arm. Russ heaved a sigh of relief. Rag smiled hesitantly and held out the basket.

'I have seen you, child. You may put down the gift. I accept it.'

She took a step forward and put down the large basket inside the enclosure, before stepping back.

'I shall sleep now. You may leave me, Morag Mia Ellis. I will remember you should we meet again.' The dragon raised its head, lifted a foot and with a claw caught the edge of the blind and pulled it down, vanishing from their sight. 'Russet of the Broons, you and your brother may approach later and cleanse the scat,' he rumbled from behind the canvas.

Russ stepped forward, grabbed Rag's hand and pulled her back with him, and all four walked away quickly.

'That was a Dragon!' breathed Rag.

'Why did you take us somewhere that dangerous!' snapped Boyd.

'A Dragon!'

'Shut up Rag!' Boyd was frightened, which made him cross.

Russ pointed to a path through another stand of trees, and they walked in that direction. 'We were fine,' he said, 'though I did think he'd be asleep. He usually has a nap about now. We'd best be ready, Peat – splat duty!'

Boyd was still too cross to speak.

'That was a dragon…' mumbled Rag.

'Yes,' sighed Peat, 'And one who will tell the Laird we disturbed him.' He gave his brother a push that made him stagger.

'We were fine,' said Russ, 'He invoked the law of hospitality.'

Peat gave a non-committal grunt that Boyd took to mean '…and what if he hadn't?'

'Russ…' began Rag, '…what's splat duty?'

They were approaching an open-sided hut with a bench and table under some sheltering trees. The threatened rain was still holding off.

Peat laughed out loud, 'You tell her brother - then she may not be so keen to hold your hand!'

Russ sighed, 'After lunch?'

'Why not now? Is this something else we should know about?' said Boyd.

Peat chuckled and slapped Boyd on the back, 'I very much doubt it.'

They had reached the shelter, Peat pointed to the bench. 'Sit down a bit. Go on then brother - explain to our guests what our illustrious duties are for today – because you upset The Broon!'

'It was not my fault entirely!'

'What is it?' said Rag, 'What did you do?'

'Doesn't matter...' said Russ, 'why don't we forget about it.'

Peat was still grinning broadly, and Boyd sensed there was a story here.

'No,' said Boyd, 'you can tell us.'

Peat started to walk towards the low wooden building that was a little further along the path, beyond it was a deep ditch, with a newly-built structure of criss-crossed lathes of pale wood and copper mesh, sloping down from the far end of the shed and reaching across the ditch.

'I will fill the water butt – we don't want to run out like last time,' called Peat.

Russ shouted after him, 'That wasn't my fault either! Sandy and Tan had not turned the sluice gate.'

Peat raised one hand, but in agreement or derision it was hard to tell.

'Are you keeping something from us?' demanded Boyd.

'No, laddie,' said Russ ruefully, 'it's just that it is a wee bit embarrassing... We have the dubious honour of clearing away, then washing the dragon's scat... his shit.'

'Oh...' said Boyd, 'so - 'splat' duty...'

Russ nodded.

'Ugh – like the buffalo thing?' said Rag.

'Fortunately no, it's really quite dry, but it is what it is... are you sure you want to hear about this?'

Peat returned, 'It's filling up, we're here for a good half hour maybe.'

'Time for lunch then,' said Russ, 'Do you want some? We have enough.' Boyd could see inside the hut there was a mesh framed box raised well off the ground, with two cloth-covered baskets inside. Russ got one out, uncovered it and held it up, 'See?'

‘I’d like some,’ said Rag, ‘have you got any water, I’m thirsty.’

There were bottles of water in the baskets, along with ham sandwiches, cheese scones, parsnip crisps, and slices of dried apple with a crunchy honeycomb crust. They divided it between them. Boyd felt in a better mood after having had some food.

‘I think you can tell us what you have to do now,’ he said.

Russ stuffed his remaining apple slices in his mouth and mumbled around them,

‘Eating… you tell…’ he muttered.

Peat shook his head, took a sip of water and put the bottle down. Rag and Boyd looked at him expectantly. Peat rolled his eyes.

‘All right – dragons… have a… delicate digestion. If they eat something hard, they will bring it up – you’ve seen a cat heave up a fur-ball?’ Rag wrinkled her nose and nodded. ‘Well you have the picture then – armour, weapons, jewellery, belt-buckles… they all come up…’

‘Wait,’ said Boyd, ‘Armour?’

‘If people go up against a dragon they tend to go in fully prepared,’ said Russ, helping himself to Peat’s leftover apple slices.

‘And they get eaten…!’

Russ shrugged, ‘You do not mess with dragons.’

‘But you have to…’ said Rag.

‘Yes,’ agreed Peat, ‘and we are exceptionally polite about it – and the end product… from his end product… is actually quite valuable.’

‘No!’ exclaimed Rag.

‘Oh yes,’ said Russ, warming to the subject now, ‘They can’t digest hair, fleece or fur; it passes straight through – if you see what I mean. Our duty of the day is to collect it, and wash it to get the fibres out'

'That's horrible,' said Rag, 'Broonie must have been seriously mad at you two.'

'We mainly all have to take turns,' said Peat, 'while his eminence is here – it's not often we have a dragon as a guest.'

'So… why is a dragon here?'

'He had been hunted. A cold-iron arrow had damaged his wing and dislodged some scales on his side…'

'I thought you didn't use cold-iron,' said Boyd.

The brothers looked at each other. Then Peat said, 'It was not one of us – it was humankind.'

'Here - on this side?'

Russ nodded.

'So how did the dragon escape them?' Boyd asked.

Russ shrugged, 'They breathe fire.'

'Oh,' said Boyd.

'But how did he get here, to you?' asked Rag

'The Dragons all know we're here - he knows Wulfric Kennetson will help him, so he came – as an honoured guest. The reason he's down here… well, there's nowhere else large enough for him to sleep. And if he was wandering around freely… the rest of the stock would be frightened to death – remember, they are meat-eaters, polite ones, even royal… but carnivores.' said Peat. 'So he stays down here – look on it as a sort of tent rather than a cage.'

'Wow…' breathed Rag, for once at a loss for questions… which Boyd wasn't.

'But why… what fibre?'

'The sheep's wool? Once it has passed through a dragon's gut it's fireproof… among other things. You can spin it, weave it into fire-proof coats, stuff it in a gambeson…' said Peat.

'That's gross,' said Rag.

'No,' said Russ, 'it is his favour to us. He prefers goat, but we feed him sheep to get the wool and he obliges us by eating them. It's all very fair in the long run.'

'Anyway,' Peat slapped his thighs, 'Broonie will be after us for slaking, so we'd best take you back.'

'Can we come again?' said Rag.

Peat considered, 'I am sure the Laird will say yes, but after such an introduction he may well hang my foolish young brother up by his heels and use him for target practise!'

'Oh no!' said Rag, genuinely concerned.

'Don't worry yourself. The Laird will bark, but he won't bite… at least, not that much,' said Russ, but he didn't look that sure about it.

'I'll say it was my fault,' said Rag.

'Lass – if it's one thing the Laird always knows, it is when you're telling the truth.' said Peat. 'My wee brother and I did this together, we'll see to it through together.'

Boyd had walked away and was standing to one side staring though the trees out onto the expanse of moorlands beyond. 'That's the world out there isn't it?' he said.

Peat nodded. 'Yes, in a manner of speaking…'

'Is it dangerous?'

'Some of it is – but danger is more the people in it,' said Peat. 'Don't think about going out there yet a while; you've plenty to discover, and to learn, before that.'

'But your brother has gone to the south – which way is that?'

Peat pointed back, past the castle, 'But you're not thinking of going, are you?'

Boyd was looking out over the moors towards the distant mountains. 'Of course not,' said Boyd. He turned, 'Look - we'll be ok getting back on our own. I know you're going to be busy – it's just following the main path isn't it?'

'That's right – you'll keep straight won't you?' said Russ.

'Sure, of course,' said Boyd with a smile, 'I can carry the baskets back for you. We'd better let you get on…'

Peat slapped his brother on his good shoulder and chuckled, 'Oh yes brother - you can rake it. I'll shovel.'

Russ gave a huge sigh that said it all. Peat handed them the empty baskets,

'Keep to the main path - they'll be someone around near the barn to let you through. Take care now.'

'Bye,' called Rag.

The two brothers walked away. Rag and Boyd set off back towards the Keep. By the time they reached it, the rain had started, not heavy but persistent, enough to take them inside for the rest of the day and evening.

Chapter Twenty-Five

In Rag's bedroom that evening, she watched the pukis struggling to drag one of her waders into its basket. There were already a number of her shoes in there. She heard a soft knock on her door.

'Rag? It's me.' Her brother paused until he heard her say 'come in.' Rag got off the bed and sat down quickly on the floor cross-legged, watching the pukis.

Boyd opened the door and stood just inside the room for a moment looking at the little, dragon-like pukis, who with a final tug, aided by some wing power, succeeded in getting the large boot over the rim of the basket. The little scaly green creature trod round and round a few times like a cat, before settling onto the pile of Rag's belongings.

'Why do you let him do that,' said Boyd, coming into the room.

'If I let him have my shoes he leaves my other stuff alone,' said Rag with a sigh. 'I miss having all of my other things from home.'

'I didn't think you'd bought those red boots with you… or those sandals,'

'No…' said Rag, taking a closer look, 'neither did I.'

Boyd flopped down on the end of her bed. He landed next to

a large hard lump, surprised, he flicked the quilt back. Hidden underneath was a back-pack, already filled.

Rag deliberately concentrated her attention on the drowsing pukis.

'Rag…'

She turned to face her brother, 'So - what?'

'You're not going!'

'Want to stop me?' She turned and was up on her knees.

'You're not going – I am.'

'No way!'

'I can find the direction Dad took. The Hippogriff showed me.'

Rag jumped to her feet, 'I'm going too. This was my idea.'

'I have a compass.'

Rag was having none of it, 'If I don't go – I'll tell Uncle Wulf.'

Boyd stood up, 'What good will that do? We'll both be banned. He could probably put a spell on us or something.'

Rag folded her arms and snorted her derision, 'He's not Gandalf!'

'Look, the Hippogriff… not exactly showed me, but there is a place he thinks Dad was going to. It's two days from here. I can camp out for one night, and then look for him.'

'I can do that. I'm not frightened of being out at night,' said Rag.

'You won't like it.' said Boyd

'I don't care. You are not going without me. Either I go, or I tell…'

'You wouldn't really say anything…?'

'Just try me,' growled Rag.

'It's too dangerous. You heard what Russ and Peat said'

Rag took a step towards the bed, and rummaging in her pack; she dragged her knife out and pulled it from its sheath.

'Doesn't mean you know how to use it,' said Boyd.

Rag waved the sharp knife in Boyd's direction, 'I can use this as well as you can use yours – and if you don't say you'll let me come with you, I'll go straight to Uncle Wulf, right now.'

She slammed the slender knife back into the leather sheath, but held onto it by the hilt as she faced down her brother.

Boyd could see he was getting nowhere.

'You have to promise,' he said reluctantly, 'if there is any trouble, anything at all, you'll run straight back to the castle for help.'

Rag grinned in triumph, 'So – shall we go tonight?'

Boyd shook his head, 'No. We better go tomorrow morning. They'll start looking for us straight away if we're not down for breakfast. We say we're going bird-watching or something. It'll be hours before anybody looks for us. In the meantime, we sneak down the stairs to our door. We can go around the edge of the pens and go from there.'

'You've been thinking about this,' said Rag.

'I had a good look yesterday, first while Gam was showing you those *skyader*... bunny things – then at the far end of the paddocks with Russ and Peat. I think we can avoid those and go to the other side of the woods and out on to the Moors.'

'Yeah... the *skyader* lay eggs you know. I wonder if that's where the story of the Easter Bunny came from? You know, half hare, half what was it... capercaille, I think he said.'

'Focus Rag – we have to do this right or they'll catch us.'

'I know - I'm not stupid. You already had this planned didn't you?'

'Better than just walking out and not knowing where I was going.'

'I was going to take the unicorn with me,' said Rag.

'Like nobody would have noticed that was missing!'

'Well he wants to leave. They only keep him here because he can go through the veil thingie.'

'How do you know?'

'He told me,' said Rag smugly, 'See, I can talk to animals as well, not just you and the Hippogriff.'

'But we don't need to go through the Veil; we are going to be on that side.'

'Yes,' said Rag, 'but we might need to get back to our side in a hurry.'

'Oh. I suppose so. But you couldn't bring a unicorn back through with you, that would make us too obvious.'

'No. I was going to leave him there, on his side.'

'He might have been in danger too,' Boyd said.

Rag considered for a moment, 'Well, I'm sure he can run fast.'

Boyd shook his head, 'I think I saw where Dad was going. I don't think we're big enough to be noticed by anybody out there. So we go straight there and if he's not around – it's a wood with a wall around it and there's a sort of cave entrance under a cliff – it leads somewhere important, but the Hippogriff was a bit hazy about what. Anyway, if he's not there, we come straight back – is that agreed?

Rag thought about it.

'Rag you have to agree. We can't wander around, we won't have enough food. If we take toast and sausages from breakfast, and whatever we can carry, we can have enough for two days, maybe three if we're very careful.'

'Two days,' said Rag, 'If Dad is that close, why haven't they found him?'

Boyd shrugged, 'Uncle Wulf said this Vandyke, the other brother, is coming back from the south, that's the wrong way.'

'Where are we going then?'

'North.'

In the morning, when Rag went down to the breakfast room – Boyd had taken all the sausages out of the tureen and put them between slices of toast. Rag found the Broons had sent up several boiled eggs as well as scrambled.

'We can take these too,' she said to Boyd.

'Yes, wrap them in a napkin – some might be soft-boiled but we can still eat them when they're cold.'

Just then the whistle sounded and the dumb waiter started to rattle its way upwards. When Rag opened it she found two small, woven cane lunchboxes. She took them out and brought them to the table to show Boyd – each contained a neat parcel of cheese sandwiches, a paper bag of cherry tomatoes, an apple and a bag of Hazel's sweet tablet.

'Great, I told them we wanted a picnic lunch – we can put the other stuff in there as well – just take the paper bags out, we can put those in our coat pockets,' said Boyd.

They went back up to their bedrooms, feeling that at every turn they would run into Uncle Wulf and he would demand to know where they were going… but they didn't. The household was busy doing its normal chores and nobody was around to challenge them.

Once upstairs, they decided to wear their new hiking boots rather than wellingtons. Boyd insisted they wore the sturdy waxed coats. He still had a plastic water bottle from their journey up to Scotland, which he re-filled from the bathroom tap. He checked he had everything he thought he'd need in his rucksack – compass, binoculars, water, food, extra sweater, socks....

He got his Scottish knife and sheath from the top drawer and strapped it to his calf; inside his sock and beneath the leg of his jeans... just in case. He had no idea what might cause him to use it, and it didn't feel good thinking he might have to... but it seemed a 'good idea' to have it.

He looked around his room before he left – bed made, clothes hanging up, a few books on the desk... yes, everything looked normal. He went and knocked on Rag's door.

'Is that you Boyd? '

He opened the door – it looked like an explosion in a clothes factory, garments everywhere... so no different than usual then! Rag was propping the window slightly open with some books.

'For Pookie – he can get out if he wants to. I feed him the apple and a cheese sandwich and he's fast asleep now.'

Boyd could see the pukis snoring contentedly on a pile of Rag's shoes and tee-shirts.

'I still don't know that you should let him do that – collect your stuff like that,' Boyd said as she half-closed the cupboard door.

'He likes it. It makes him comfortable to have my things around him. I wish I had more of my own stuff here.'

'Maybe we can ask Uncle Wulf to take us to get some more things, or have them sent by post. Auntie Carol would parcel them up.'

'But she doesn't have a key anymore – I don't think,' said Rag sadly.

'We'll ask when we get back,' said Boyd, 'though we might have to wait a bit. We're probably going to be grounded after this.'

'But we have to DO something to help Dad!' said Rag.

'I know. Have you got everything? Got your knife with you – just in case?'

Rag nodded, 'I put it in my backpack.'

'Ok – let's go,'

They tried hard not to tip-toe - because that would look suspicious, but they walked as quietly as they could. They went down the passage, down the long, spiral staircase leading to the tiny courtyard at the bottom of the Keep's tower. They had already decided on the place they could slip away from most easily - across an empty paddock, where they could see the shelter-belt of trees beyond. Through those and make their way out onto the moors and go north.

Beyond that neither of them had much of an idea. Boyd wasn't all that happy about taking Rag with him, but he knew he couldn't leave her behind because she'd go and tell on him straight away. She'd said she would, and he didn't doubt her.

Rag wasn't really thinking very far ahead – they would have to walk a long way, and Boyd thought he knew where - and they would find Dad. She wasn't going any further than that in her mind. Once they had him back everything would be fine again. They didn't have Mum... but they would have him, and that was all she wanted.

They checked carefully, the way was clear – nobody was around, although they could hear some distant laughter that might have been Russ and Peat. It came from the top end of the enclosures, and they decided if they crossed quickly they wouldn't be noticed. They climbed the railings, slipped over the top and ran across the paddock; climbed the fence and raced into the trees that now hid them from view. They paused, out of breath from excitement. They could see across towards the path that led to the dragon's tent and the 'dangerous creatures'.

'This is it,' said Boyd, 'Are you sure you want to come? You can still go back.'

Rag shook her head, 'If you're going, I'm going.'

The sky was a little cloudy, but it didn't look like it was going to rain. They started to walk through the woods, towards the moorland to where they had a clear view so Boyd could take a compass reading to find north.

Chapter Twenty-Six

North turned out to be beyond the woods they'd just left. They retraced their steps through clusters of silver birch. There, the trees lessened in number, but became larger and older, ash, alder and oak… and then mainly oak trees. Boyd had sort of got his direction but they had to make detours around bushes and scrub and old fallen trees.

It was also feeling much warmer underneath the leaf canopy. Rag took her coat off, took her hoodie off and stuffed it in her backpack and put her coat back on. Boyd was a little way ahead, but stopped for her to catch up; there was a large fallen tree nearby that looked like a good place to sit down for a moment. He waited for his sister, and took out his water-bottle for a drink. Rag caught up with him and flopped down on the log.

'Warm, isn't it?' she said.

Boyd nodded. He felt in his pocket and found the bag of cherry tomatoes, and took a couple out to eat.

'The wood looks thinner over there – I think we should go that way and then take another compass reading. It should be easier walking outside of the wood,' he said.

Rag nodded – she dug a packet out of her pocket, but she chose the sweet tablet. Just then she heard a tiny rustle in the dry leaves.

'Boyd...'

There was another rustle.

'I know...' he said quietly. 'Pick your bag up... in case we need to run...'

They were both looking at the same place when there were more rustles... and a sharp muzzle with a black nose peeked out from a thick tangle of briars, followed by a triangular face with bright eyes and pointed red ears – a fox! The pair of them sat very still, not frightened but wary... the fox watched them, saw they were still and hopped out a little further holding its front paw up so it had to walk on three legs.

'It's hurt its foot,' whispered Rag.

The fox looked very sad and lowered its head and hopped painfully forward making little whining noises. It came closer then lay down a few feet away from them.

'It seems friendly enough,' Rag whispered again.

The fox lifted its nose and sniffed a few times before giving another pathetic little moan. Rag and Boyd sat very still... it edged a little way forward, not taking its eyes from the youngsters.

'Do you think I can stroke - her?' said Rag. 'I'm going to stroke her.'

'Wait,' said Boyd, but she'd already put her backpack on the ground and begun to stand slowly. The fox didn't take its eyes off her.

'Rag – foxes have a nasty bite. Be careful!'

The fox sniffed again and edged towards the backpack on the ground. Rag took a step forward and bent over, just running her fingertips across the top of its head. The fox laid its ears back, but edged another fraction closer to the backpack – still sniffing inquisitively.

'I think she's hungry. I bet she can smell those sausages,' said Rag.

The fox moaned like a dog waiting for a treat and gave a little yip of agreement.

'Is that what you want, eh?' Rag carefully sat back down and unfastened her pack and took out her lunchbox without making any sudden movements.

'Rag, if you must feed it, make sure you throw the sausage on the ground. You don't want your fingers bitten.'

Rag took a sausage and tossed it a little way away. The fox moaned and pulled itself painfully towards the sausage on its belly – which when she got to it, she wolfed down in one mouthful.

'Ah, she's hurt – that's why she's hungry!'

She threw the next one down a bit closer to where she was sitting. That was eaten quickly, along with two more. Rag was nearly out of sausages.

'Boyd, give her one of yours.'

The fox turned its face to Boyd and blinked adoringly, giving a pitiful little whine. She looked so forlorn. Boyd sighed and also took out his lunchbox and peeled a couple of sausages away from the toast.

Just then, they heard more little rustles and tiny sniffles and out of the briar crawled four little fox cubs. The rolled on their backs and looked up adoringly at Rag. Mother Fox gave another pitiful moan and having crawled closer to Boyd, laid her head on his foot, looking up at him imploringly. He couldn't resist her pleading look and fed her a sausage.

The four cubs gambolled at Rag's feet alternatively mewing

and sniffing the air. 'They're hungry too. I've only got one sausage left - give me some of yours for the other cubs.'

Rag put her lunch box down on the log, and stood to reach over to Boyd. In a sudden flurry of movement, Mother Fox jumped up and snatched the sausage sandwich from Boyd's fingers, knocked his lunch-box off his knee scattering the contents over the leaf mould and dirt, and bolted – using all four legs!

The cubs jumped for Rag's lunch box, knocked it over and cleared it out, apart from the apple, and chased after their mother – one paused to grab a cheese sandwich of Boyd's... another snatched up a hard-boiled egg, before all of them disappeared back under the thick briar-patch in an instant

'What...' yelped Boyd, shaking his nipped fingers.

'Oooo... they've eaten all of it!' said Rag.

From the bushes came a tittering series of high-pitched wheezy little barks, which only diminished as the foxes ran away.

The two youngsters were stunned.

'Those foxes was laughing at us!' said Rag.

'I think you're right,' said Boyd. 'Let's get out of these woods and start walking.'

'But that was just mean!' said Rag.

'Yeah... well...'

Boyd looked at the scattered remnants of food. The remaining buttered toast were covered in dust and twigs; he retrieved two hard boiled eggs that seemed ok, put his lunch-box away and fastened his back pack up and slung it on. Rag crossly gathered her nearly empty lunchbox; the apple had rolled away, but didn't look too bad... She polished it on her sleeve and took a bite – it seemed pointless putting it back in the box on its own. She put the box in her pack and stumped after Boyd, who was heading for where the trees seemed thinnest.

'Foxes!' she muttered in disgust.

It had turned out to be a sunny day with just a scattering of small woolly clouds drifting across the clear blue sky. They walked for some time; the moor wasn't that easy to cross, the undulating ground was uneven, and the tough sedge grasses grew in big thick tussocks that you had to walk around, rather than risk turning your ankle by treading on them. The heather spread its branches widely and although quite low, it could catch your toes and make you stumble. Come mid-morning, they were hungry and ate what little remained of their food.

Later, the sun was high overhead; the clouds had thinned, leaving a heat haze around the edges of the moor so that far-off rising hills looked misty blue and all very much alike. The woods were far behind them, no more than a darker smudge against the distant grey stone towers of the castle. Even that was barely visible in front of the bluish line of hills on the horizon, beyond the moorland that rose and fell in great sweeps of grey-green ground.

Rag had taken off her waxed jacket and buckled it to her backpack. She was hot and thirsty. She stopped to take off her pack and pull open a side-pocket, looking for her water-bottle. When she took it out, it felt disappointingly light; she gave it a shake discovering it was almost empty. She drank the last mouthful and gave a heartfelt sigh. She looked across the moor towards Boyd, striding ahead of her.

'It's alright for him,' she muttered aloud. 'He's got long legs!'

Boyd had loosened his coat so it flapped open as he walked; having decided it was easier to wear it than carry it. He slogged doggedly down a narrow animal-made path that was little more than a wavy line of bare ground between coarse grass and low-growing heathers – until he realised his sister was not behind him anymore. He'd started to think that he should have done this by himself.

As he waited for her to catch up, he put the binoculars hanging around his neck to his eyes, adjusting the focus as he tried to find some sort of landmark they could aim for; he scanned the horizon all around them, but nothing seemed obvious. Rag came to a stop a few feet away from him.

'You don't know where we are, do you?' she said accusingly.

Boyd let the field-glasses drop to hang by their leather strap and turned to carry on walking down the faint path.

'Boyd! Wait!'

He slowed a little but didn't stop. Rag trotted forward and caught him by the sleeve. 'We have been walking for hours.'

Boyd didn't reply. He took the brass compass out of his pocket and checked the direction, turning it around and around to get the metal spindle inside to settle on a bearing.

'You're not fooling anyone with that!'

Finally irritated enough to reply, Boyd blurted out,

'I told you not to come!'

'You said you knew where to go,' said Rag, dropping her pack to the ground.

'I said I knew which direction, I didn't say 'where'.'

'I'm thirsty,' said Rag.

Boyd looked through his binoculars again, scanning the moorland near at hand. A tiny flash of reflected light attracted his attention and he refocused the lenses to get a better look.

'I think there's a stream over that way – we can fill the bottles.' He pointed to a fold in the ground someway away where the moorland dipped down; a narrow rill of water fell over the rounded edge, glittering now and again in the sunshine. He moved off the path towards the little stream. Rag picked up her bag wearily and followed him, kicking through the heather sullenly as she walked.

'Do you think they've missed us yet?'

Boyd didn't say anything. He was concentrating on the shiny glitter so he didn't lose sight of the tiny waterway amongst the monotonously brownish-green heathers.

Having shouldered her back-pack, Rag stumbled after him, she was tired and she wanted to sit down, and was hoping that her brother would agree to rest for a bit when they got to the stream, because her legs were aching, and her back.

It took a little while to get to the tiny stream, which they found rippled over and down through a little cleft of rocks, before dropping much further to flow on through a long, narrow gully caved by water running over it for many long ages. They could see that further down it widened out considerably; small trees had rooted and grown among the splintered rocks and steep sides, providing dappled shade. The sides of the little ravine were quite steep at the beginning, but the thought of taking a breather in the shade seemed very appealing.

They walked along the rim until they found a place to scramble down where the descent eased from being near vertical, to just steep. They had to hold onto rocks and straggly bushes, and the occasional exposed tree-root so they didn't fall and roll all the way down. When they reach the bottom they could see the clear water widened into an inviting stream that flowed over a base of shingle and pebbles; kept clear of mud by the tough grass-roots that held the earth tightly in their grip along the banks.

They gratefully leaned down to fill their bottles and scooped up water in their hands to drink.

Rag suddenly looked around, 'Boyd…' she mouthed.

He nodded; he could hear the mumble of voices as well. He beckoned to her and pointed to a thick clump of nearby bushes. They scuttled behind them; trying to hide, but still get a look at what was happening further down the gully.

On the other side of the stream, a troupe of half a dozen very small men came into view, smaller than the Broons, not even as tall as Rag. They wore old-fashioned clothing … almost like they were in historical costumes, thought Rag.

'Those are Polewiki,' whispered Boyd. Rag raised her eyebrows. 'Dwarves?' she mouthed at him. Boyd shook his head, 'The Hippogriff showed me them – something about 'field spirits', but I didn't quite get what he meant while he was thinking about them.'

Rag nodded and stared at the men; all their clothing was either black or white, but that could be black sleeves on a striped black and white shirt, or white collar and cuffs on a black coat. They had lots of ornamental silver buttons, up their sleeves or down the outside seams of their breeches. They all wore soft black boots to the knee and some had patches of black leather on their clothes at the knees or elbows. The most startling thing was their hair – it was vivid green and looked like big tufts of healthy grass. They were evidently here for the water too; some filled leather bottles or stooped to drink from the stream with cupped hands.

Rag and Boyd watched from their hiding place afraid to come out, but not knowing how to escape, because the Polewiki were clearly intending to set up camp.

On the other side of the stream where the ground was flat and more open, two began to gather stones to make a hearth, others picked up dry sticks. They'd put down their packs and shook out leather hides to sit on - they were going to be here for some time, maybe even all night!

One stood up from filling his water-bottle and looked directly at their hiding place; he raised his head like a hunting dog and sniffed the air.

'You may as well come out,' he said. 'We can smell you are there.'

Rag and Boyd stayed as still as they could, trying not to even breathe.

'Oh well… if you do not want any food, all the more for us,'

The polewiki turned on his heel and walked back towards where the others were getting ready to start a fire in the make-shift hearth.

Rag and Boyd looked at each other helplessly – they couldn't stay here, neither could they easily run. Boyd shrugged, Rag nodded her head, and then they both stood slowly upright and edged out from the bushes.

The polewiki paused, half-turned, then carried on walking. He said over his shoulder loud enough for them to hear.

'Good. You can fill the buckets with water and bring them over.'

Then they noticed he'd left two small leather buckets at the stream's edge. They walked a few paces upstream to where a couple of large rocks formed convenient stepping stones and crossed the stream, then walked to the buckets.

'What do we do?' hissed Rag softly.

'Be careful and see what they want – and be prepared to run for it if we have to,' whispered Boyd.

They picked up one bucket each, filled them and took them over to the campsite.

Chapter Twenty-Seven

The two little men at the hearth had got a fire started. Another arranged a bronze tripod over the fire, hanging a large copper cauldron from its hook; the outside of it was burnt black, showing it was well used.

The first polewiki, the one who had spoken to them, made signs for them to pour the water into the copper pot over the fire.

'More,' he said and shooed them back to the stream.

'Are we safe?' whispered Rag as soon as she thought they were out of earshot.

Boyd whispered back. 'The Hippogriff wasn't clear – something about them looking after the fields, helping farmers… He didn't seem to think of them as dangerous, but we'd better be careful.'

Another polewiki came by them with more wood.

'Come – stop whispering. There is work to do. We need more water if you want to eat.' He strode back to the camp with his load of kindling.

The children struggled up the gently sloping bank with the buckets filled to the brim, the water slopping over the edge with every step, and emptied them into the cauldron.

'Again!' commanded the first polewiki who was sitting by the fire with his legs stretched out in front of him. His grass green hair, Rag noticed, had a little daisy growing in it.

Rag opened her mouth to say something, but Boyd gave her a nudge and they walked back down to the stream once more. When they came back with the third bucket each, that seemed to satisfy the polewiki who was giving the orders, but now he stood over two coarse brown sacks. He handed a small knife with a wooden handle to Rag, and pointed at the sacks.

'You peel,' he said, then beckoned to Boyd. 'You come.'

He took Boyd over to an old tree stump and showed him the small axe laying there was for chopping up the larger branches. After chopping a couple of small bits, he gave the axe to Boyd and left him to it, returning to sit at his ease with the others by the fire.

One sack was full of onions, the other of potatoes; Rag sat on the grass between them. Somebody dropped the two leather buckets at her side.

'You fill, one for onions, one for potatoes, and cut them up for boiling,' he said and sat back down again with the other polewiki who were doing small tasks; one was sharpening a knife, another was whittling a piece of wood into a whistle; another sewed a button on his coat – small things to do as they relaxed and put their feet up.

Rag made a start on the potatoes, but she wasn't used to a knife, her mum had always used a peeler, so she was slow and the peel she took off was in thick chunks. There was nearly as much peel on the ground as there were potatoes in the bucket.

One polewiki looked over towards her after a few minutes and saw the potato bucket was only a quarter full and there were no onions at all.

'More speed – we need both to make soup.'

'It'd be quicker if I had some help,' retorted Rag.

They all paused in what they were doing, glanced at each other, the one sewing rolled his eyes at hearing her complain. 'If food you want, you must earn it,' he said and bit the thread to break it, before preparing to sew another button in place.

Boyd came back with an armful of chopped kindling and dropped it in a loose pile near the fire.

'No, no – be tidy. Make a stack, big at the bottom, small above,' said the one threading his needle to sew another button.

Boyd looked rebellious but knelt down and did as he was told and tidied the wood into a small stack.

'Then…' said the same polewiki, 'help your sister peel, or we won't have nuncheon 'til suppertime.' He bent his head to his sewing. When Boyd had finished stacking the wood, another polewiki offered him a small knife. He took it in silence and went and sat down by his sister. Boyd pulled the sack of onions towards him and took one out; tearing some of the flaky brown skins loose.

'Why do we have to do all the work,' whispered Rag crossly.

'My hands have got blisters from all that chopping,' Boyd grumbled. 'We're going to get our share of the food and then we're going.' He cut up and peeled some of the onions, which made his eyes sting and water. He tried to wipe his eyes but the onion juice on his fingers made it worse. He sniffed loudly.

One of the little men came over to the campfire with a wide wooden bowl and a sack of flour.

'Chitter chatter, chitter chatter – work harder, eat sooner!' He tapped Boyd's arm, 'I must have water to knead the bread – you fetch.'

Boyd wiped his stinging eyes with the back of his hand, 'No – fetch it yourself!'

All the polewiki stopped what they were doing and looked at Boyd.

He looked back at them defiantly. His eyes were sore and the onion juice on his blistered hands was making them sting. 'We're doing everything – why don't you help us!'

The first polewiki who invited them to eat, and seemed to be the leader, clapped his hands twice. The others immediately put down what they were doing and the camp became a flurry of activity.

One took the knife from Rag and shooed her backwards away from the fire, another took Boyd's knife off him, and both polewiki began to peel and chop, rapidly filling the leather buckets with neatly cut vegetables. Another of them fetched water for the baker, who kneaded the dough before tossing it from hand to hand and spinning it in the air to make it round and thin. One produced a little box of salt and spices and sprinkled a few good pinches into the boiling water as the chopped potatoes were tipped from the bucket into the copper pot.

All of them were active and busy; Rag and Boyd were taken aback at the speed and agility as they worked around each other to bring out wooden spoons and bowls, and put a skillet on the fire and feed more wood into the flames. The children got chivvied to one side to make room for the polewiki to get on with the cooking and baking.

Very soon the spiced onion and potato soup was bubbling; the flatbread was puffed and browning on the skillet. The Polewiki passed around the bowls, ladled soup for themselves, and tore off chunks of the flatbread. They didn't offer any food to Rag and Boyd who were left on one side to sit and watch them.

Rag was hungry, and the soup and bread smelled very good; eventually she spoke up.

'Excuse me…'

They ignored her.

'Excuse me! Don't we get any?'

One of the polewiki who had his back to them looked over his shoulder and said, 'Those who work get to eat.'

'But we did work!' said Rag, indignantly.

The polewiki chewed his bread and thought about that. 'Ummmm… maybe. A little… Here.'

He leaned over towards the youngsters and handed them some scorched flatbread.

'Is that it?' said Boyd.

The one with the daisy in his hair nodded at another polewiki, who took the copper cauldron off the tripod and walked round and put it on the ground in front of the children, along with two wooden spoons. It was nearly empty, but Rag and Boyd eagerly scraped out what remained, including what had stuck to the bottom of the pot. They were famished, and even scorched bread and crusty soup tasted good.

Soon, two of the polewiki come over, as the others started to tidy up their camp and put out the fire.

'Come. You want to go – we take you. Now,' said one.

The youngsters were still scrapping the remains of the soup and charred vegetables out of the cauldron with bread, but the two little men were already walking away, down the bank following the path of the stream, to where the gully widened and the sides were much shallower.

'Where… are you going…?' Boyd mumbled, still chewing his last mouthful of bread. The polewiki showed no signs of stopping; they didn't even turn around to see if they were being followed. Rag was licking her fingers; her brother turned to her.

"Come on Rag, looks like it's time to go,' he said.

They both grabbed their packs. Rag still had a piece of crust in her hand as she trotted off after Boyd. The two polewiki climbed the shallow slope of the gully, and set off across the heathland.

The remaining four polewiki grinned at each other and shook their heads, as they cleaned up the campsite and re-packed their knapsacks.

Out on the moors, the two little men had set off at a fast trot and were some way ahead. Boyd was in front of Rag, jogging after them.

'Wait,' he shouted. 'Slow down a bit.'

One of them stopped and looked back to where the two youngsters struggled to keep up.

'Tired? Already? We go to that rock over there.' He pointed to a large outcrop of granite quite some distance away that Boyd hadn't noticed before. 'Then you can rest,' the little man said. They set off at a fast loping run that soon left Boyd some-way behind.

Rag followed, trying to catch up the best she could. Sometimes she stumbled when the heather caught her feet. She had to slow down when she developed a stitch in her side that soon became a painful ache. She stood still, and tried to breathe it away; when the pain dulled enough, she ran after them, but not very fast.

I'm sure Mum told us not to run straight after a meal, she thought. And remembering that all she had left of her mother were memories made her feel sad.

Boyd slowed his speed, and waved for Rag to catch up with him. She was nearly there as he reached the huge, wind-sculpted boulders that lay in a great pile tucked deep into the earth among the tall clumps of rough shrubs growing around the base. The rocks sat at the top of a rise, and a long slope of moorland fell away gently on its far side.

The two polewiki were sitting on a wind-smoothed rock with their feet up, watching as the two exhausted children arrived and threw themselves to the ground panting from the effort.

Rag looked up, shading her eyes to see the two green-haired little men stand and stretch. One took a long drink from his leather flask that he'd had hanging from his belt, while the other gazed around the wide-open landscape.

It was mid-afternoon now and the sun was just beginning to get lower. Around them the moor stretched in all directions; occasionally there was a bright glint as the sunlight reflected briefly from the surface of a watery bog.

In the far distance was a long lake half-surrounded by straggly trees that drifted down towards the shores, and beyond that, rounded foothills covered in dark woods, rolled away to rise into bare mountain-sides, already shadowed with evening purples in the clefts and high valleys below their still bright peaks.

Boyd finally got his breath back and sat up, and asked,

'Where... are we?'

The one at the height of the rock jumped down; his companion took another drink and shook the flask; there was not much left. He handed it to Rag, who took it eagerly and drank. The two polewiki began to walk away, back the way they had come.

'Wait,' shouted Boyd after them. 'You were going to help us.'

The two little men didn't even pause as they strode over the moorland.

'Wait!' shouted Boyd.

One stopped and turned around, but the other was jogging away.

'You would not help us – now you must help yourselves.'

'But... but... we did help you,' cried Rag.

The polewiki had already started to trot away after his companion as he called back, 'Not enough. And not with a willing heart.'

And all of a sudden they were gone. Disappeared.

Boyd jumped to his feet and shouted, 'Wait! Wait!'

Rag struggled to her feet beside her brother, yelling, 'Come back!' She scrambled up onto the rock to look for them – but no one was in sight. 'Come back...'

She stamped her foot. 'Come back...' she gasped, as she slid down the rocks and slumped to the ground. Her eyes brimmed with tears that rapidly overflowed and trickled down her face.

CHAPTER TWENTY-EIGHT

Boyd was numb with shock... how could they do that? He had trusted them. As he looked around them, from far horizon to far horizon... he realised they were lost. They were in the middle of nowhere... They were truly, completely lost, and the sun was going down - in a few hours it would be dark. And an awful thought suddenly struck him - the Hippogriff can fly! A day, two days and a night for the winged creature... could be a couple of hundred miles or so flying in a straight line - it could easily be much, much further for the two of them on foot!

'Ooooo... nooooo...' he whispered.

'What's that? What did you say...?' said Rag, wiping her face with her sleeve.

'Nothing,' Boyd said quickly. He climbed up onto the rocky outcrop to try and get a better look – in the distance he could see a large lake and a shining reflection of the darkening sky... which means water, and trees nearby, they could find some shelter...think about what they can do next.

All of a sudden he felt very much out of his depth. It had all seemed so reasonable when he had thought this up and planned what he could do... but now...

'Come on, Rag – we have to go,'

'Go where? We don't know where we are. They just left us and walked away. No, they didn't even do that, or we could have followed them. It was worse, because they just… vanished! Just like that – Gone! It's not fair!'

'We can't stay here… we need to find some shelter for the night.'

Rag miserably cuffed more tears away, but didn't move.

'There is a lake over there – it looks a bit like the one near the castle. Maybe they took us back through before they dumped us. Maybe that's why they disappeared so quickly,' said Boyd.

'You think so?' Rag struggled to her feet and looked where Boyd was pointing.

'See? Over there – it's a long way, and it might take us a couple of hours, but at the very least we'll get some water, we can fill our bottles again. And there's bound to be somewhere to shelter until the morning, and then we can work out where we are and what we do.'

Rag nodded, and wiped her nose on her sleeve.

'Besides – Uncle Wulf will be looking for us by then. Maybe he's even looking for us right now,' said Boyd.

'He doesn't know where we went.'

Boyd shrugged, 'I don't think that matters. We can't be that far away, how far can we have walked in a day? Twenty miles, thirty?'

Rag shrugged her pack onto her shoulders. Boyd took a reading on the lake's position with his compass before he clambered down from the rock.

'Come on Rag. If we get going, we should get there before dark,' he said cheerfully, and started walking in the lake's direction – not feeling half as confident as he hoped he sounded.

Rag followed him and then stopped dead. 'Just a minute - you said we've walked maybe thirty miles at the very most. The hippogriff travelled for two days, and with an injured leg – that's sixty miles - so why can't they find Dad? Uncle Wulf has had months!'

Boyd turned slowly to his sister, 'I forgot something,' he said, then turned and carried on walking.

Rag trotted forward and grabbed the sleeve of his coat.

'What did you forget?'

Boyd pulled his arm away.

'What?' demanded Rag.

'I forgot he could fly.' Boyd walked on ahead again.

Rag stamped her foot. 'He can fly… he can fly. Boyd, you idiot!'

Boyd spun around to face his sister.

'I know! But arguing now won't help. I'm sorry, but that's how it is – We need to keep walking and get to the lake before it's too dark to see.'

He turned and headed across the moor. Behind him he heard her inarticulate snarl of exasperation, but he also heard the rustle of her footsteps as she followed him. The moorland rolled up and down in parallel folds of land. He only hoped they would have enough light for him to keep to his compass bearing. If not… well he didn't want to think of 'if not...'

Rag's thoughts were a jumble of punching and ripping… but after fifteen minutes or so they crested another rise in the ground and she could see the distant lake clearly, but it was still a long way off. She wasn't at all sure if it was the one by the castle, but then, there were other lakes nearby. They'd passed them as they drove up to the Keep after Alice left them with Uncle Wulf in Inverness.

She sighed as she plodded on… that whole life seemed a long while ago, and then she realised she had barely thought of her mother for over a day – which made her both sad and cross with herself.

But Mother had lived here as a child…she thought. More than that, she and Dad hadn't left until after Boyd was born. She had been born in a hospital in England, she knew that. Which made her wonder for the first time… why had they left Scotland? But Dad didn't really leave this place – he had been going away 'on business' for as long as she could remember. He was coming here. And sometimes Dad stayed and Mum went away for a few days… Or Auntie Carol looked after them when both of them left 'on business'…

The more she thought about it, the more she realised there were lots of things she had never questioned, just accepted as normal. How sometimes Dad would bring back bright feathers that almost looked artificial they were so colourful, and there were pretty pebbles of unusual striped stones, and coloured crystals. And sometimes pieces of jewellery for Mum that looked quite strange; intricate and beautifully made, but different from anything you saw in the shops.

She had a bracelet herself he'd given her for her eighth birthday. It was woven from white metal; it had eight small, rounded stones held in silver collars, and if you turned the clear stones in the light, they had rainbows inside… And for her tenth birthday he brought her another one; a bigger crystal made into a pendant… it looked like a smooth, fat teardrop, coloured with rainbows.

That was the time he had a broken arm and a bandage round his lower leg that made him limp… Mum had said he'd fallen down some stairs… It struck her now that nobody said where the stairs were, and she hadn't asked… But what if there hadn't been stairs at all, or even a fall! Look at Russ and Peat; they went out looking for creatures… Look at the Ogre… and the Dragon! That pulled her up short for a minute. Even Boyd realised she had stopped.

'Are you alright?' He called back to her.

Rag nodded, 'Fine.'

She started to walk after him again, and another thought struck her. She remembered her mother's watercolour box and how she used to do beautiful drawings of the funny plants and flowers she bought home with her after she'd been away. 'Rare specimens,' Mum had called them… Some of the drawings were in dark brown ink and delicately shaded. Rag had always been fascinated by the printed names on the little paint cube packages, which included, Russet, Sepia, Gamboge… and Vandyke! She trotted up behind her brother.

'Boyd – do you know that all those people who help Uncle Wulf are called by the names of shades of brown?'

Boyd rolled his eyes, but he just nodded - what else would a Broonie be called? Boyd had read the bit in his book of mythical creatures about brownies a few days ago – the household spirits, *fae,* who help with chores and farming… only Uncle Wulf's 'broonies' were very real.

'Boyd…' said Rag,'… do you think we'll get into trouble when we get back?'

Boyd sighed, but said more hopefully than he felt… 'Nah – we'll just tell them we got lost.'

Chapter Twenty-Nine

As they tramped across the moor the ground got wetter, dipping down into hollows that held soft earth that once they put their weight on it, oozed water, and in two steps more, became thick mud sucking at their feet. Again and again they had to detour from their planned path, because the direct way was blocked by scummy standing water edged with tall stiff grasses. In the golden afternoon light these often seemed to be in shades of green that were unnaturally vivid.

Boyd looked back, he could see the outcrop of rock they had left and realised it was a considerable height above and behind them now.

This ground must all be bog-land, he thought – which was worrying because the continual detours took time and the sun was almost dipping below the far off hills on the horizon.

They had to give up only looking for the dry paths because there didn't seem to be any anymore. They were forced to walk through sticky black mud, trying not to shudder if they went ankle-deep into a particularly deep patch of wet ooze.

Boyd led the way, checking his compass bearing to make sure he could get them back on the right course, because now they just seemed to be wandering from side to side. The bog lay at the bottom of what seemed to be a shallow, basin-like depression; he couldn't see over the rim, or see the lake at all. They were almost in the middle and all the paths looked as if they were dissolving into dank pools of stagnant water when Boyd heard a gloopy splash behind him.

'Rag? Was that you – are you all…'

He turned around and Rag was standing stock still. It looked like her ankle and boot had caught in a wiry branch of old dead wood. She looked petrified.

'Come on,' he said.

'I can't – move - it grabbed hold of me.'

'You're just got it stuck in a bramble – here, I'll pull it off.' He shuffled back to her.

'Boyd, I can't move!'

'Ok – I've got it.'

He had to go down on one knee at her side because the sliver of dryer ground they'd walked along was very narrow; his knee sank down unpleasantly into the wet mud. He bent forward to get a grip on the clinging grey twigs, but as he prised it from Rag's ankle it seemed to twist and grab his hand and wrist so tightly he couldn't get loose.

Rag jumped past him once she was free and scampered on a few steps before she turned and looked back. Boyd couldn't get to his feet. The knobbly finger-like twigs held him fast and were pulling him down. He could feel his knee and leg sinking deeper into the pooled water and black mud. He tried to unwind the clinging stems with his other hand, but they gripped tighter and pulled his hand further down into the stinking mud.

'Boyd, come out, don't mess around,' called Rag.

'I can't! It's pulling me in!'

There was a belch and pop of fetid air as a bubble rose through the thick liquid mud and burst, followed by another, and another.

'No, no don't say that, you're scaring me!' said Rag.

The ground under his knee was becoming softer and his calf sank under the filthy water, mud oozing upwards around his foot. He frantically clawed at the thing holding tightly to his wrist, pulling him down, when the water and mud heaved and shifted and a slobbery voice spoke…

'What are you that walksss my mere?'

'Nobody, nobody – let me go,' shouted Boyd.

'Nobody. Nobody mussst …give me a presssent,' said the mud.

'Boyd, Boyd, what is it?'

'Nobody hasss a friend. …That is two pressssentss…' The mud bubbled with awful glee.

'What do you want? We haven't got anything!' shouted Boyd.

'But I have you…'

… and Boyd felt his hands slide under the surface of the bog nearly up to his elbows.

'Let us go and we'll never come back!' Boyd shouted, as he was pulled slowly forward and downwards into the slimy foul-smelling water.

More mud bubbles popped in front of him, the noises they made sounded like thick slobbery laughter.

Rag staggered, she could feel the mud under her feet becoming more slippery. She was sinking too and she tried to find some firmer ground, stepping towards Boyd.

'Presssent… Give me…' hissed the mud voice.

'Rag – throw something in the water!' cried Boyd.

'What?'

'Anything! Give it a present!'

Rag whimpered… she could barely think; she could feel her feet were sinking, and, so was Boyd. The mud was halfway up his arms, and he'd been forced to put his other knee down into the bog that was very slowly swallowing him.

Rag searched her pockets; suddenly realising she still had the polewiki's leather water-bottle. She fumbled it out and threw it into the muddy pool. It sank slowly with a slurping noise, and moments later the voice bubbled up.

'Tasssty… more!'

'No,' said Boyd. 'That was one gift. Let her go!'

There was another belch of fetid air from the mud, 'Nobody mussst give me sssomething… or I takesss Nobody down to be with me forever…'

Thick mud was oozing up, forcing Boyd's face closer to the water. Rag unslung her back-pack; the empty lunch box was at the top. She flung that into the swampy mud, it floated for a moment before sinking slowly, as if the mud was tasting something unfamiliar to see if it liked it.

'More… Arghhhh... it bitesss. It isss biting!'

The black mud and water roiled and bubbled around Boyd's calf, suddenly drawing away from one sodden leg of his jeans, and once again his knee was almost on solid ground.

'Throw something else!' yelled Boyd, still struggling to free his hands.

'I haven't got anything!'

She searched again and found a notebook and pencil in a side pocket, and a crumpled old programme for somewhere she'd been and forgotten about. She threw them into the water. They floated on the rippling surface, before being spat out by rising bubbles of fetid gas. She searched frantically - found some old sweet wrappers in her backpack, and the paper bag that had held tablet in her pocket; she flung those at the bubbling mud.

'It bitesss!' burbled the mud, wet bubbles seething away from Boyd's knee, like water spluttering on hot metal.

Boyd couldn't see what he was grabbing under the churning, greasy water as he tried desperately to prise his wrist free. He got a grip on something thick and solid deeper in the mud below the twigs. He curled his fingers around it and pulled at it with all his strength in an attempt to make whatever it was release him. He rocked backwards and his free knee and leg went into the water again.

'Aarrrrgh,' screamed the mud. 'It bitesss! Go… Go!'

Suddenly, whatever was holding Boyd let go and he shot backwards, still hanging onto the large loop of something hard, dirty and cold, covered in slimy mud. It felt like metal, but he was too startled to look at it closely. Under him the clinging twigs and roots pulled back as the water and the mud retreated with sickening slurping noises. Rag caught him by his shoulder and back-pack and hauled him up. They turned and hopped from tussock to patch of slippery ground, slithering and sliding as they tried to get as far from the oozing stagnant mud as they could.

Behind them the dank mud started bubbling and hissing like a pan of filthy soup - mud blisters popping, spluttering and spitting.

'Nobody hasss it. Nobody hasss it! Arrrrggghhh!'

They both felt big gobbets of mud and scum hit their backs, but they didn't stop to look. They scrambled away as fast as they could - sometimes ankle and more deep in pools of green scummy water. They splashed their way upwards until the ground became soft, then dryer, and then hard under their feet - stumbling on until there was just heather and ordinary grass underneath them - then they both collapsed to the ground, panting.

'What – what was – that?' gasped Rag, breathing hard.

Boyd shook his head. He had been sure he was going to be drowned as his face was pulled nearer and nearer that awful fetid water. He shuddered at the thought of sliding under the surface, so thickly slicked-over with green slime and algae. He just could not get free until he pulled… he looked down at the large loop of dull metal he still clutched tightly in his fist. It was an oval, big enough to go around a wrist, with small balls on each of the open ends.

He wiped the mud off on the grass, wiped his hands till they were free of slime, and automatically stuffed the metal loop into his coat pocket without thinking anymore about it.

'I don't know what was in there, and no way am I going back to find out!' said Boyd.

'No, I'm never going back there!'

Boyd took a deep breath and stood up, he felt a bit shaky. His legs were wet and cold were his jeans clung to his skin. He had to pull the fabric up to adjust the sheath of the knife he had strapped to his calf, because it had twisted around as his knee had sunk deep into the mud.

'Oh – you brought your knife?' said Rag.

'Of course – you've still got yours haven't you?'

Rag nodded, 'In my pack.'

'Good job you didn't throw that in.'

'Oh no – that mud-blubber didn't deserve that!'

They looked around them. They had come out of the bog facing in a slightly different direction, the sunset sky, though bright with pretty pinks and mauves, was off to one side and there was no reflection off the water to guide them towards the lake. Just then Rag spotted a distant tiny flicker of light, she pointed.

'What's that?'

Boyds' binoculars had been zipped inside his coat so fortunately they had stayed relatively dry and clean. He got them out, put them to his eyes and focused the lenses.

'I think it's a fire – somebody is camping there - and that should be the general direction of the lake.'

'Do we go?' said Rag.

'We might as well. We can try to get a look at them before they see us. They might be ok…'

Rag nodded. They both felt very unsure about meeting anybody else, but the sun was near to setting, and it didn't feel comfortable to be walking around in the open – not anymore. Wet and bedraggled, smeared in slimy black mud, they began trudging towards the little dancing flame of the camp-fire lying in the lee of a wooded mound.

Chapter Thirty

Boyd and Morag crept closer. Near the trees, inside a ring of carefully placed stones was a cheerful fire; little licks of flame emerged from wood that had mainly turned to red-hot embers. They could see the small wisps of drifting smoke mingling with the steam rising from the blackened copper pot perched firmly on the fire.

A large man with a tanned, outdoor face and thick, curly black hair reached forward with a long stick to scrape a baked potato out of the hot ashes. Once free of the fire he reached to pick it up, but huffed and puffed when it scorched his fingers; fingers that momentarily morphed into black hooves and back to hands and back again to hooves as he juggled the hot potato before dropping it on the grass beside him. It rolled a little way into the shadows away from the firelight before coming to a stop against a tussock of grass. The 'man' at the fireside had a strong Irish accent when he spoke.

'Now where are yer, yer liddle… are there ya're!'

He spotted the potato, leaned over, and prodded it back towards the edge of the fire, before the hoof shimmered back into a large hand again.

Rag and Boyd had followed the flickering light from some way off, but decided to approach as quietly as possible - in case whoever had made the fire didn't look friendly. They peered at the strongly-built man by the fire-side. His clothes looked sturdy and old-fashioned: corduroy knee-breeches, thick socks and strong boots, a knitted jumper, under a tweed jacket with big pockets. He looked normal... until they thought they saw his hands change shape. But now they were definitely back as hands... and he didn't look that bad... and it was getting very dark... They looked at each other, and nodded agreement.

The Buggane sitting at his camp-fire heard somebody clear their throat. He whipped around to see who'd made the noise – and saw two very dirty, dishevelled youngsters, streaked with thick mud and looking exhausted. He shot to his feet.

'Excuse me,' said Boyd. 'Where are we - please?'

The Buggane swayed a little, he was nearly speechless, 'Who, wooo... whoowooooh!' was all he managed.

Boyd took half a step forward and pronounced his words very slowly and carefully, adding hand signals where he could.

'Can. You. Tell. Us. Where... is this?'

Boyd smiled and nodded... which he hoped made him seem friendly.

The three of them gazed at each other in silence for a few moments.

'I don't think he understands us,' said Rag quietly. 'Try again.'

'Do. You. Under...' began Boyd.

'Yes, all right, all right, I gotcha the first time! Now I know exactly where I am – which is obviously more than can be said for you two. What yer doin' out here? Childers like you shouldn't be about this time o' night, 'specially way out here.'

'Oo – you're Irish,' said Rag.

The Buggane drew himself up to his full height.

'I – am Manx! From the Isle o' Man,' he said.

'Um... sorry,' said Rag.

'No offence taken. The Mammy's family are all from the Green Isle and what with herself around, I always had the accent. Not that we have much to do with that side of the family – awful stiff-necked and self-righteous so they are. My Auntie Carmel now – she has a sharp word for everything that's not right - to her way of thinkin' that is - about everything that comes her way, daft old cow that she is... and I do mean that literally!' The Buggane paused for breath, 'Which isn't tellin' me who you are, an' what yer doin' here?'

'We're lost...' began Boyd.

'I can see that!'

Rag sniffed the air, 'Is that chicken stew?

'Pigeon actually, but near enough...' The Buggane sighed. 'Where's me manners? The Mammy is always tellin' us 'guests are a blessing you haven't yet wished for' Come on, come on – you two look like yer need to sit down, before yer fall down.'

Rag looked at Boyd, who shrugged his shoulders – do they, don't they?

'Ah come on – I won't bite! And you two don't look like yer going much further, not tonight anyhow.'

The Buggane laughed, but it sounded more like a bull's

bellow, then he cleared his throat and his voice took a more serious tone.

'Listen here – I promise, on me sacred grandmother's grave, that as my guests I will not harm a hair on yer heads… and you twos will not be under any obligation to me and mine for the hospitality I freely offer, or the supper you shall now partake of… Mind yer, what me cookin' will do for yer is another thing.'

Boyd took a tentative step forward, Rag was just behind him.

'That's right, that's right. Come closer – sit down. I'll put another 'tatar in the fire for yer.'

He laughed again and smiled as he sat down by the fire again. He reached deep into his huge leather pack and brought out two potatoes.

Rag and Boyd shuffled forward and sat down. The fire's warmth was very welcome. Their feet and clothes were still wet from stumbling into the filthy bog on the moors.

Thinking about that made Boyd shudder; he could still smell the stench of stagnant water on his clothes, and almost feel the tightening grip around his wrists as that thing had pulled him down. Now he thought about it again - whatever it was had been laughing through those bubbles in the mud. He remembered the sounds… Then pushed the thoughts away… at least now things seemed to be looking up again – he hoped.

'Um… So are we here… or are we… there?' Boyd didn't know how else to ask the question.

'Now that's a fair question…' said the Buggane. 'Where would you like to be?'

'Back with Uncle Wulf!' said Rag fervently, 'at his castle.'

'Aaaah… castle you say? Then that would make yer uncle,

Wulfric Kennetson?' said the Buggane.

'You know him?' Boyd asked.

'The Liosalfar? Everybody knows The Liosalfar! Sure himself is himself!'

'Oh…' said Boyd, not really understanding.

'Uncle Wulf is this 'liosalfar'?' said Rag.

'He is *The* Liosalfar – at least round these parts.'

'And… liosalfar are…?' asked Boyd.

'Tough buggers when they have to be, and evil bastards when they want to be!'

'That doesn't… really sound like Uncle Wulf…' said Rag, puzzled.

'Oh Wulfric Kennetson is fair as fair – or so I hear; I've never met him. But there's others, who shall we say - don't have the same patience with those who's not of their kind.'

'There are others like Uncle Wulf?' Rag wanted to hear more. She turned to Boyd, 'See? I said he was different… and not really human…?' she whispered.

'Hush now!' Buggane raised his hand, turning his head to listen.

'What..?'

Just then they too heard the distant jangle of metal and dull rumble of wheels.

'Hush! Well would you believe it, twice of an evening – and all the way out here! There's somebody else passing – over t'other side that rise. Now, you twos get behind me and we'll just have a wee bit of a walk through the spinney up there, and take a quiet look at who's out there.'

They knelt under the trees. Over the rise, through the gathering twilight they saw two high-sided wooden wagons with curved roofs, one glossily painted with coloured patterns and pulled by two heavy horses, the other plain timber and weather-beaten, pulled by two enormous oxen. Driving the painted wagon was a tall, slim man in a dusty red leather coat, which fell open from where his feet were propped up on the foot-board. They could see his dark trousers were tucked into knee-high red boots - out of which poked a knife handle that looked like it belonged to a sizable blade; a thin blue scarf was loosely twisted around his head and neck and over his mouth, making it impossible to see his face clearly.

The ox-cart rumbled behind the first wagon, driven by a big man with wide shoulders, his dark skin was almost as black as his supple leather coat. Another man, smaller than both of them; olive-skinned, with long, oiled curls that bobbed and glistened in the last of the setting sunlight, trotted alongside the wagons, mounted on a lively horse with dainty features.

'Ah…now then, isn't that her?' said Buggane. 'At least - I think it is…'

'Her…?' Rag said '…they all look like men.'

'Driving the horses – that one, so I believe, is the Salt Woman. She only looks and dresses like a man because she chooses to.'

'Why?' said Rag.

Buggane pulled a face. 'Easier to drive a wagon – safer than travellin' as a woman – more threatenin' if she were to pick a fight… she's very good with her knives, I hear… I don't know; pick any reason or all of them.'

'Will they help us – get back to Uncle Wulf?' said Boyd.

'Well… I don't know about that. Though I could do with some salt… and she's always keen to trade, so I heard… that's why they travel so far. I can't see it'll do any harm to ask.' Buggane got to his feet. 'Come on, let's stroll down nice and quiet like and maybe make her acquaintance.'

Rag and Boyd scrambled to their feet and walked after him.

The painted wagon pulled to a halt as the driver saw the three walking slowly towards them, the other wagon stopped close behind. The dainty horse skittered sideways as her rider turned the horse's head in their direction, then horse and rider came towards them at a canter. Buggane halted in his tracks as the horse passed them at speed.

Morag and Boyd stopped close behind the Buggane, sheltering at his back.

'Just keep still and let me do the talkin',' said Buggane out of the side of his mouth.

The horse reached the top of the rise, turned and trotted back. 'They're alone,' shouted the rider. 'They've a camp-site over there, I can see the fire.' He wheeled his horse around them, circling several times at a steady trot, not taking his eyes off the buggane and the two youngsters.

'Heads up, keep still,' muttered Buggane.

The Salt Woman gave a piercing double whistle, and beckoned.

'You can come down to us,' said the rider, and trotted back leaving them to follow.

Chapter Thirty-One

The tall black man had climbed down from the ox-cart and was standing near the driver of the painted wagon. He had a long club made of dark wood in his hand, which he smacked lightly against his open palm. His scowl was made all the more ferocious by the intricate patterns of fine scars over his face. As they approached, the wagon's driver unwound the scarf from her head and face. Now Rag was able to see that she was a woman… although her features were strong and angular enough that she could have passed as a beautiful man; you couldn't call her pretty, but handsome was a good word for her.

She pushed her elaborately plaited hair back and looked down at them from the wagon's driving seat.

'We don't meet many people in the middle of these moors,' she said.

'Ah, we was just passin' through, milady.' Buggane gave a little nod that wasn't quite a bow.

'Don't 'milady' me. You can call me Melleth – and you would be?'

'Just Buggane will do me – And this is…

'Boyd, and my sister, Morag,' said Boyd.

'They are wards of The Liosalfar, so they are,' said Buggane.

'Out here? Alone? Or is His Honour in hiding hereabouts?'

'Alone – Yes, that's just what I first thought, and very soon we'll be heading back his way… though they did wonder if you…' said Buggane picking his words carefully.

'We're looking for my father,' Rag blurted out. 'He came this way – we think. Have you seen him?'

'Did he now? Not many cross the moor to come this close to the mountains. Buggane – you know whose realm you're skirting?'

'I had heard they weren't usin' that ol' Keep these days,' said Buggane slowly.

'You have old news, Buggane. We saw a troop yesterday, but we kept our distance and they let us alone. They must have their own business nearby.'

Rag and Boyd listened quietly.

'Ah… Is that so?' said Buggane.

'Yes, Buggane.'

Rag couldn't wait any longer: 'Could those people know where my father is? Could they have seen him?' she said.

Melleth looked down and looked the girl in the eye. 'You do not ask their business, unless you want to be part of Svartalfar business - and believe me, that is not something to seek lightly.'

'But…' began Rag.

'No 'buts, child. You should hope your father is elsewhere.'

'His name is Lachlan Ellis,' said Boyd, taking a step forward. 'Have you heard of him?'

'Lachlan Ellis – you're free with his name Boy,' said Melleth.

'My name is Boyd!'

Melleth laughed, the black man grinned, showing perfect white teeth. Just then the curly-haired rider walked up behind the children and Buggane, knocking against Boyd's shoulder in passing.

'Oops, sorry lad,' the rider said, steadying him with one hand, brushing Boyd's coat down with the other, 'There - Ok are you?' Then he continued towards the wagons.

Boyd frowned. His coat felt different… lighter… He thrust a hand into his pocket – the metal loop was gone.

'Wait – you took it – from my pocket!' Boyd said loudly.

The rider turned towards him with a look of surprise, holding out his empty hands. 'Me?' he said with an innocent smile. 'No, not me – Did you drop something?' He bent down and seemed to pick something up from behind a tussock of grass. 'Oh was this it? You dropped your bracelet – here it is.' He offered it back to Boyd, his delicate face a picture of sunny smiles.

Boyd snatched it back with a scowl.

Melleth gave a snort of laughter, 'You're getting careless Besim if a boy can spot you.'

Besim raised both hands, which Boyd saw were long-fingered and slender – pick-pocket's hands; the young man turned to them with a beautiful smile that lit up his brown face and big brown eyes. Placing one hand to his chest he bowed his head so his shiny cork-screw curls fell forward and hid the mischievous grin.

'I get so little practise these days, my queen,' he said, and sauntered back to stand by Melleth's wagon.

'I apologise for my crewman. He shouldn't steal from my guests.'

'We're yer guests are we?' said Buggane.

'The least I can do is offer you some tea - and break our bread with you- if you choose to,' said Melleth. 'Will you have us at your fire-side Buggane? Or shall we remain here?'

'My camp is humble enough, but you're welcome to share it,' Buggane gave an awkward bow.

'Don't worry, we will not stay long. We still have a way to go before we rest for the night.'

She turned to the tall black man, 'Tamir – bring the cart and follow me, we will take a break. Besim – you can water the animals.' She shook the reins and turned the horses' heads to walk the wagon around the edge of the rising ground.

Rag watched her.

'She hasn't told us anything about Dad!' whispered Rag.

'Slowly, slowly me girl… She won't tell us nothin', not just like that,' Buggane replied quietly. 'Now you two, back with me - they'll round that top in a few minutes.' He hurried them back up the small hill, through the trees and down to his fire-side.

They'd not been at their camp-fire long before the wagons pulled round the edge of the rise and stopped a short distance away. Rag watched curiously as the Blackman, Tamir, immediately jumped down from the ox-cart and went to offer his hand to help the Salt Woman down from her wagon.

She was very tall, Rag saw as she walked towards them; her long coat was full-skirted, the dull red leather heavily embossed with ornate patterns of swirling leaves and stars. When she got closer Rag could see she had light blue eyes, a bit like Uncle Wulf's, but hers were more greenish-blue than grey-blue.

'You examine me intently, child.'

'I'm not a child!' snapped Rag.

'Neither are you grown enough to know better.'

Boyd nudged Rag's shoulder and gave a slight shake of his head. Rag folded her arms with a frown.

'Your fire is for one, Buggane – you are courteous, but we'll start another.'

Melleth returned to the back of the painted wagon and dropped the back board; revealing some folding steps that she dropped down so she could climb up to open the back doors.

'Young cubs – here - help us set camp,' said Melleth.

Rag was curious in spite of being cross, she followed the woman. She had seen gypsy wagons that looked rather like this in a museum – painted wood, with an arched wooden roof, fitted out inside with benches and cupboards like a tiny house.

Melleth passed down a set of bronze tripod legs to put over the fire to hang the kettle on. Rag did as she was bid and took them to where Tamir had swept some ground and was laying kindling for a fire. Boyd stepped forward, one hand outstretched to take the large copper kettle from her.

'That bracelet - can I look at it?' she said. Boyd hesitated. 'I will not steal it. I buy and sell - I have a reputation to think of.'

Boyd reluctantly handed the open loop of metal to her, 'I didn't know it was a bracelet,' he said. Melleth nodded, turning it over in her hands.

'Where did you get it?'

'I found it.'

Melleth raised an eyebrow, but said nothing.

'It came out of a bog where something nasty lived,' said Rag, who had returned for the kettle. Boyd scowled at her.

Melleth handed her the blackened kettle. 'Tell Tamir I will be there in a few moments,' said Melleth. 'Go on, he needs it to boil the water for tea.'

Rag walked away, struggling a bit with the large kettle.

'Can I have it back?' said Boyd.

'You don't want to sell it?'

Boyd shook his head and held his hand out. Melleth polished the torc bracelet against the skirt of her coat. It began to shine dully as the dried mud rubbed off.

'...Then if you're keeping it you should wear it.' Before he could say anything she had slapped the torc about his wrist.

Boyd yelped in surprise as the metal cinched about his arm. It felt cold and heavy. Melleth smoothed it into place with both hands, polishing it with her palms. When she took her hands away, Boyd was surprised to find it felt warm... and now a comfortable fit that nestled tightly against his skin, not heavy and awkward like at first.

'What did you do to it?'

'You do not keep a warrior's torc in a dirty pocket. Wear it with pride – somebody else did, a very long time ago.'

'Really? A warrior?'

'Once. You took it from the grip of a Peat Hag, they wouldn't have been very pleased.'

'Will they want it back?' said Boyd.

'Of course – that was once an offering... or from a victim, or maybe stolen from a dragon's hoard. However they got it – now it has come to you - look after it.' Melleth climbed down the wagon's steps carrying a basket. 'But if you want to sell it, let me know.'

'It's just an old metal bracelet...'

'A solid gold bracelet,' she corrected him, and walked towards the fire.

Boyd walked behind her, peering at his wrist hard, rubbing the bracelet with his other hand; already it felt smoother and shinier. Rag was waiting for him.

'What did she say?' whispered Rag after Melleth had walked passed her towards the newly flickering fire Tamir had already got started.

'I'll tell you in a minute,' said Boyd.

'I'm sure she knows something,' muttered Rag. Boyd nodded, 'I agree, but she's not going to tell us just like that. She's like Uncle Wulf, half of what she says sounds like she's telling you a lot less than she knows.'

The woman put down her basket next to Tamir, 'Oh - I forgot something,' she said, and turned towards the wagon. Tamir caught hold of the hem of her coat; he nodded to her, and flicked some signs with his fingers. 'Yes, we will not stay long,' said Melleth and left him to return to the open door of the wagon. The man took out heavy pottery cups and packets of dried teas from the open basket.

'Will you look at that – real tea!' said Buggane, rubbing his hands in delight, 'Can yer see yer way for us to have a bit of a trade? I could do with a wee pack of salt...'

Inside the wagon, Melleth rattled the bars of the large brass cage hanging from the ceiling. Inside it, a pair of ravens dozed on a perch. 'Hugge,' she said sharply.

One bird stirred, she poked the cage again, making it swing. The bird opened dark beady eyes and looked at her. 'Yes, you heard me. I have an errand for you.'

The bird appeared to sigh, his fellow nestled down to go back to sleep. Hugge leaned down, pulled out the peg that kept the cage-door shut and dropped it to the floor of the cage. He hopped to the edge of the bars as the door swung open.

'Hugge – I want you to fly to the Liosalfar's Keep and tell him his cubs are here.' The bird gave a quizzical croak. 'Yes – I'm sure they will feed you.'

She held her left arm out; the raven sidled from the cage to her wrist and fluffed its feathers. She opened the half door at the front of the wagon behind the driver's seat. The raven stretched his wings and grumbled a few more croaks.

'Of course he has hobs of some sort to help him – they will have corn for you. We will move on soon. The Buggane and the cubs will stay somewhere around here for the night. We will make up time, drive to the foothills tonight and camp there. You can meet us in the Stoneman's Valley - we should be there in two days' time. Tell the Liosalfar to look for them near the long lake. No… he can come for them after dawn, they should be safe enough 'till morning.'

The bird huffed. She stretched her arm out of the door; the raven launched himself into the air and flew away.

After they'd been given cups of strong tea by Tamir, Rag and Boyd murmured 'thank yous' but the man simply nodded, remaining silent. But when Besim tapped his shoulder and made quick signs, he broke into a broad grin showing his large white teeth. Melleth picked up on their visitors' unasked question.

'Tamir has no voice - but his hearing is perfect. Besim just likes to sign to him - usually when they're talking secrets,' she said, frowning in disapproval, 'Even when to do so in front of guests is discourteous.'

Besim grinned at her, then touched his chest and bowed his head, still grinning.

Rag could see that just above the neck of the large man's shirt was a scar, curving around his throat nearly from ear to ear. Tamir saw her staring and pulled his neckerchief tighter. Rag quickly looked away.

Melleth spoke to Rag and Boyd, 'Our path lays the opposite way to The Liosalfar's Keep, and we have customers waiting for us. We will not be able to take you that way.'

'Oh…' said Rag.

'We have obligations.' The woman sipped her tea, 'I dare say the buggane could help you, for a price.'

'Well we hadn't got that far…' said Buggane.

'We'll be ok,' said Rag.

Melleth looked them up and down pointedly in silence; they were both covered in drying mud. Eventually she said, 'Stay by the buggane's fire tonight and see what tomorrow morning brings.'

'Now isn't that the sensible thing for the two of yer? We'll all sleep on it and start again tomorrow,' said Buggane.

CHAPTER THIRTY-TWO

Soon afterwards, Tamir stood and collected the cups back up, Besim poured the water remaining in the kettle over the fire, and they prepared to leave.

'Could I offer you some good potatoes for a wee packet of salt?' said Buggane.

Melleth nodded, she called to Tamir, 'Buggane has something to offer for one of the small bags, see you're satisfied.'

Buggane hurried off to do his trade. Melleth turned to Rag and offered the girl her hand to shake. Rag felt a little odd taking the hand of an adult like that, but stood up straight and shook hands. Melleth ignored the fact the girl's hand was still filthy. She turned to Boyd. He shook her proffered hand, but she also reached forward to clasp the bracelet around his wrist with her other hand.

'Take care of it. Things like this come to you for a reason, even if you don't know it yet,' she said, then stood back and gave the slightest of bows, hand on her chest. 'Go well, both of you. If you travel the moorlands in future I dare say we may meet again. Keep safe.'

She turned on her heel, back towards her wagon, climbed up, took the reins and turned the horses away. They hadn't seen the men get them out, but now there were closed lanterns hanging from both sides of the wagons' seats. Besim turned to them and gave an extravagant bow before climbing up to sit beside Tamir on the ox-cart; his horse now tethered to the rear of it. Buggane walked back to the youngsters holding a red cloth bag, weighing it in his hands.

'Not bad,' he muttered. 'Not wonderful, but not bad at all…'

The wagons rolled around the mound and the noise of the quietly jangling harness soon died away.

They returned to the buggane's camp-fire. 'Here now - let's get some o' that stew down us. I meself am near barkin' from hunger,' he said, reaching to unhook the lid of the quietly bubbling stewpot - the fragrant aroma of hot cooked food wafted out. Boyd's mouth began to water.

'Sit yer down,' said Buggane, rummaging in a brown linen bag hanging from the outside of the enormous black leather pack beside him. He produced deep wooden bowls and pewter spoons, 'Now let's get to the important bit - and we'll save the rest of the whys and wherefores for afters.' He had a brass ladle by the fire and started to spoon thick broth into the bowls - to Rag and Boyd it smelt like the best stew ever!

A while later - they had nearly finished their stew and were busy mopping the bowls clean with chunks of flatbread. Buggane had the cooking pot on the ground in front of him and was scraping the last drops out of it with a wooden spoon, smacking his lips as he ate. Rag and Boyd listened raptly to the tale of his travels…

'...Rhyme we spoke in time to time - if you talk so, they'll stay benign. For a thing from them you do desire, you must speak in words they do admire... Around the rocks we quoth and then... Ah, yer don't want to hear all the gory details. We did the deal and I came away from the Blue Men of the Minch with me prize. And now I'm on me way home.'

'Everything you say to them has to be in rhyme?' asked Rag.

'All of it – and you really need to have the last word. Otherwise they may see fit to drag yer down to their sea-caverns and that'll be the last of yer.'

'They sound dangerous,' said Boyd.

'Not if yer have the gift of the gab, like I have.'

Buggane has finished with the cooking pot and licked his spoon with a surprisingly large, thick tongue.

'De-licious – if I say so meself. Now – I've told you about me and I've heard some little bits from you. You are Morag, but yer brother calls you Rag, and you are Boyd, and yer sister calls yer Boyd outloud. Mmmm... you're mighty free with yer names yer know.

'Why shouldn't we? And you haven't told us your name,' said Boyd.

'Ooo – ooo... I don't know if we're that well-acquainted just yet, even for all yer in The Liosalfar's keeping. You can just call me Buggane, as that's what I am. Now you might have heard tales of fearsome ogres and great hairy beasts and such, but that is absolutely not on me Da's side of the family. The Mammy's side ... well, there's some that I wouldn't trust out on a dark night... Nuncle Mulligan - he's a great lurker, and I did mention the nasty sharp tongue Auntie Carmel has on her… But no, Mammy'd be most upset to hear me casting aspersions like that'

'We hadn't heard anything like that,' said Rag.

'Had yer not?' said Buggane, sounding a touch disappointed. 'Well, no matter, cos that's not all my family like that!'

Rag yawned hugely.

Buggane nodded, 'I dare say the Salt Woman was right, anything else yer have to say can wait 'til mornin',

'Um, Rag… maybe we should…' began Boyd.

'Go?' said Buggane. 'And where would yer be goin' to? Yer don't know where you are in the first place and it's too dark to see a hand in front of yer nose out there. Look, I know the way to The Liosalfar's Keep – but there are too many bogs and boggarts between here and there to take yer in the darkness. Settle down. You and yer sister should stay here - you can stay that side o' the fire and me on this. See – after you've shared food with a guest you're beholden not to do them a mischief in the night. The Mammy says that is very bad form!'

Buggane sat back, smiling encouragingly.

'Really?' said Boyd.

'On my life,' said Buggane solemnly.

'Really, really?' said Rag

'Hand on heart and hope to die! Curl up together there. I'll find you a couple o' wee blankets after I put the last few bits o' wood on the fire – we'll have them last 'tatters for breakfast, and then we'll take a wee detour and I'll set yer both back where you belong.'

'Thank you,' said Rag.

'Yes, thanks very much,' said Boyd.

Buggane stood up and stretched his arms and flexed his shoulders.

'Ah, don't mention it. I dare say Himself might have a wee acknowledgement to make, for the favour like…I'll get that wood – I'll be back in two shakes…'

He walked away towards the trees. After a few minutes he returned with an armful of small branches. Rag and Boyd were fast asleep curled up next to each other by the hearth.

The Buggane searched deep inside his big leather rucksack, leaning in further than seemed possible, until he sat back and pulled out two folded shawls, each one woven in intricate patterns around the borders and heavily fringed. He laid one over each of the youngsters.

Buggane shook his head and began to feed the last of the thicker pieces of wood into the embers of the fire to keep it smouldering into the night. He muttered to himself as he laid the branches.

'Whish, whish… d'ya ever see the like?'

His head shook violently and morphed into the head of a black bull… before shaking hard again and turning back into a 'human'.

'Settle down you – they're our guests. Mammy would scorch the hide off our back if we broke the Rules of Hospitality.'

His head shook again, but the bull couldn't get the mastery. Buggane blew hard - which sounded like a cow exhaling, and gave himself another shake, like boxers do before a fight. He reached inside the black leather pack for another blanket for himself, before pulling the drawstrings tight. Then he lay down on his side of the fire with his head and shoulders propped up on the rucksack and settled down to sleep.

CHAPTER THIRTY-THREE

Late at night in the moorlands all was quiet, disturbed only by the small hops and splashes as the creatures of the bogs came and went; soft noises barely heard. Overheard, a multitude of stars burned fiercely bright in the blackness of the night-sky. Any thin mists rising from the lake barely reached to the tops of the trees; they certainly didn't hinder the solitary night-hunting bird, near silent, pale-feathered, as she swooped out into the bogs to catch a frog for her brood of chicks.

Across the surface of the lake a new mist was forming, thickening swiftly, moving with gathering purpose across the water, growing ever denser as it neared the shore. By the time it reached the shingle at the water's edge it was almost tangible; a seething, greasy-looking cloud that revealed glimpses of fangs and claws. Exploring tendrils crept out across the shallows, and then slithered over the ground, reaching out towards the sleepers beside the dimly glowing fire.

Rag mumbled something, and rolled over in her sleep, pulling her coat closer to her. She mumbled again, and became more agitated, twitching and... She suddenly sat bolt upright.

A short distance away, a huge spider confronted her. She screamed. She looked down – centipedes, spiders and shiny, scaly crawling insects twitched and scurried, covering her in a thick, disgusting mass of twitching creatures. She screamed again and jumped to her feet trying to shake them off the shawl that had been over her legs.

Boyd groggily came awake. 'Wh…? What…?'

'Help me!' shrieked Rag. 'Get them off me!' She threw the shawl away from her.

Boyd shook his head; it felt wet, like he had a layer of mud across his face. He tried to rub it away from his eyes, but it thickened under his fingertips. He sat upright in a panic.

'Rag! I can't see! I can't open my eyes!'

He struggled onto his knees but his legs got tangled in the borrowed shawl and he couldn't stand up properly. He stumbled, and accidentally put his hand in the hot ashes by the fire's edge, making him shout out in pain.

Rag tried to brush the mass of creeping insects away, but they clung to her hands, and crept up her legs as she tried to stamp on them. The enormous spider came closer to her, one step at a time; she could see the glitter of its multi-facetted eyes. She screamed in panic.

'Rag – where are you? What's happening? I'm blind! I can't see you!' shouted Boyd.

Boyd tried to crawl, but the shawl tangled around his legs hindered him. He clawed at his face, but the smear of mud had become a thick mask of solid earth.

Buggane shuddered, before jerking awake, wild-eyed. He jumped to his feet with the wild bellow of a bull, flailing his arms around him trying to ward something away. He screamed like a man in pain, and dropped to his knees shaking. His hands trembled to hooves and back as he tried to unlace the side-pocket of his pack; eventually he managed to fumble a long-bladed knife out of its sheath.

'No... No nonoooo...' he bellowed; slashing at the rising wall of shapeless dirty grey mist that had now grown ragged, needle- sharp teeth and vicious claws that slashed at the Buggane.

Rag shrieked, frantically brushing herself down, trying to rid her arms, body and legs of the crawling horror that was enveloping her. Suddenly, the mass of insects drew back and scurried towards the enormous spider, crawling up its legs, becoming part of it, making it grow, and grow...

The spider clacked its jaws and came close, closer... Rag was petrified with fear. She couldn't move, she stood rooted to the spot, feeling wild screams of panic welling up inside her... but she couldn't make a sound.

Boyd finally managed to pull the shawl off his legs and scrambled onto his hands and knees, trying to feel his way across the ground towards Rag.

The gathering mist from the lake sank into the ground around him and the earth became like liquid quicksand, clinging to him, holding him down – and burning. Each time he dragged a hand free, painful red blisters appeared on his skin. It felt like he was being buried alive! He shouted out in fear and pain.

Buggane flailed and slashed at the snarling mist. 'Come to me,' he shouted. 'Come to me both of yer!'

'I can't see you – I'm blind!'

'Come to my voice!' Buggane yelled. He slashed deep into the mist which momentarily pulled back. 'It's *Fuath*!' He slashed wildly again. 'They take the shape of what yer fear most!'

Boyd struggled to crawl free of the clinging mud, but every time he put his hand to the seemingly near-liquid ground it was like dipping it in acid. He cried out, whimpering as he tried to crawl free.

Morag was petrified as the huge spider stalked slowly forward, clacking the palps either side of its mouth as it prepared to bite… rearing up and back to leap on top of her…

A wild swing from the stumbling buggane and his long blade sliced through one of the spider's front legs. It wailed, and the mesmerising spell it had over Rag was momentarily broken. She stumbled backwards and fell over her back-pack. The buggane bellowed like a charging bull, swinging wildly at the curdled mist with his knife.

Boyd screamed. He shuddered with pain and reached down with a now raw and bloody hand to try and push the acid-mud off his legs. His hand accidentally brushed against the knife still strapped to his calf. The blade rang out clearly like a struck bell as his fingers brushed the sheath. The mud on his fingers curled away from it and the raw blisters faded. Boyd gasped in relief as the pain disappeared from his fingers. He touched the sheathed blade again and suddenly realised it must be something to do with the knife and fumbled it free. Once the blade was out, it glowed; enough for him to see a light through the congealed mud plastered over his eyes. He tried to crawl, the knife clenched in one fist. As he did, he plunged the blade into the soft ground. The mud-mist hissed and withdrew from the blade's bite, and the quicksand became ordinary earth and grass again. His hand and knee came free. Boyd stabbed the ground again and again until the earth beneath him felt normal. The mist-monster howled and rolled back from his attack.

'Rag, Rag – get your knife!' he shouted. 'Your knife!'

He struggled up, repeatedly stabbing the ground until it freed him completely.

'Come to my voice,' bellowed Buggane.

Morag rolled over to fumble inside her pack as the huge spider, its once severed leg now renewed, stalked towards her. Her fingers curled around the hilt... the knife zinged as she drew it from the sheath, gleaming coldly. The spider halted. She thrust the shining knife in front of her and the spider cringed back. It skittered to one side to get around the shining blade. Rag backed away from the grotesque monster towards Buggane.

He was slashing and jabbing at the roiling cloud of thick oily fog, biting fangs and slashing talons. The buggane bellowed with every winning cut that made the cloud recoil.

Boyd staggering up from his knees; he held the glowing knife-blade flat across his eyes, the mud dropped away into dust. He wiped the flat of the blade down his arm. The mud curled back and dropped from him; freed from the cloying filth, his skin healed instantly. He rubbed the remaining mask off his face with his hand... he could see! He staggered towards Buggane and Rag.

'Face them. Face outwards and stand with yer backs together with me.'

The spider collapsed into a fetid cloud; the dirty mist rose from out of the ground that had held Boyd, and both streams trickled towards the grumbling fog that widened and moved to try and encircle the three of them.

It heaved itself into barely formed monstrous shapes. Rag

and Boyd's two glowing blades lit a growing nightmare of chaotic forms.

Suddenly – they heard the deep-throated baying of hounds. A horn sounded a sweet note, high and clear. The *Fuarth* halted its writhing, and hesitated...

They could hear pounding hoof-beats, nearer, nearer... Out of the darkness leapt Freki, snarling and snapping at the edges of the cloud – instantly followed by Geri. Hunting in their own world, the *Cu Sith* looked even bigger and far more fearsome. They savaged the fraying edges of the glutinous mist-monster, snapping and growling as they tore pieces away that fell from their jaws and dissolved into the ground.

A great black horse with fiery red eyes galloped up, skidding to a halt. Wulf sat astride it, dressed for fighting in a long, studded leather coat, with strong leather bracers buckled to his forearms and a quiver of arrows at his belt - his curved hunting bow was already nocked. He loosed pale arrows repeatedly into the roiling mass, which howled and retreated from him.

Wulf leapt from the prancing horse's back, dropped the bow and drew two long knives from the harness on his back. The blades glinted fiercely as he slashed his way through to where Buggane was defending Rag and Boyd. Shoulder to shoulder, Wulf and Buggane forced the *Fuarth* to retreat, carving and stabbing at whatever they could as the *Fuarth* extended twisted claws and snapping jaws.

On the other side of the monstrous mass, the black stallion reared, kicking out and biting, bringing its great hooves crashing down onto patches of glutinous fog, which howled and dribbled away as he pounded them into the ground. The fight was turning. Wulf and Buggane forced the monster to retreat towards the lake.

The black horse had vanished into the darkness beyond the dim circle of firelight, though they could hear stamping and snorting nearby. The *Fuarth* abruptly collapsed to the ground, withdrawing like a tide of fetid water rapidly draining away. The dogs snapped and snarled at its edges until Wulf called them back.

Drawing a deep breath, Wulf turned to the buggane, who leant down, hands on knees, panting hard. Boyd and Rag had collapsed at his feet. Rag was nearest to Wulf… still deeply shocked by the attack out of the dark… for a moment all she could focus on was that Uncle Wulf had changed his customary Doc Martins for knee-high, brown suede boots – wrapped with bands of soft leather that kept them tight to his leg… Cool… I wonder if I can have some like that… she thought in a random sort of way. Her legs felt like jelly, her stomach felt hollow… and she wasn't sure she could lift her arms up, let alone stand up.

Wulf stood over them, breathing a little harder than normal from the exertion… but still sternly in command as usual. He looked down at them before finally speaking…

'Well met.'

'Well…' managed the Buggane, blowing hard, 'Well… well… Dayz…!' He pointed behind Wulf with a shaking finger towards a tall figure, head high, striding purposefully out of the darkness.

Rag tore her gaze away from Uncle Wulf's transformation into warrior mode and stared at where Buggane was pointing…

She shook her head… what… have these two stepped out

of a fantasy game! Rag blinked and rubbed her eyes… No – still there!

The tall man walking towards them had the striking good looks of a romantic hero from the movies: lean, muscular, moody dark-eyes; his long black hair flared loose down his back. He was completely dressed in soft black leather: sleek fitted trousers, knee-high boots and a form-fitting, long-sleeved jacket. He stalked towards them with the elegance of a thorough-bred racehorse – apart from one hand was tangled in the filthy matted hair of an unearthly child-like being covered in slime. The man was strong enough to easily keep it at arms-length, forcing it to walk ahead of him.

The dogs gambolled joyfully around the new-comer, but bared their teeth and growled at the filthy creature he had to half-drag as it twisted in his grip. The skinny creature hissed and snarled, struggling to bite the man; who suddenly shook it unmercifully hard until it cringed and whimpered.

'*Each Uisage!*' Buggane breathed, staring in horror and instantly raising his knife in a fighting stance.

Wulf half-turned to block the buggane's raised knife with his own blade, from which the gleam was rapidly fading.

'Peace. This is Muirdoch. He is with me,' said Wulf.

Buggane slowly lowered his knife and took a step back, looking wary and uncomfortable.

'I caught this Brollachan,' said Muirdoch.

'*Fuarth* spawn,' spat Buggane, his attention turning to the slime covered manikin.

The Brollachan renewed its snarls and struggles, but Muirdoch had a firm hold and gave it another shake that momentarily took the creature off its large flat feet.

'Its parents have retreated to their lair – let it go,' said Wulf.

'It might have something to tell us,' said Muirdoch.

'Go cringe under your bridle Water-horse! Saddle-maid!' shrieked the Brollachan.

Muirdoch gave it another fierce shake.

'Fester and burn!' cursed the creature.

'Enough!' commanded Wulf, 'Or I change my mind.'

Muirdoch twisted the creature's head by its hair and bent forward to snarl in its ear. 'I wear no bridle and kneel for no one.'

'Dayz!' murmured Buggane.

'Take it to the far side of the water - I do not want it creeping back to make more mischief before dawn,' said Wulf.

The Brollachan twisted furiously and kicked out at Muirdoch.

'Lick-spittle codling! Cockhorse!' it shrieked.

'Hold your tongue or I'll fly you up and see how long it takes you to fall from the clouds!' growled Muirdoch.

The Brollachan howled like a furious banshee as Muirdoch shook it again.

Uncle Wulf turned to Morag; he touched her shoulder, 'Are you well, Morag?'

She nodded. She wasn't sure if she could actually think about what had just happened, not yet anyway.

And then to Boyd, 'And you, Boyd… how do you fare?'

The Brollachan abruptly whipped its body into an arch and spun itself round and round, leaving a hank of straggly hair in Muirdoch's fingers. It leapt away - then paused to shout.

'They fare better than the Milkskin's sire. The Svartalfar have him thralled in a place well beyond your reach!'

The creature leapt into the air with a cackle of harsh

laughter before scuttling away into the deep shadows along the lake-shore.

'Muirdoch...!' said Wulf.

Muirdoch sprinted after the disappearing Brollachan. Just as the man got to the far edge of the firelight's reach, he changed form. Huge black wings appeared from his back as he leaped into the air and vanished into the darkness, but they could hear the swish of great wing-beats in the air.

There was a moments silence before Buggane spoke. 'Erm... are you sure he's with you?'

'Muirdoch will not harm you,' said Wulf mildly. 'I have his pledge.'

'Oh... Ooo...' said Buggane.

'Have you other doubts? If not - we need more wood for the fire,' said Wulf.

Buggane nodded and hurried to round up branches and brushwood, keen to escape Wulf's scrutiny. Uncle Wulf crouched down beside Boyd and Rag, who had collapsed to the ground. He spoke quietly.

'What you did was very rash. I do not doubt your bravery, you are your father's children, but you must also heed what you inherited of your mother's wisdom – to blunder into this world... There are things out here that do not love Humankind.'

Rag nodded. Boyd swallowed and tried to speak, not sure if he was ready to talk about what happened to him, or to his sister.

'I... Sorry. ...How did you find us?' he said.

'Muirdoch came upon a messenger. I had planned to introduce you to him shortly, hopefully under more congenial circumstances.'

Rag felt a little hesitant, but had to ask… 'Did he… Just change into a bird?'

In the distance they heard a thin, high scream and moments later a faint splash. Wulf stood, turned and looked towards the sounds, then shook his head, before speaking to Rag and Boyd again.

'Muirdoch… is rare. He is *Each Uisage* – a Water-horse. He can be a man when he chooses, and also a great bird.'

Buggane walked back with some more brushwood. 'Yes – and they eat people!'

'I told you – he is pledged. Do you choose to believe I lie?' said Wulf coldly.

Buggane backed away from Wulf's stern frown and the icy anger in his eyes.

'No, no, Liosalfar. If yer say what yer say, what yer says is the truth!'

Wulf raised an eyebrow. Buggane wilted under Wulf's gaze.

'Just sayin' is all,' he mumbled, and busied himself building the fire and keeping his head down.

Wulf turned back to the children.

'I know you will have many questions, but rest now as much as you can – sun-rising will be in an hour or so. Then we will return home, and I will answer all I can – and you will tell me all that has happened to you.'

Chapter Thirty-Four

Boyd and Rag had curled up together, and despite their questions, exhaustion won out and they were soon asleep. Uncle Wulf retrieved the buggane's shawls to lay over them. The buggane was now snoring gently on the other side of the make-shift hearth, his back against his pack. Geri and Freki lolled near the camp-fire and snoozed, snuffling gently and occasionally having a bit of a twitch and a scratch.

Muirdoch returned, he and Wulf sat a little way apart from the sleepers, speaking together in whispers. Muirdoch told him what he had learned from the Brollachan – dropping him repeatedly from a great height had loosened his tongue considerably and he'd reluctantly told his secrets.

Now and again they glanced at the children then returned to their conversation. Shortly, as the sky began to lighten, they stood up and faced each other, clasping forearms in a warrior's pact and nodded agreement. Muirdoch walked away from the little camp-site towards the water. Wulf walked over to the sleeping buggane, he knelt at his side and put his hand firmly over the buggane's mouth.

Buggane woke with a start. His eyes widened as he tried to struggle, but Wulf was too strong for him.

'Hush Buggane – do not wake them.'

Buggane nodded and Wulf relaxed his grip and took his hand away, he jerked his head for Buggane to follow him. A short distance away, and out of ear-shot of the youngsters, Wulf gripped the buggane's sleeve and leaned forward to speak with quiet intensity.

'Do you want my thanks, Buggane?'

'Oh it was nothin'...'

Wulf shook his sleeve, 'Do you want my thanks...?'

Buggane realised this wasn't a simple question and paid more attention.

'Oh – Well, of course, if there is anything more I can do...'

'Thank you, Buggane. I will not forget this. The children cannot stay here, and Muirdoch and I have an important task. I want you to guide them back to my Keep. We will catch up with you as soon as we can. I will leave the dogs with you, they will help.'

The dogs' heads were up; they wagged their tails slowly, but remained lying down.

Buggane nodded doubtfully, but ventured a question.

'Will... erm, will yer be long?'

'As long as it takes,' said Wulf. 'Get them to the Keep safely and you may ask the Broons for the reward of your choice – even if I am not with you. Especially if I am not with you.'

Buggane opened his mouth to ask another question, but realised he'd get no answer at all, or worse, an answer he really did not want to hear. The Liosalfar was about to do something dangerous and the less he knew was probably for the better. So he just nodded.

'Good,' said Wulf.

Muirdoch walked back with a handful of white-fletched

arrows he'd gathered; some were blackened. Wulf handed him the quiver and dark-haired man walked away to look for more. The dogs stood up, giving little whines, aware that something was about to happen.

'Geri, Freki, stay – guard Morag and Boyd. Go with the buggane, back to my Keep.

Geri woofed in a low tone from deep in his chest. Freki, nodded, tongue out, looking from one to the other, then sat on his haunches.

Wulf, nearly a head taller than Buggane, took him firmly by both shoulders and looked him closely in the face.

'Keep them safe and you will have your heart's desire. Abandon them, and there is no place you can hide.'

Buggane stood stock still - at a loss for words.

'Good,' said Wulf. 'We understand each other.'

There was a snort and a breathy huff from the lakeshore; the great black horse stood there pawing the water impatiently. Wulf clapped Buggane on the back with an open palm – which made Buggane stagger a little, before he strode down to the water's edge.

The Liosalfar scooped up his quiver of arrows, left waiting on a rock at the edge of the lake, and leaped up onto the horse's back, winding a fist into the long black mane. Horse and rider charged away – across the surface of the lake; small splashes of white spray marked their path across the dark waters.

The dogs leapt into the shallows after them and yipped a few times, wanting to go, but knowing they'd been ordered to stay. They paddled slowly back to the shore and came towards the dying fire; flopping down on the grass, all eyes on the buggane, tongues lolling.

Buggane, open-mouthed, watched the two galloping over the lake's ripples for a few moments... and whispered to himself.

'To think I was this close to *Each Uisage* – The Mammy always said I was reckless... Dayz!'

His head shook violently and for a second morphed into the black bull – who gave a deep and mournful 'mooo' – before changing back to Buggane.

'Now don't you start!' Buggane muttered. He looked towards the remains of the fire and saw Rag and Boyd stirring. The dogs pricked their ears up, alert and waiting.

'Well now – who's for breakfast?' Buggane said, rubbing his hands together. 'I've got bacon, and to have some flat bread browning on the skillet won't take long, sure it won't.'

'Where's Uncle Wulf gone?' asked Boyd.

'He and yer man have something they must do in a hurry.'

'What? They left us behind?' said Rag.

'I don't know what - it's not my place to ask that sort o' question. Sure you don't ask alfar their private business without you not being worried about keeping the hide on your back!'

'But...' said Rag. 'What about Dad? What about us?'

'I think they have something they're plannin' on doing that you can't be part of. Something dangerous...'

Rag opened her mouth to speak, but Buggane cut her off.

'Don't fret yourself – I believe they are going where you can't – arguments will do no good at all! Come on now - yer Uncle says we're to go ahead and they will be catching us up. In the meantime – breakfast! After that, we'll make a start at heading for yer Uncle's Keep.'

He sat down to rummage deep in his pack before producing a large muslin wrap of sliced bacon and a bag of flour. Rag and

Boyd looked at each other; Boyd frowned.

'I don't think it's fair… but I suppose there's nothing else we can do,' he said.

'They should have told us before they left – not just gone off,' grumbled Rag.

'And when has a grown-up ever done that for yer?' said Buggane.

Rag glowered and folded her arms.

'Rag, we can't go on anymore. They may come back with good news. We - just have to be patient,' said Boyd

'I suppose… OK - and I do feel hungry,' said Rag.

'Me too… That pack must be really heavy, all the stuff you have in it, Buggane,' yawned Boyd.

'It's not so bad… salt, salt, where's me new bag?' He dived back into his bag, groping so deep inside the edge of the rucksack's opening was up to his armpit. 'Ah, got yer!'

He withdrew his arm and brought out the fist-sized, red cloth bag of salt. 'Can yer pass me the water-skin, Boyd – and we'll need to fill these at the wee spring over there afore we go.'

Boyd shook off his borrowed shawl, and reached for the leather water-skin lying nearby and passed it to Buggane. 'Is it all right if I wash my hands and face in the lake?' he said.

'Sure,' said Buggane, 'The *Fuarth* are gone. They won't come here in daylight. Heh, do yer want a knob of soap and a towel?'

Boyd nodded. Buggane thrust an arm back into his pack and felt around inside until he found what he wanted – a neatly folded, white linen towel, and after a second search, a large knob of pale brown soap.

'Thanks,' said Boyd, before walking over to the lake shore.

A tumble of rocks provided somewhere to leave the towel

while he knelt down at the edge and splashed water over his neck and face. Geri followed him slowly down towards the water and lay down on the grass nearby. Freki stayed where he was - sitting up, looking around, keeping an eye on things.

CHAPTER THIRTY-FIVE

Rag came over to sit closer to Buggane, close enough to try and peer into his pack as he lifted a large, tinned-copper skillet out of the depths. It looked dark inside… and only half-full at best. She frowned.

'Buggane – you got us blankets out of your pack… and the cauldron and food… now that pan. And still that towel was all nice and folded… that's an awful lot of stuff for you to carry.'

'I'm as strong as an ox… as the sayin' goes. And this is me special travellin' pack – an heirloom passed down from me Granddaddy's Da. I might be away from home for weeks at a time. Yer have to keep everything yer need to hand.'

'Even so…' murmured Rag.

He ignored her and started mixed flour and water in a wooden bowl along with a good pinch of salt, kneading the mixture into soft dough. He stopped to put the skillet on the fire. 'Here,' he said, and handed Rag the pack of bacon, 'Put three rashers for each of us into that pan.'

Freki gave a deep 'woof'. Buggane looked at him, the dog looked back, and slowly wagged his tail.

'And yer better put out some for them dogs an' all – you can leave it on the grass, they don't mind it not bein' cooked.' He reached into a side pocket for a long-tined fork with a wooden handle, 'Use this,' he said, handing it over.

Rag laid bacon in the pan, then took another half dozen strips and divided them into two piles for the dogs. She lifted the heavy pan and balanced it on the fire.

Freki crawled forward and one at a time, wolfed his slices of bacon down, but left Geri's share alone.

'We could do with another fire, if you want to bake the bread. I don't think there's enough room on this one for two pans.'

'We could at that… do yer want to start one?'

'I don't know how.'

'Oh it'll be easy for yer. You're a natural fire-child if ever I saw one.'

'You're just saying that because I've got red hair.'

'Ah there's more to it than that, besides - you have the temperament. I bet you have the skills too – have yer tried lightin' fires?'

'No – Mum always told us not to play with matches.'

'Wise lady. But watch me – I just needs me tinderbox…'

He rubbed his hands together hard to get rid of the dough flakes, wiping the remainder off on his trousers. He stood up, patting his jacket pockets and then took out a small brass box. He opened it to show Morag a narrow oval of crosshatched steel with two loops to put your fingers through, and a shiny flint.

'Now the strike-a-light will feel a bit tingly like, but here, put your fingers in the loops and hold the stone in yer other hand. I'll get some tinder ready.'

He searched through the dry branches until he found a large piece of peeling bark. 'This here is Birch bark, good for raising a fire 'cos it has oils in it.'

He took a small knife out of the tinderbox and proceeded to scrape the inside of the bark to make a little pile of dusty curls. Then he swept the earth free of loose leaves and laid a few small straight branches side by side; on top, he piled a thick layer of dry twigs. 'Yer always clear the ground so the fire won't spread… Now, take the flint and hit it against the striker…'

Rag did and produced a flash of sparks. Freki moved away and gave a puzzled whine.

'Knew you would,' said Buggane. 'Now again, but downwards, right close over the tinder, you want the sparks to drop and catch the wee scrapings.'

She did and at the third strike a tiny ember glowed.

'Good - tip the bark and blow gentle to raise the flame… then take the flame to the kindling …'

Rag laid the piece of flaming bark down quickly before she burnt her fingers. The fire snapped and crackled into life.

'Yes, you're a Fire-child all right.'

Boyd walked back to the campfire; his hair was still wet, but his face and hands were clean of yesterday's bog-mud, and he'd also done his best to wipe it from his clothes. Geri walked with him, spotted the bacon on the grass and quickly finished it off.

'Look Boyd – I made a fire!' said Rag, pleased with herself.

'Yeah…? Be careful you don't burn your fingers.'

'Nicely done, young Morag – give it a bit more of them twigs. Now your brother here, he should learn to use a strike-a-light too, 'tis a useful skill – have a go.'

Boyd sat down by the fire, 'The towel's wet, where shall I put it?'

'Drape it over me pack, it'll dry out in a bit,' said Buggane.

'There - take the loops over yer fingers and hit the steel with the stone.'

Boyd tried it several times, but the sparks were thin and sparse.

'I did it first time,' said Rag.

Boyd gave her a dirty look.

'Don't be hard on yerself, it takes practise, but you'll get the knack of it. For the little heifer here it comes natural. See – I bet yer the one who could dowse for water, that's your bonding,' said Buggane.

'What's that mean?' Boyd asked.

'He says I'm fire-bound,' said Rag, 'Is he Water, then?'

'I'd say so. We can try it maybe – just need to find a bit o' Hazel, or find what tree suits you best…'

'Finding water – that'd be cool. What sort of wood… shall I look for one?' said Boyd.

'What are you? And what's Uncle Wulf ? And Muirdoch - what's he?' said Rag.

'Slow down. Let's eat first and I'll get to yer questions after.'

He'd turned back to the dough. 'We need to get this baking or we won't have breakfast 'til nuncheon.' He put the large stewpot on its side in the bigger fire, the open top facing him, then took a chunk of dough, stretching it out, and slapping it between his palms. 'Is that fire going, Morag me girl?'

'Yes, I think so.'

'Build it up a bit, then put that skillet of bacon on the top - that should finish it off.'

In the meantime he slapped the piece of stretched dough onto the curved inside of the hot stewpot. Geri and Freki watched in rapt attention, in case something else by way of food was coming their way.

'Not long to go. Yer'll keep an eye on them rashers, won't yer Rag?' he said. 'Here Boyd, you've nice clean hands now – try makin' the bread.'

'I don't know…'

'That's only cos nobody's learned yer – here, take a lump and give it a bit of a pat, then stretch it…'

Boyd stretched too hard and put a hole in it.

'Doesn't matter – roll it up and start again.'

It took a few tries before Boyd got the knack of making flat sheets of dough - which Buggane slapped inside the pot as the previous ones cooked and lifted away from the hot metal. He had a small stack of flatbread in a bowl, and the bacon was sizzling nicely.

They were happy to sit and eat hot bacon, sandwiched between sheets of camp-bread, in near silence. Rag put her questions on hold, at least while they ate. The dogs watched them with their tongues hanging out, until Rag took pity on them and wiped the remaining bread that was a bit over-cooked, in the bacon grease on the skillet and fed them. The dogs didn't care if the bread was burnt; they cheerfully wolfed down what they were given.

CHAPTER THIRTY-SIX

Buggane wiped his hands on the grass. 'We'd best be off then.'

'What about Uncle Wulf, and Muirdoch?' said Rag. 'What about Dad?'

'He told me to take yer home to his Broons and he will follow. Sure, he'll probably be right behind us. But... we're not to wait for him.'

'Why not?'

'Because he doesn't know how long he'll be. Now, he made me promise to take yers back for him. Yer wouldn't want me to break my word would yer?'

'Ok... if you say so.'

'I do. Now – clearin' up – we needs to wash the pans and get some more water. Boyd - did yer see the spring flowin' down into the lake there? Good lad! Fill up the water skin and whatever bottles yourselves have. Morag – take a pan and we'll clean up.'

He picked up the stew-pot - leaving Rag to bring the skillet, and then he walked down to the shore, looking for a patch of clean shingle. Rag sighed, and eyeing the dogs and the skillet, pushed it towards them. They eagerly took the hint and licked up the remaining bacon fat.

Buggane called back to her: 'Come on, me girl – that's not clean enough to cook in again, even if those two have near licked the tinning off.'

Rag picked up the skillet and slouched down to the lake.

'Why do I have to do the girlie stuff?'

'Cleanin'? Well do I look like I'm a girlie? No – we has to do what needs doin'.'

He hadn't taken his boots off, but was ankle deep in the water. 'See? Here the little stones are nice and clean so you scoops some into the pan… swirls it around… then you pour it out and do it again…' He swirled the pan in circles, Rag could hear the shingle scouring round and round in the pot.

Buggane showed her the inside. 'See – not perfect, but very respectable.'

Rag tried. The dogs had taken the fat off the metal, so a couple of swirls with fine shingle and water took the rest, but she still felt resentful about doing the girlie chores.

'Still don't see why I have to do this. I could have fetched the water.'

'Sure you could, but yer brother is doin' that, so you do this,' Buggane said, rinsing out the remaining sand from his wooden bowl. 'Anyway, there's no such thing as a boy thing or a girl thing – apart from having babbies of course - yer just have to do what's needed at the time.'

Rag snorted, splashing the skillet from side to side in the water.

Buggane stood up and shook the bowl dry. 'I suppose yer really askin' what can a girl do – the answer is whatever they want to - providin' they can do it. If yer want to be cuttin' down oak trees yer have to be big enough, and strong enough, to swing that sort of big, ol' axe – So you lift weighty things, eat meat and grow bigger... or - yer find a different sort of tree and yer wields a littler axe.'

'Mmm...' Rag wasn't entirely convinced. 'I don't want to cut down trees.'

Buggane rolled his eyes. 'Listen, all these things are more to do with temperament. If a man wants to weave cloth and make dresses, sure he can weave and sew. If a woman wants to plough, or be a stonemason, she can be, as long as she can handle the horses, or lift a stone – if she can't heft the great big blocks of stone around, she can still carve the dainty fiddly bits. If he has hands and fingers too big for the delicate silks and lace-makin', then yer man can weave wool, and knot carpets... The only thing that's expected of yer is, whatever you chose, yer can make a proper job of it.'

He rubbed his hands together to dry them. '...But if yer no higher than a fawn's eye and you want to wrestle giant horses... well maybe yer little arms and legs ain't suited for that, but you can make yer trained ponies be the very best in the world.'

Buggane stooped to scoop water into the stew-pot.

'So – can girls fight? Could I learn?'

'If yer have a mind to - but learnin' how to fight – use a knife, a sword even, or a bow, or lance... means yer can defend yerself. Doesn't mean yer have the right to attack other people.'

'Oh no, I wasn't thinking that,' Rag said quickly.

'Good. 'Cos we have laws here, the same as both here and there – stealin' and killin' is wrong. Cheatin' and swindlin' can be punished. Being cruel and hurtin' things for yer own amusement is wrong – some still do those things, but it doesn't make it right – yer understand?' He walked back towards the camp-fire.

Rag nodded. She shook the water from the skillet and followed him. Buggane poured water over both fires and put them out. Then he fully opened the top of his pack and started packing the pot, skillet, bowls and blankets away. Each time he reached deep inside and put the things down carefully. Rag watched in fascination… it was almost like he was stacking shelves inside there! When he'd finished, Boyd was back with the water-bottles. The dogs had been swimming in the shallows. They gave themselves a good shake and water sprayed everywhere.

'Looks like we're ready to go then.'

Buggane hoisted his huge pack onto his back, tightening the leather straps around his shoulders; he led them away from the lake.

'Didn't we come from the other way?' said Boyd fumbling in his pocket for his compass.

'No – I think them Polewiki led yer a fair bit of a ways out yer way. It's what they like to think of as a 'sense of humour'. We're goin' in this direction .'

The dogs gambolled around them, first ahead, then to the side, as the youngsters trudged after Buggane, who set a fast enough pace so they had little breath left for talking.

They walked up a rising incline of moor for an hour without saying much, but the final push up a rock-strewn boulder slope left them all panting and Buggane called a halt for a pause and a drink leaning against a large boulder.

'Buggane,' began Rag, 'you know you called me a fire-child?'

'You are.'

'But what does that mean?'

'It means that's what you are.'

'I don't get it.'

Buggane rolled his eyes, 'sure your Mammy must have said.'

'No.'

'Well… I suppose you're a bit young for the talks…'

'Woah… if you're talking 'birds and bees', we've had those talks at school!' said Boyd.

'What birds and bees?' said Buggane. 'Though I suppose they must have some bits of it too…'

'What have they got to do with fire?' Rag still wanted an answer.

'Rag…!' Boyd gave her a warning frown.

'No…' said Buggane. 'It…it is a fair question. You, little heifer, are fire-bound. Yer Brother here, is water-bound, and I am Earth, of course - big lump like me, what else? With just a touch of water!' He snorted with laughter.

'I'm… not sure…' said Rag.

'You mean like the old elemental stuff, Earth, Fire, Air and Water? We did that in history,' said Boyd. 'But isn't that all make-believe?'

'Aye, well somes may be inclined to think so, but 'tis the general thought, at least over here – that every livin' thing has the bind – most are a bit of this and bit of that, but there's your main binding - who you are, like… it's that that can help you… if you need it to – that said, if it's too much, it can also hinder.'

'And I'm Fire – that's cool!' Rag was pleased with the idea. 'And of course you're Water, Boyd - look how long you spend in the bath!'

'Uh… glad that's sorted. Let's be goin' then.' Buggane stoppered his flask and pushed up from the boulder and looked around. In the distance was a domed hill topped by a ring of ruined wall and a wide tower. 'That's the way we need to go.'

Buggane strode off, the dogs gambolling ahead of him.

Boyd checked his compass again, 'I don't remember seeing that ruined castle before.'

'Ah, probably not – you were on yer own, so you wouldn't necessarily see it if it wasn't remarked upon.'

'What's that got to do with it? It must have been behind us, and we just didn't look back,' Boyd said.

'Wouldn't have helped – not all landmarks are clearly visible, not until you've seen them with somebody who knows them, otherwise they can be a bit sort of hazy.'

'That can't work! How do you find a place you've never been to!' exclaimed Boyd.

'Yer can do, but best you have a map that is marked for where to look… or someone guides you.'

'What if you've never ever been there, nobody has,' said Rag

'Then there'll not be much there until you have the thought that… whatever it is you are seein' in front of yer, is a waymark – then it becomes a waymark. That castle there, I know that hill and wall exists on the other side, so to say, and I can see it here because it's sort of… bled through. When there's something built in that exact same spot here, then you might have an echo of it over there – and same coming the other way.'

Buggane thought for a moment. 'It's why some new places you go to can feel familiar - and sometimes you'll go to a place yer've never been before, and yer don't like the feel of it. That's often because there is, or was, something nasty happened there, bad enough to leave a… stain, on both sides.'

'That's very strange.' said Rag.

'And impossible,' said Boyd.

Buggane paused and turned around. 'Not impossible, and remember, this world is old. Somebody has seen everything here, so that a memory remains in the place, an echo of being seen and known and thought about. It's just you have to learn those memories – you attune to them, so you do. Or you can find out about it with that quantum fizzy stuff your mages and alchemists use'

'Now I really don't understand,' said Rag.

'I think he means quantum physics,' Boyd said quietly to his sister.

'That'll be the fella,' Buggane said cheerfully. 'Look – back there, behind us, is the big lake right? If there was a rift in the Veil and yer went through it, then on your side it would still be water, but it might not be the same sort of water, could be a river or a pond or a marsh, the only thing it wouldn't be is salt-water, cos salt goes to salt and fresh to fresh. Do yer see?'

'Not really,' said Boyd.

'Well you'll never go straight from dripping wet rain-forest directly to desert or t'other way around, or middle of the ocean to mountain-top. The only time the two places adjacent to each other, here and there, are so completely different is down to some great disasters, like a terrible earthquake. Or a volcano erupted and drowned the whole place in ash and fire.'

'I can see that part… but I don't know…' said Boyd thoughtfully.

'I'm no alchemist. I don't know why, I only know is. I know

that once you have seen and acknowledged a place, then that place is fixed like it is. If somebody else comes along, with yer, or sees it because they are told it is there, it is there for them and you, and yer can't impose another view of it on top of something else - cos it is what it is.'

'That's stupid! What if somebody built a city all over the top of a place you once saw?' said Boyd.

'It would still be there underneath. Anyways - you have the very big cities – we don't.'

'What - nowhere?' said Rag.

'You have more people over there. Humankind are very prolific.' Buggane started to walk away. Boyd and Rag had to follow.

'Do you have our sort of people here?' asked Rag.

'Humankind? Yes, there are a few small villages up here, and way over on the coast, but there are lots and lots more further south, where the Salt Woman comes from.'

'And do they know about the mythical animals and the people who... aren't... people.' It sounded a bit weak even as she said it.

'Course they do – even if they haven't really met more than one or two, they've heard stories, and maybe seen some of the creatures. But I suppose I must say that Humankind, 'specially down south, tend to keep mainly to themselves. And there's very few of them here, other than wizards and shamans and such, who knows or cares about *your* side of the Veil.'

'Wait – you have wizards?' said Boyd.

'Well, they're not my wizards – we don't have use for them... though we'll ask a few mages when they're needed.'

'But... but... wizards!'

Buggane came to a stop. 'Look – this is not truly my place to tell yer the likes of what this place is. Yer needs to ask The Liosalfar. These are the sort of questions he needs to find the answers for.' Then he strode away again, leaving Rag and Boyd behind him.

'Wizards!' said Rag

'I don't know…' said Boyd doubtfully.

'Do you think they have pointy hats… and wands…!'

'Yeah, and maybe we'll all end up at Hogwarts!'

'Oh Boyd, don't be a spoil-sport – I'd like to meet a wizard.'

'And with any luck he'll turn you into a frog and I'll get some peace.'

Rag tossed her head and sniffed disdainfully.

'Salamander.'

'What?' said Boyd.

'Salamander, it's a fire-lizard – I saw it online, and I'm Fire.' said Rag.

'Oh give me strength…' sighed Boyd.

'Are you twos comin' or are yer takin' all day?' shouted the buggane over his shoulder; he was quite a way ahead of them. The dogs loped back to finds them. The sun was well up the sky now, and they still had a long way to go.

Chapter Thirty-seven

Buggane kept them walking fast. They stopped for a brief rest at noon; water, and some bread and cheese from Buggane's pack, before he had them up again. He did point out more landmarks, hills and crags, valleys and watercourses, but he gave up trying to explain why the two worlds operated under different rules, 'they just do!' was all he could say.

Places were similar, but not exactly the same, people were Human, like the Salt Woman and her men, '...though I has the suspicion there's more to her than she lets on...' - and then there were folk like him, and the Polewiki, and dozens and dozens of other kinds too.

'Like Liosalfar?' said Rag.

'Yes – the Liosalfar and the Svartalfar, they are like, but unlike...'

'Are they Fire? Or Air, I bet they're air!' she said. 'And what are svartalfar – will we meet them?'

'Oh, no, oh nonono... those are the ones you don't want anything to do with!'

'No?'

'No!' Buggane shook his head and rumbled at the back of his throat, but kept his inner bull under control. 'My Dayz... No.'

'Um… so those are the bad guys…? And they have Dad…?' said Boyd.

Buggane tried to reply, but avoid answering, and it just came out as a string of 'ah…oh… err… arhhh…'

'They are like Uncle Wulf, but different… Is that it?' said Boyd.

'Mmmmm…. You know I told you the liosalfar can be tough, and they can also be mean buggers sometimes – well depending on who you ask. Svartalfar are mean all the time, at least to anybody who is not of their kind. They…have their own way of doin' things and they've no time for what doesn't go their way – but I suppose it all depends who yer talk to.'

'And the elemental thingie?' said Rag, 'Are they Fire?'

'Now that's the thing – both of the alfars are all the elements equally balanced like… plus they each have an extra binding, so to speak, that makes them *lios* or *svart*. Svart are metal-bound, which can be useful for gadgets and mechanicals and such, but it's also hard and unforgiving, like weaponry and armour.

'And Uncle Wulf?' asked Rag.

'The *lios* have… best yer can call it is 'wood-bound' maybe. They have empathy with living and growing things of every nature.'

'Don't other people… or creatures, have wood and metal?' Boyd asked.

'No, not so much… maybe a bit once in a while,' Buggane frowned as he thought about the question, 'though tree spirits, they must be all Wood, and then there are Tommy Knockers in the mines… they're Metal for sure. But what was the word The Mammy uses… those are not so *corporeal* as other fellas are. Apart from them, it's usually only the alfar and their offspring, and even there the one svart might have a touch of wood, and the lios a bit o' metal without going the whole hog, as they say.'

'Does Uncle Wulf?' said Boyd.

'Oh yes. He has a particular wood-binding - and I'd also say he has a strong touch of metal in him as well.'

'Is that bad?' said Rag.

Buggane shrugged. 'Neither bad nor good - it's more how yer man uses it.'

'Iron,' said Boyd, 'can they use iron? Only in the castle it's all bronze, brass and copper pipes.'

'Only the dwarves use cold iron – they bein' miners of ore like. They roast and smelt it and turn it into steel. Everybody but them... well it hurts when you touch it; it can make you feel sick to your stomach – though you can learn to use it after a while. I don't know – maybe it hurts dwarves too, but they're used to it – I never asked one.'

'You have proper dwarves?' said Rag.

'Well I wouldn't know what an improper dwarf was,' said Buggane. 'Though I have heard a few tales I won't be tellin' you two!' he laughed.

'What's that mean?' said Rag.

'Forget it,' said Boyd. He reached for the knife strapped to his leg and pulled it out for the buggane to examine.

'This is steel? From here?'

Buggane peered at it, 'Oh yes, that's alfar made – you see the ripples shinin' like little rainbows?'

'I've got one as well,' said Rag, stopping in her path to get her backpack off.

'Ah, you can show me later; we need to get on now, or you'll never be home. And neither will I.'

'Ok...'said Rag, rather disappointed.

He handed Boyd's knife back. 'See there?' The buggane tilted the blade from side to side; Boyd could see wavering lines shimmering with rainbows in the sunlight. 'Steel like that is what they call 'tempered', and the hilt being bound in wood and leather holds it safe – so yer can handle it easy like. I can run a steel razor across me chin, but it feels funny, not altogether painful, but a bit prickly, yer know what I mean?'

'Like static electricity?' said Boyd. He took the blade and bent to put it back safely in its sheath.

'Well if I knew exactly what that was, I might agree with yer.'

'Like lightening, but much, much smaller and weaker - we can make electricity in generators,' said Boyd.'

'Yer don't say?' said Buggane, 'And what do you do with it?'

'We use it for lights and stuff,' said Rag.

'Mmmm... yes, I seen those when I've been visitin' – in a little glass bowl?'

'Yes. And computers, telephones, trains, television...' Rag listed them off on her fingers.

'Ah no, me gal. We don't have those over here, whatever they are. Not that I've heard anyway. On the other hand – the Svartalfar – they have very cunning things made of metals – they might have somethings like, I suppose... and then the humankind down south... But I don't go that way so's I wouldn't know.'

They walked on for a short while without speaking, but Rag still had questions.

'Where are they – the Svartalfar?' Rag asked.

'They have their own places, same as the Liosalfar do,' said Buggane.

'Do they have keeps and castles - like Uncle Wulf does?' asked Boyd.

'Not so much – they favour caverns, not like a troll cave, no… theirs are – so I'm told, I've never been there, nor want to… more like a palace underground, carved from stone… and they go up through the mountain to the very tip, as well as down deep below… as I say, so I'm told.'

'And they can come through the Veil into our world?' asked Boyd.

'I hope not,' said Rag.

'They can, if there's a rift for them to use, but they're, shall we say, more takers than givers. If they go through the Veil it's because there's something there they want to bring back for themselves – I've never heard of them stayin' over long, not like Wulfric Kennetson.'

The ground was level and dry as they trudged on, topping a long ridge stretching across the moorland. The sun was high, but a breeze made walking quickly comfortable. Boyd thought more about what the Buggane had said.

'That stuff about them, the Svartalfar coming through to us… doesn't sound very good,' said Boyd.

'No. Sometimes, I've heard say, they visit just to cause trouble – a vexation. It amuses them.'

'Really? Do we, Humans I mean, know about that?' said Rag.

'Not so much. But likely as not, a Human that's causin' major troubles – he or she might easily have a svartalfar whispering in their ear.'

'Would they know it was a svartalfar?'said Boyd.

'Sometimes - or it might be they thought they heard a voice in their head. But I dare say some svartalfar could be there in person. Yer Uncle Wulf now, he can travel between can he not?'

'Yes. And the Broons, and Muirdoch too - we've seen him as a bird,' said Rag.

Buggane threw his hands up and shrugged expansively. 'Well so can they, where there's a place that's open.'

'Can they make a place to go through?' said Boyd

'Nobody makes a place – there's just places that tears. Some can be kept wide open, like where yer Uncle's Keep is built. That's apart from unicorns, of course, they can poke their way in with their horn. It's special – don't ask me how special, I don't know!'

'Uncle Wulf has a unicorn – it's chained up.' Said Rag

'Ah well, they are flighty beasts. I'll bet he keeps one for when he might need a shortcut making.'

'Couldn't he just keep an old unicorn's horn – use it to make a tear, like a knife?' said Boyd.

'Has to be a living unicorn – although… I have heard tales of taking a unicorn's horn along with its power… but that's Dark Magic, forbidden…' Buggane shook his head, looked around him and whispered, as if even saying it aloud was wrong, '… yer have to eat it… the beast's essence – its heart and soul! It's not natural!' Buggane shuddered at the thought.

'Eat it… Really?'

'Now then - that's enough of that nasty stuff.' said Buggane

He stopped to look around him, shading the sun out of his eyes and peering into the distance until he spotted the waymark he was looking for.

'This way,' and they set off again. '…It's just good for yer lot,' he continued, 'that most of them svartalfar think it rather beneath them to mingle with the lesser orders – in their opinion.'

'Is that what we are – lesser?' said Boyd.

'No… well, a bit… sort of… yer different is all. Yer don't quite see what we see… But then Dayz Above! I would not want to take on an alfar, light or dark - not without a good part of me head thinkin' it through, and even then it would have to be a calamitous life or death event to be a part of.'

'Wow…' said Rag, 'but Uncle Wulf… he's just Uncle Wulf… isn't he?'

'Dayz, dayz… I hope that's all yer ever have to see of him!'

'Why?' said Boyd.

'Because – well there are things… Oh he must explain himself should he need to, it's not my place.

'But…'

'No buts or beasts! How long have yer been out here? A day - two, three, four? Well yer have a lifetime ahead of yer for questions. Now how about we find a nice wee hollow and settle in for some nuncheon?'

They found shelter below an outcrop of rocks. Buggane opened his pack, reaching in deeply to bring out cheese, apples and some bread wrapped in a cloth. It was only as they finished eating, and started down off the top of the ridge that Rag began again with fresh questions that had occurred to her.

'So this Fire and Water thing… what's Muirdoch?'

'The Water-horse – he's a rarity because he's all of them too, that's what makes him special. He's Air as a bird, Water as a horse and Earth as a man, and all of his nature is Fire as well.'

'And you said - he eats people. Is that like the unicorn horn thing?' said Rag.

'Mmm… no. The one is somethin' you cause to be done by yer own will. With *Each Uisge* that's their nature - eating people – at least they used to. But if Wulfric Kennetson says yer man doesn't, then he doesn't... I suppose,' Buggane said thoughtfully, before continuing.

'It's not so much the actual physically eating people...' he said, 'though maybe they did once. It's more... they sap the life out of yer, which may or may not kill your body, but at best it'll give yer a terrible, terrible hangover, so I've heard. The worst is they leave yer perched on the knife-edge of livin' or dyin', and yer never knows which side the body's goin' to fall 'til it falls.'

'That's what Russ said, remember Boyd?' said Rag. '...It doesn't sound very good.'

'It's what I heard - I wouldn't know more – I never met one before.'

'Still...'

'Trust yer Uncle Wulfric – if he's vouchsafes him, then accept what it is. Me, I just keeps me head down and tries to stay out of it.'

'Out of what?' said Boyd.

'War. Struggles. Politics... whatever yer want to call it.'

They trudged along through the heather, dropping a pace or two behind Buggane, Geri and Freki, running back and forth and around them. Eventually Boyd caught up with the buggane again.

'But you're in it now, the politics?' said Boyd.

Buggane shrugged, and gave a great sigh.

'Buggane,' said Boyd. 'If you tell us which way to go, maybe draw a map with the way-marks, I'm sure we can get back from here on our own. You've helped us enough and we are truly grateful.'

'No, no, nononono! I couldn't do that. I promised The

Liosalfar to take the two of yer home, and take yer home I will. Besides – I get to do a deal with his Broons – that's a prize worth the having. I shall have to give some deep consideration what to dicker for.' He smiled.

Rag, walking on the buggane's other side, reached up and gave him a hug.

'Thank you,' she said.

'Ah, go on, go on, with yer…' Buggane said, blushing, but pleased.

Suddenly, they heard distant dull thuds behind them; a horse was pounding across the moorland - hidden from them by the long ridge of rising ground they had just crossed.

'Hide! And not a word!' hissed Buggane, he turned to the dogs, 'You two – go!' He hustled Rag and Boyd down into a corrie's bowl-like shape that dipped into the top of the hillside. Along one rim a thicket of scrub was growing around and over a tumble of cracked boulders.

The *Cu Sith* slunk off between the rocks, disappearing from view. Buggane took his pack off and chivvied the youngsters into the undergrowth, where they crouched between the split boulders. They could hear the thudding hooves getting closer… closer. Buggane put his finger to his lips and eased his long knife out… They heard a horse neigh loudly close by…

'Buggane!' It was Wulf's voice.

'Stay here while I make sure 'tis yer man for real,' Buggane whispered. He shuffled through the undergrowth away from Rag and Boyd's hiding place.

'Buggane!'

Buggane parted the scrub and saw Wulf standing in the hollow – holding up an injured man with dirty bandages around his head and hands. The great black horse beside them snorted loudly and trotted out of sight over the top ridge of the corrie. The dogs had their master's scent; they crawled out of hiding, rushing over, to greet him with small yips and whines. Wulf clicked his tongue and signalled them to follow the black horse.

Buggane hurried over to help Wulf with the fainting man.

'Are they safe?'

'You can come out now,' called Buggane over his shoulder.

Boyd came out of the bushes first, followed by Rag. They watched Wulf and Buggane carry the half-conscious man and sit him down, propping him with his back to a rock.

'Dad! Oh Dad! What's the matter with him?' shouted Rag, running forward and throwing herself down on her knees beside him.

Chapter Thirty-Eight

Lachlan Ellis was not only injured – he was also clearly very ill. He was pale and sweating, every so often a spasm shook his whole body. His head rolled back against the rock, and the youngsters could see his eyes were filmy, clouded blue-white…

'Nooo…' breathed Boyd. 'What's happened to him?'

'He's thralled,' said Buggane.

'What's that? What does that mean?' sobbed Rag, trying to take her father's hand without hurting him.

'He's ill,' said Boyd. 'But you can fix him, can't you Uncle Wulf? Can't you?'

He wanted very much to hug his Dad, but he daren't touch him, afraid of doing more damage in some way… afraid his father might also be going to die...

Wulf stood up and looked around him.

'Get him some water.'

Buggane hurried off to retrieve his pack and the water-bag.

'Yes, we can help him – but not here. We need to get back to the Keep and we need speed. Those holding him felt secure enough to leave very few guards, but they will have sent word by now…'

'And they're coming after us…?' said Boyd.

Wulf nodded. Buggane rushed back with the water, handing it to Wulf.

'But you're hurt too...' said Boyd.

Wulf shrugged and took the leather water-bag from Buggane.

Boyd could see Wulf had superficial cuts on the arms of his leather coat, and one heavy slash through the padded leather across his shoulder – his white hair had come loose and hung down around his face...a trickle of blood seeped from a scratch across his cheek-bone that ran back to make a wider bloody line through his pale hair.

Muirdoch scrambled down the steep side of the hollow and jumped the final few feet to land beside them. Geri and Freki loped down after him, to run back and forth, silent, but obviously unsettled.

'We have circled the hill. I cannot see them, but they will come,' said Muirdoch. He has a superficial cut near one ear; a thin trickle of blood had dried down one side of his neck. He moved closer to Wulf and spoke quietly.

'You need her. You must call for her help.'

Wulf shook his head. He dropped to one knee to try and get Lachlan to drink. The man managed a mouthful, but the rest ran down over his chin.

'Oh Dad... Dad,' sobbed Rag, clinging to his hand.

Boyd knelt down beside her and put his arm around her shoulder. Buggane came to stand behind the youngsters, unsure what to do next – he patted Boyd on the shoulder encouragingly.

'Here Boyd,' said Uncle Wulf, 'see if your father will drink a little more.'

He handed the water to Boyd, nodded to Buggane, then

stood, and faced Muirdoch.

'You know it,' said Muirdoch. 'We cannot get them off the moor on our own.

Wulf's shoulders slumped a little. 'I know.'

'Do it. I can fly back. Raise the alarm.'

Wulf nodded. He straightened up, he and Muirdoch clasped arms briefly.

'I'll return soon,' said Muirdoch.

'Soon,' replied Wulf.

Muirdoch scrambled up and disappeared out of sight over the crest of the hollow.

Suddenly, a great bird with huge black wings flew up into the sky from beyond the ridge. He beat his wings hard as he rose, circled above them once and gave a single harsh cry, and then swiftly flew away.

'Go!' commanded Wulf pointing after Muirdoch. Geri and Freki raced away over the moorland after the bird, rapidly disappearing from sight.

'What's happening?' said Rag.

'Just what I was goin' to...'

Wulf quelled the Buggane's unspoken question with one stern look.

'...no, I'm sayin' nothin', nothin' at all...'

Lachlan had swallowed a little water, but his head lolled forward to his chest.

'What's the matter with him?' said Boyd. 'Is - is he going to die?'

Wulf shook his head. 'He is thralled... a spell holds him, one that is not easy to break...'

'But you can - can't you?' said Rag. 'You can do that?'

Wulf looked at his feet before speaking. 'We must get him home.' Wulf looked around him, and took a deep breath as he made up his mind. 'But… we cannot do it alone. There's something I must do – wait here – I will return shortly.'

He strode across the hollow, up the shallow slope and out of sight.

'What do we do?' Rag moaned.

'We wait,' said Buggane. He put his big hand on her shoulder and gave it a gentle squeeze. 'Yer man knows what he's doing.'

'Here,' he said, taking the water-bag from Boyd's numb hands. 'Let's see what we can do for this fella.'

He produced a large, red handkerchief from his inside pocket and gently poured a little water over Lachlan's face, mopping it away with the hanky. He eased off the dampened grimy bandage to get a look at the cut on his scalp - it had had stitches in it once, but was now largely healed into a raw scar. Then he looked at the man's hands, washing them, removing the bandages; the ragged cuts and grazes there were newer, but fairly shallow.

'There's no poisoning; they're raw, and some bones might be broke, but they'll heal,' said Buggane. 'I should have a bit of ointment that'll help.' He moved away, crouching down to open his pack and search for the salve.

Rag very gently touched her father's arm. 'Don't die Daddy,' she whispered.

Boyd had shut down, he simply knelt at his father's side, his face frozen, his eyes unfocused, staring ahead of him without really seeing anything.

Buggane came back with a little stone pot and the linen

towel Boyd had used previously. He sat down at the man's side and tore the towel into strips.

'Marigold, chamomile and bee's wax...' Buggane said, as he delicately dabbed the raw knuckles and joints on Lachlan's hands, before winding strips of towel neatly around them. He dabbed some onto the scalp wound, but judged the cut had healed enough not to need a bandage.

They heard a horn call from beyond the rise – then again, the same series of high, clear notes repeated twice more...

'Is that them...?' whispered Rag.

Buggane shook his head. 'He's calling for her.'

'Who?' said Boyd.

'Saive.' said Buggane.

They heard the horn again – a different series of sweet notes... repeated and left to fade away across the moorlands. Buggane abruptly lifted his head and sniffed the air.

'What is it?' asked Rag.

'She's comin' ...oh Dayz, she's heard and she's comin'!' he said.

'Is that good... Or bad?' said Boyd slowly.

'Depends which way you look at it – Saive is the Queen of the Moor. She's the Deer-woman. This is her realm, and we pass through it because she lets us. If you call on her for help, you won't get it for nothin'. She'll have her price – and it won't be small change.'

In the distance another horn sounded, low and ringing, then moments later, it sounded again, closer... and closer. They could feel the earth thrumming beneath them, and heard the pounding of many hooves galloping towards them...

'Dayz – she's comin'!'

CHAPTER THIRTY-NINE

It seemed to them that suddenly the top edge of the corrie was surrounded by bare branches - rising slowly, until they recognised them as mighty antlers – slowly they were ringed by a herd of huge stags that stood in silence, watching them. Several minutes passed under the gaze of the silent guard.

'Oh this is reckless… Reckless… reckless.'

Boyd grabbed the buggane's arm. 'What! What will she do?'

'She will help us.'

Their heads turned on hearing Wulf's voice. He walked slowly towards them; he'd tied his hair back tightly from his face, but the rest hung loose down his back. At his side walked a tall, finely muscled woman dressed in cream-coloured deer-skins. Her wildly tangled white hair was studded with dry leaves and heather flowers, and there were glints of crystals and pearls threaded there; it foamed up into a great dandelion cloud of pale hair around her head.

Saive paused, stood her ground imperiously and looked them over, one at a time in silence.

'Buggane,' she said. 'You have a pearl.'

Buggane spluttered, unable to say his words clearly.

'What else would you ask of the Blue Men of the Minch?'

Buggane shrugged and tried to look innocent.

'A pearl will buy your passage. Only one – you may keep the rest… Or would you rather wait for the Dark Ones?'

The buggane got to his feet, stood before her and made a deep bow.

'Lady Saive – it would please me greatly if you would accept a small gift from my travels…'

He stood upright and searched the inside pockets of his jacket, bringing out a drawstring velvet bag. He loosened the strings, and poured a quantity of fine, creamy-white pearls into the palm of his hand and offered them to her. She stepped closer, looked at all of them carefully and selected the largest as her price for his safe passage.

Buggane slipped the rest back into their bag and tucked it back in his pocket, muttering… 'Small, I said…'

'What was that?' said Saive sharply.

'Nothin'! Nothin' at all your Highness,' said Buggane quickly.

Saive turned to Lachlan and his children - Rag and Boyd both crouched nearer to their father, hoping to protect him, but not sure how. Saive smiled down at them.

'I am not come to hurt him,' she said.

She dropped on one knee and leant forward, taking his head in both her hands, moving him gently until she could look directly into his eyes. She eased her grip and letting his head lay across her palm, passed her other hand across his face, her fingertips pausing to press lightly against his fluttering eyelids for a moment or two. When he opened his eyes they were slightly less opaque.

'Aurelia?' he breathed the name, little more than a sigh on his lips.

'She has passed. You have your children to take care of now.'

'Gone?' he whispered. 'She's really gone…? They… told me. I… I thought they spoke to torment me…'

'The Wheel turns. Your passage is paid. Will you let me raise you up?'

He nodded once. She leaned forward and slipped her arm under his shoulders and gathered him up. With her other arm under his knees supporting him, she stood up with Lachlan cradled across her arms.

'We ride,' said Saive, walking towards, then among, the stags standing shoulder to shoulder around the corrie's rim.

Rag tried to grab her father's drooping hand as she past. Wulf reached out and held her back.

'She will not let him fall' he said.

From a distance they heard a far off, brassy horn, followed by another calling, and another – war bugles approaching them from across the moorland beyond the ridge.

'Come now,' said Wulf urgently. 'We must ride! Buggane – you too!'

Wulf gripped both the youngsters and ran, pushing them ahead of him, around and over the hollow's rim to where the huge stags were gathered. Buggane slung his pack across his back and was only a step or two behind.

They saw Lachlan, lolling forward over the neck of a huge white hind – Saive in her deer form.

'Quickly,' Wulf lifted Rag and put her on the back of one of the enormous stags.

'I can't ride!'

'We will,' says Wulf, 'I shall be with you.'

He helped Boyd to mount, 'Lean forward, not back, hold

on with your thighs and knees, and grip the rough hair of his neck mane with both hands. He will not let you fall – trust me!'

'Buggane?'

'Yes, sir – I'm right. The beast says he'll look out for me... I hope he's right for the job.'

Wulf leaped up behind Rag, tangling one hand in the stag's shaggy pelt and putting his other arm around her waist.

From atop the stag's back Rag could see across the moorland, a dark line of mounted riders were in the distance, their brassy horns brayed again and again – they had sighted their quarry too.

The White Hind lifted her head, bellowed – and lead her herd away. They broke into a thundering run as they streamed across the moor, so swiftly it seems they could barely be touching the ground, though the thunder of their hooves striking the earth proved that was just an illusion.

Boyd was terrified, he has never been on something moving so fast over which he had no control. He gripped hard with his knees and crouched low over the stag's neck, holding on tightly with both hands. At his mount's shoulder, Buggane held on tightly to his stag's neck with both fists, but whooped with excitement, eyes wide, his face alive with exhilaration – he was thoroughly enjoying the ride!

Rag was shielded by Uncle Wulf's body, but because her legs weren't quite long enough to get a grip across the stag's wide back, she was jounced up and down; it was only Wulf's grip around her waist that kept her securely in place. She was glad to feel his warmth and strength at her back, and realised she too had to grip the deer's coarse mane, which steadied her a little. It was scary and magical to ride a giant stag so fast that the wind in her face took her breath away... she had to screw her eyes up to be able to see against the rushing air.

The herd were at full gallop across the moor; leaping over tiny streams and splashing through boggy ground, jumping hollows, running at break-neck speed, westward towards the soon to be setting sun. Other, rider-less deer ran with them, shielding the White Hind and Lachlan, who lay across her back, barely moving; his head hung against her neck, but his hands were buried in the shaggy white fur.

The low sun made it difficult for Rag to see clearly. She looked to one side and saw Boyd and the Buggane both holding on grimly to their galloping mounts, though the Buggane was grinning with delight. Another stag blocked her view as it ran between her and her brother's stag. Abruptly – a black arrow pierced its neck. The stag crumpled to the ground and was left behind them.

Rag gasped in horror. Uncle Wulf held her tighter and urged their mount onwards. Another black arrow thrummed through the air close by, but missed them. Wulf hunched over Rag to shield her. She saw Boyd shift on the stag's back to try and look behind him. She turned her head and glimpsed riders in dark clothes, wearing high-peaked helmets and shoulder armour that glinted metallically in the low sunlight. They were still at a distance, but near enough to loose arrows as they rode. One zinged past her brother. His mount bellowed and stretched its neck out, galloping even harder.

'Hold on!' Wulf shouted to Rag.

He took his arm away, reaching to unsling his short bow from his shoulder. Keeping Rag against his body as best he could meant he could only half turn, but he nocked an arrow, loosing it towards the mass of dark riders behind them. Another arrow…

Rag screamed as she felt herself slipping sideways from the stag's back. Wulf grabbed her, but holding her meant he couldn't use his bow.

The White Hind led her herd in a zig-zag path, making it harder for them to be hit by the bolts of the Svartalfar chasing them, but the dark arrows still thrummed in the air, slicing past the running stags, burying their cruel barbs into the turf and heather. Another deer was wounded and somersaulted headlong into a crumpled heap the others had to leap over.

Then, pale flickers in the air streaked down from above - arrows! Rag squinted up, and caught a glimpse - white arrows. She turned her head and saw a dark rider off to one side; he had gained on them, but suddenly he tumbled and fell to the ground from his wild-eyed horse, struck in the chest by a pale fletched arrow. She looked up into the sky…

The great black horse, Muirdoch, lead a phalanx of flying animals: hippogriffs, griffins, three enormous eagles… each had a Broon on its back, loosing arrows at the Dark Alfar. She recognised Peat and Russ among the riders, their faces grim as they fired their hunting bows – now they were all dressed like Uncle Wulf, in stiffened leather body armour, their hair streaking behind them in the wind.

Over the rise of the hill ran Geri and Freki, howling in pursuit, but they were dwarfed by a pack of enormous white hounds with red mouths and huge red ears. The *fae* hounds were belling and baying as they hunted, storming down the slope, streaming through the racing deer towards the pursuing dark riders.

'Gabriel Hounds!' shouted Buggane, 'My Dayz – Gabriel Hounds!!'

The Svartalfar riders slowed, reining their mounts in, now under the onslaught of arrows from above and the great hounds descending on them, they were now outnumbered and their pursuit faltered.

Until abruptly, the air behind and around them appeared to waver in huge swirling circles that rebounded against each other. More dark warriors suddenly appeared; even the air seemed to bristle with long, metal-tipped lances - they'd come to support their comrades in battle.

'Hold on fast!' Wulf shouted to Rag. He brought one leg up and leapt clear of the deer's back, rolling on the ground and coming up onto his knees, bringing his bow around, nocking an arrow to the bow-string, firing rapidly towards the dark horsemen… arrow after arrow from the quiver at his hip.

The stag with Rag on its back galloped onwards; she clung on with every bit of strength left in her arms, almost sobbing with fear.

Muirdoch had changed form, back from bird to horse; he galloped towards Wulf, who swung himself up on to the Water Horse's back. They charged down towards the dark riders, who were already wheeling about, surprised by the unexpected onslaught that met them.

The White Hind slowed and lead her herd over the crest of the hill and out of sight of the conflict. There was a slight hollow, a dry corrie that once held a small pool. Saive wheeled into this space, allowing Lachlan to slide from her neck to the ground. She bellowed loudly, then morphed back into her human form. The herd of stags milled around the edge of the hollow, while the three ridden animals descended to the smooth grassy floor .

'Dismount!' Saive commanded.

Rag almost fell off, as Boyd quickly slid from his stag's back and hurried to catch her. Buggane was already on the ground and running to Lachlan.

'We will be back,' Saive shouted to Buggane. 'Keep them safe!'

The largest of the stags came forward, pawed the ground, Saive leapt onto its back. In her hand was a great trident made of sharp antler tines; she ululated a fierce battle cry. The huge stag charged away, carrying her into battle. The rest of the herd bellowed and followed her, thundering back the way they had come.

Boyd and Rag heard the bellows diminish, but there were many distant shouts and cries, and furious baying, out of sight, beyond the rise of the sheltering ground.

CHAPTER FORTY

Buggane had his arm under Lachlan's shoulders and pulled him up, half carrying, half dragging him to the deepest side of the hollow in the hillside. The rim of the turf curved out above their heads, forming a shallow cave - with a slab of bare bed-rock on one side, and tumbled boulders worn smooth by the rill that used to flow over them on the other.

Boyd had Rag by the shoulders, steering her because her legs were still weak with shock and fear, he followed the buggane. Boyd's chest was still heaving with the effort of clinging to the stag's back. Buggane had laid Lachlan down, before looking around him. Rag threw herself down beside her father. Boyd stood in silence, looking to Buggane for guidance.

'What now?' he said eventually.

'We wait,' said Buggane.

They could still hear the distant clash of weapons and shouts, muted by the wall of turf around and above them.

'And?' said Boyd.

'Until it all goes quiet. When it all goes quiet - then we worry.'

Lachlan mumbled, then managed to whisper, 'Help them…'

'Hushshshsh… we're safe enough in here…,' Buggane did his best to sound reassuring.

He turned around and held out his hands, made some complicated passes in the air as he muttered words the youngsters couldn't understand. They blinked – the entrance to the shallow cave was covered by a smooth gauze curtain stretching from the overhead rim above them to the ground - from the outside it looked like a large oval on the hollow hill had become a smooth grassy bank. He sighed, 'well …as long as the big boyos don't come lookin' too hard… Now – I do believe I've a bit of a snack in me knapsack.'

He unslung his rucksack, loosened the leather cords and opened it wide enough to reach in and rummage around; soon producing something wrapped in a cloth, a big chunk of paper-wrapped yellow cheese and a silver hip-flask. He spread out the wrapper revealing the cheese, which he broke up into nuggets and laid beside the cloth, which held some very dark, solid-looking bread already cut into slices.

'Who's for a bite?'

'You want to eat at a time like this?' said Boyd barely believing his eyes.

'You eat when yer get the chance, me lad,' says Buggane. 'Move over chick,' he said to Rag. She slid away from her father's side so the buggane could get closer to him.

Lachlan was propped up at the back of the hollow. Buggane raised the man's head to coax him to sip from the flask.

Rag sat, hugging her knees in silence, her eyes barely focused on the here and now. After a few moments, almost without thinking, she reached over and picked up a small piece of cheese and nibbled it, staring at the open leather pack… which still looked half empty.

'Buggane… how come you have so much inside your

back-pack… but it's still not full?'

Lachlan swallowed a mouthful of the liquid from Buggan's flask; he coughed a little. Buggane lifted him up a bit and encouraged him to take another sip. The man swallowed some more, then coughed again, waving his bandaged hand vaguely – *enough*.

Lachlan could barely see, it seemed everything was hidden in a thick fog and now and again a distorted shape drifted out of the mist and into view, and then vanished. He heard Rag's voice, but as if she was far away, almost as if she was speaking from underwater… he could only catch one or two words at a time. But at least he was not… there… His mind plunged away from the thoughts of what had been… He could feel the reviving heat of the liquid at the back of his throat… strong, distilled spirits… He swallowed and again for a brief moment he heard his daughter's voice clearly…

'What is it… is it like a Tardis, so it's bigger on the inside? All the stuff that you take out of it… What's it made of – it looks like black leather – is it special?'

Lachlan had some idea… he'd seen something like it before. He tried to speak, but could only whisper before the chuckle that welled up inside him let him give the ghost of a smile…

'Poach… poacher's pack…' Lachlan's chuckle turned into a racking cough and he drifted slowly back towards unconsciousness.

'What..? said Boyd, 'what did he say?'

'Not a lot,' said Buggane.

'He did, he said something!'

'All right – calm down… He said… poacher's pack.'

'Why did he say that? What does it mean?' Boyd was becoming frustrated by all the mysteries.

'Well if you must know – that's why me travellin' pack is big enough for three months provisions. It's… linked, to a special cupboard at home - and that's where I have everything stacked where I can lay me hands on it.'

'Like a little doorway…?' said Rag.

'Sort of.'

'How did you make that – and how does it stay open?' she said with a frown.

'It's not open at the other end. I have to be there, at home, and open the locked door from the outside.'

'So you could go back that way – if you could get inside the pack,' said Boyd.

Buggane shook his head, 'No. I have to open the door from the outside – anything that goes in from here, can't get out until I let it out.'

'Oh – Poachers…' said Boyd.

'What's that mean?' said Rag

'It means if he wants to steal something, or catch an animal, it's hidden inside until he gets it out when he gets home.'

'Steal is a harsh word!' said Buggane sniffily. 'I trade.'

'But could we… hide inside…'

'Not really, me girl, yer might get in… but if I'm not there to let yer out… that's the end of you… And we don't need to be mentionin' any of this to The Liosalfar, do we?'

'Why?' said Rag

'Because poaching is illegal,' said Boyd. 'Can I have some cheese?'

Rag handed him the paper to pick from. Buggane took a swig from his flask and grimaced. 'It's not for poachin'! At least not anymore – that was back in my Granddaddy's time…'

Boyd handed the cheese back. Buggane leant forward to inspect the food. 'I think I'll have some of this meself – soda-bread?' He offered Boyd a piece of dark rye bread - it smelt slightly sour, 'Go on – try it, it's good.'

Boyd took a piece – it tasted better than it smelt. He chewed reflectively. 'So how did your Grandad make it – and I thought you said it was your great-grandfather's,' Boyd said around a mouthful of bread.

Buggane nodded, he chewed his bread and cheese for a moment… 'Well - If yer must know – it IS me great-grandfather… his skin anyway.'

'What…!' Rag yelped, spraying bits of cheese crumb across the cave.

'Rag…!' said Boyd brushing his sleeve.

'It's nothing like that, not yer Dark Magic! He gave his permission. In writing. And Grandaddy waited until after he died.'

'Eeeuww!' said Rag, wrinkling her nose.

'This…' said Buggane, patting the pack, 'is a rare and precious thing, made with love and respect!'

'And…' said Boyd, 'I bet it's against the law, or lore, or whatever you have here…'

Buggane looked away and sniffed, and picked up another slice of rye bread. 'It's a family heirloom, part of my ancient heritage and tradition.'

'Yeah, right,' said Boyd.

'Skin…' said Rag, '… so that's made out of cow-hide, right? Like proper leather… but you're related to it?'

Buggane nodded. Rag continued, 'Is that a … thing. That people do here?'

Buggane turned to her, 'No. It is special. And you were grateful enough for bread and bacon out of nowhere before, weren't you?'

'Yes… I was,' she said, 'I only wondered… it's just there's so much that is… different.'

'Hummphh!' the buggane snorted huffily.

There was a small silence between them, broken after a few moments when Rag thought of another question she wanted to ask.

'Buggane…' said Rag.

'What?'

'What will she want from Uncle Wulf? What does he have to give her?'

'For this? A life for a life most likely.'

'She's going to kill him? Or us?' said Boyd, alarmed.

'No… nonono… She wants him. Has done for… years, I'm told.'

'Him?' said Rag.

'She wants his babby. It would be what do yer call 'em… A Hero. Yer know - like that Greek fella in the stories…'

Rag and Boyd looked mystified – they had no idea.

'Ah you'll have heard of him… Achilley-thingy…'

'Achilles?' said Boyd.

'That's yer man! A Hero.'

'Why does she want that?' said Rag.

Buggane shrugs, 'Every mother wants a son to be proud of… I dare say she'll ask for a daughter too – one for each of yer.'

'That's weird,' said Rag.

Buggane chewed the last of his bread, 'No. The wyrd thing is – a Hero is the only thing can kill *Each Uisage* in a fair fight. That's part why The Liosalfar has denied her all these years… so I've heard anyway…'

'Buggane…' said Boyd

'She wants Muirdoch dead?' said Rag, puzzled.

'Buggane…'

'Who knows what goes on inside a queen's head? Power games, chess pieces, pawns… The Liosalfar is a powerful one himself – Don't be kiddin' yerself he pays this obligation lightly… But at the end of the day, as me Mammy says… keep yer tail up and yer head down…'

He wiped his hands on the bread cloth.

'Buggane… listen… It's gone quiet,' said Boyd.

They all listened – there was silence outside.

'Didn't you sa…' said Boyd.

'Tutututut… Sssshhhhh…' hushed Buggane, listening, - turning his head from side to side in an effort to catch the tiniest sound.

They scarcely dared to breathe as they strained to hear what might be happening out there…

Then they did hear something - the swishing of footsteps through grass and the dull clank of metal on leather…

Chapter Forty-One

Lachlan lifted his head weakly and tried to struggle to sit up. Buggane gently pushed him back; he waved the children back behind him to sit with their father – then put a finger to his lips… and drew his knife… shuffling forward, holding it out in front of him.

Boyd went down on one knee beside his father, so he could ease the leg of his jeans up and draw his knife from its sheath. He held it down at his side where Rag couldn't see it – if it came to a fight… he wanted to be ready. He swallowed hard, realising his mouth was bone-dry.

Outside the filmy green gauze they could dimly see shadows approaching… coming closer…

'Buggane – come out now. I see you.'

It was Wulf's voice.

'Great Dayz Above!' declared Buggane. He made wide slashing movements with his knife-blade, and the fine green gauze split apart and dropped away, evaporating to nothing.

Wulf was outside – his white hair caked with dark blood on one side. He had his arm around Muirdoch's waist supporting him; the Water Horse's arm hung heavily at his side and he limped badly as he was guided by Wulf to sit on a boulder outside the shallow cave.

'You've a flask, Buggane? I dare say it has more than water in it!' Wulf demanded, holding his hand out.

Rag and Boyd stood and came forward to see what was happening. They watched as Buggane hurriedly fumbled open the silver hip-flask, and handed it to Wulf, who passed it first to Muirdoch. He took a large mouthful; the strong liquor must have burned the back of his throat, it made him catch his breath and cough. He wiped his mouth on the back of his hand – the knuckles of which were grazed and raw - then handed the flask back to the alfar.

Wulfric took the flask and bent forward to dribble the golden-brown liquid over the deep and bloody gash that ran the length of Muirdoch's thigh. The man's face screwed up into a grimace and he hissed in pain as the fiery spirit ran through the raw wound on his leg.

Wulf loosened his own belt and pulled his shirt loose, before taking his dagger and nicking the cloth so he could tear off wide strips from the garment's hem. He quickly wound the makeshift bandage tightly around Muirdoch's thigh, knotting it in place. The man tried hard to suppress his groans of discomfort as Wulf worked on the injured leg.

'More!' Wulf commanded, holding out the flask to Buggane.

Buggane took it quickly, muttered over it, blew over the mouth of the flask and gave it a shake… before handing it back to Wulf – who now drank a few swallows himself. After which The Liosalfar, inhaled deeply and closed his eyes for a moment, holding it inside - before blowing out a long breath through pursued lips. He opened his eyes again, handed the flask back, and looked around him.

'You can put your knife away now Boyd.' The youngster

looked down at his hand, half-surprised to find he still clutched the knife's hilt firmly. 'Your grip should be under, rather than overhand, we will show you how to wield it properly when we get back.'

Wulf looked over to the buggane. 'Have you a length of cloth, Buggane, or a leather belt or some such?'

Buggane nodded and hastily searched through the pockets of his pack, finding another large crumpled handkerchief of red cloth and a spare leather belt. He offered them to Wulf, who nodded his acceptance.

Rag crept forward to get a close look at what was happening.

'Help me Buggane – here,' said Wulf.

Buggane took a swig from the re-filled flask himself and handed it to Rag to hold.

'It fills itself? Cool!' she said, giving it a sniff, and pulling a face at the strong fumes.

Wulf took hold of Muirdoch's limp arm and lifted it slowly and gently, until the arm was bent at the elbow across the man's chest, with the hand near to the opposite shoulder. Muirdoch closed his eyes, flinching as Wulf manipulated his damaged shoulder.

'Here Buggane – hold his arm steady while I bind it,'

Buggane hesitated, and cleared his throat. He flexed his fingers, and slowly reached forward to touch the *Each Uisage*, but not quite getting there... He moved around to stand behind Muirdoch, so he could reach over the seated man's shoulder.

'Come, come – he will not bite!' Wulf said crossly.

'Are yer sure about that?' mumbled Buggane, leaning forward and reaching to hold the arm in place. As he did so, Muirdoch turned his face towards Buggane, bared his teeth and gave a fearsome snarl.

'Aaarrrgghhhh…' cried Buggane, jumping back and loosening his grip on the man's wrist.

'Muirdoch.' warned Wulf.

Muirdoch yelped with pain as his arm dropped, then chuckled, 'It was only a jest.' But he caught his breath, gasping as Wulf had to readjust his arm, before the alfar could use the cloth and belt to put together a make-shift sling to hold his shoulder immobile – with Buggane's nervous assistance.

Saive walked down into the hollow, her stags crowded the rim of the grassy dip, but kept their distance.

'The Svartalfar are fled and your helpers gather themselves to return to your Keep.

Wulf nodded without speaking.

'Your bird cannot fly, and the little ones are too tired. I will have them ride with me…'

Wulf looked at her sharply and stood up from kneeling at Muirdoch's side.

'They are safe – I have your pledge do I not?' she said.

Wulf looked down at Muirdoch then back to Saive. He nodded.

'Good. My cart is waiting. Buggane – you prove loyal and you have paid your fee, will you go on, or accept my gratitude to take you home?'

Buggand stumbled forward and bowed deeply before straightening up and speaking. 'Erm… Ma'am… Lady… If I could get a ride to the coast that would be more than gracious of yer.'

'Granted. One of my Sianach will carry you.'

Buggane turned and solemnly shook hands with Boyd, and then Rag. He pulled the strings of his pack tight and slung it over his shoulders. 'Remember now – tail up, head down.'

He winked at them, before he turned and bowed to Muirdoch, and then to Wulf. The Liosalfar took the buggane's hand in both his hands in a formal hand-clasp of fealty given and received.

'I owe you a service, Buggane.'

Buggane was both embarrassed and flattered by the attention and tried to wave it away. 'Ah, that's all fine, yer Honour.'

'I will remember,' said Wulf. 'You may call on me.'

'Sir.'

Buggane gave a little half bow, he turned and waved a hand at Rag and Boyd, and started to walk away. One of the giant stags left the others of the herd to walk at his side; straight away they were hidden from view by the other deer crowding forward.

When the herd parted again, two stags appeared and walked slowly forward towards Saive where they paused and bowed their heads to her. They were harnessed to a wide, almost fragile looking chariot with two large wheels; the floor was made of strips of woven hide, while the curved frame and waist-height uprights were constructed of slim struts of white wood. Saive nodded in acknowledgement and the deer edged forward and around, until they faced outward again, the chariot behind them.

'Mount,' Saive commanded, before striding off to one side where her stag waited.

Wulf gathered Lachlan up, and with Boyd's help, guided him forward to stumble up and into the cart. They managed to seat him on the floor with his back against the frame. Boyd and Rag got in and sat either side of him. Wulf aided Muirdoch to stand, and helped him forward. The man was able to balance awkwardly, but could barely put any weight on his damaged leg. Wulf helped him up so he could stand at the rear of the cart and lean on the surrounding rail.

Saive smiled to herself; she motioned another stag forward, then turned to address Wulf.

'Mount and follow us. Beyond the range of hills I can fold the veil and gather the rifts together briefly for you all to pass. You will find yourselves a mile or two from the village near to your Keep. Does your *Each Usiage* agree?

'Muirdoch will accept your hospitality.'

'I sincerely hope so. Come! We ride!'

Saive bounded up onto the back of her sianach, she called out to the stags pulling her cart to follow her. They moved off at a walk that gathered pace.

Rag and Boyd drew their feet up and holding their father with one hand each, held onto the upright struts of the cart with the other.

Rag could see that Muirdoch frowned in pain and hissed through his teeth as the jouncing jarred his injured leg. He leaned forward to rest his good forearm against the waist high rail, gripping it tightly with one hand, without turning his back on Saive. She rode beside the heads of the stags pulling the cart. She half turned to address Wulf, who was now beside her, mounted on another of her giant stags.

'I will send word.'

Wulf inclined his head slowly in acknowledgement as she moved to ride ahead of him.

The stags pulling her cart followed their Queen across the moor at a steady trot, the rest of the herd gathering on either side in a protective phalanx.

The sun had long dipped below the horizon and the light was rapidly fading from the skies as the first stars of evening showed clearly in the darkening vault of night above the travellers' heads.

Chapter Forty-Two

The night was pitch-dark now. They were still quite high on the hill, but they could see the lights of the village down in the valley below. Saive had been as good as her word, and if they had all been fit and in daylight there would be no problem clambering down the steep hill of rocks, rough grass and heather… But Lachlan was drifting in and out of consciousness and Muirdoch was struggling. Wulf had given the water-horse his bow to use as a stick, but it flexed too much to be useful and he stumbled repeatedly, which made him cry out, before quickly stifling his groans. They had barely managed a few hundred yards when Wulf called a halt. He and Boyd carefully laid Lachlan down.

'It is too dark,' said Wulf, 'and the ground is too rough. We will have to wait for day-light.'

Rag shivered, the wind was getting up. Muirdoch saw her; he shook his head.

'They cannot stay outside for long; the night will get colder yet. Leave us here and go back to the Keep – bring help back with you,' he said.

Wulf frowned, 'I am loath to leave you out in the open, if we could find a sheltered place perhaps…'

'What's that?' Boyd pointed back up the hill.

A row of half a dozen small lights bobbed up and down in

a line, descending the hill parallel to them, perhaps a quarter of a mile away.

'Is something coming after us?' cried Rag.

'There should not be anything out here…' Wulf said.

Just then one of the lights wobbled and slid to the ground. The lights behind halted, and across the moor drifted voices and laughter.

'They are only Men,' Muirdoch said, relieved.

'You can ask them for help,' said Rag.

'I…' began Wulf.

'Ask,' said Muirdoch. 'The children need help, as does Lachlan. I can stay out of sight and you can come back for me later.'

'Your leg needs stitches as much as Lachlan needs my aid.'

'Hello!' shouted Rag. 'Helloooo – help, help!'

'Rag! Shut up!' hissed Boyd.

The lights stopped moving and wavered as the group looked for the source of the sound.

'We need them,' said Rag. 'We can explain later – we were walking, Dad and Muirdoch fell, people are always falling down mountains.'

'Hello? Who's there?' came a shout from the darkness.

'Do it,' said Muirdoch. 'Walk towards them and leave me here – they will not see me in the darkness.'

After a moment, Wulf lifted his head and shouted. 'We are here – we need your help.'

'Aye, aye – keep shouting till we get a bearing…'

'We're over here… here… Here we are!' Rag yelled at the top of her voice.

Muirdoch did his best to slide away from them, retreating

from the bobbing beams of the head-torches that were rapidly coming towards them.

They arrived in no time, a group of six walkers, on their way back down the mountain to the village pub where they were staying.

'What on earth…' began the leader at the sight of them. 'What are you doing out here at night…? You're not exactly dressed for it.'

'Oh, I know what they are,' said one of the walkers, 'I bet they're some of those LARP-ers – you know, dress-up game-playing in costumes - but see laddie, you're well off the beaten track.'

'Photographs!' Boyd blurted out. 'We came to get some pictures with a wild background – got lost.'

Wulf looked puzzled, but followed Boyd's lead, 'Yes, photographs… their father became ill and fell, hit his head.'

'Aye and so did you by the look of it!'

Wulf touched his hair, still stiff with dried blood.

'A scratch – if you can help us down to the village, I can get help to get us home and tend him.'

'Och, of course, no problem!'

'Once we get down to the road, we will be collected shortly,' said Wulf.

The other men were making an improvised sling out of ropes and hiking sticks.

'Should we call for an ambulance for him?' another man said.

'Thank you, no – we have medication for him. He needs that and rest,' Wulf replied.

'Ok if you're sure –and how's the wee girl and boy?'

'We're fine, said Boyd. 'Once we get to a path.'

'Oh you were near enough - missed your way in the dark, did you?'

'Yes, that's right,' said Rag.

Wulf had edged backwards into the darkness as the climbers fussed around Rag and Boyd. He found Muirdoch some way back, out of the walkers' line of sight.

'They are curious, but think we are play-acting. They will not pay attention other than you are injured. Come, put your arm around my shoulder. We will follow them down and keep in the shadows.'

Muirdoch nodded. His face was pale as he gritted his teeth against the pain when Wulf helped him stand.

'Lean on me,' whispered Wulf. 'I won't let you fall.'

When they hobbled back towards the walkers - they were ready to carry Lachlan on a make-shift stretcher.

'There's another one – and the laddie's hurt too!' said their leader.

'I can help him. You go first, we can follow,' said Wulf.

'Well if you're sure about this… We're staying at the pub. They can call someone to take you to the medical centre…'

'No. We have medical assistance on the way. I just need to get them down.'

'If you say so, pal… let's get going. Can the bairns manage?'

'We'll be fine,' said Boyd.

Four of them set off carrying Lachlan, the other two walk behind. One of them offered his hand to Rag.

'Come with me lassie, the path's down here a-ways. Out walkin' were you?'

Rag took his hand. 'Yes, just out for a walk.'

Boyd dropped back a few paces, 'Can I help you Uncle Wulf?'

Wulf shook his head, 'Thank you, Boyd, but the path is too narrow for three – just carry my bow.'

'How will we get back to the castle?' Boyd whispered.

'They already know we are here – Broonie will send the car for us.'

'Oooo…' Boyd decided it was pointless asking *how* they knew; Uncle Wulf clearly had ways of communicating with the Broons.

The path down the hill was rough and the going was slow. Wulf held Muirdoch up, with one arm around his waist, and the man's good arm over his shoulder, but he could only hop slowly and painfully down the hill on his uninjured leg. Boyd walked between them and the climbers, doing his best to block their view when any of the men turned around to look back out of curiosity.

They were able to pick up the pace a little when they joined the paved lane leading from the village towards the hills, and where the lane met the main road… the shooting-brake was waiting for them, parked on the wide verge at the side of the road.

Russ and Peat were outside leaning against the car, having changed back to hoodies and camo trousers, blankets at the ready. They called out to the walkers to bring Lachlan over to them. The rear door of the car was raised already so the huge space was open. They praised the men for their help, thanked them and assured them that Lachlan would be fine; they had everything they needed at home…

The men were tired after a long day, and having been repeatedly told by a smiling Russ and Peat that they could do everything medical that was necessary, the men turned and set off to trudge back to the village inn and left them.

Wulf had hung back, supporting Muirdoch, he nodded reassuringly from a distance. Boyd had stood tall, and taken responsibility; he'd stepped forward to shake the walker's hands, added his thanks, and sent them on their way, 'yes, they just needed to get him home as quickly as possible - they'd all be looked after there. No – they were fine now - thanks very much. Goodnight… goodnight'.

Russ and Peat helped Lachlan to lie down in the pile of blankets in the back of the car.

'Laird?' said Russ as Wulf slowly came forward holding Muirdoch around the waist. He took Wulf's bow and empty quiver.

'Well done. The children can ride in the back with their father. Help Muirdoch get onto the back seat so he can sit with his leg straight.'

He carefully handed the man over to Russ and Peat for them to help Muirdoch hobble around the car and prop himself up in the rear seat.

Wulf climbed into the open back of the car with Lachlan. A leather bag was open and waiting there; Wulf pulled out a small glass flask checked the label and poured a few drops onto Lachlan's lips coaxing him to swallow. The injured man opened his eyes and mumbled, '…are they safe?'

'Yes,' said Wulf, 'sleep now. Sleep – you are home and you are safe. You can safely sleep…'

Wulf passed his hand across Lachlan's forehead gently and

the man sighed and appeared to relax back into a proper sleep.

'Sit beside him,' Wulf said to Rag and Boyd, 'we will do more for him as soon as we can.'

Wulf searched the leather bag again and produced a silver hip-flask that he handed across the open back to Muirdoch, who was now propped up with his leg along the seat. 'Here, it's laced with a little poppy oil,' he said

He nodded to Wulf, took it and swallowed deeply before handing it back.

'Keep it. I can wait,' said Wulf. He scrambled out of the rear and allowed Peat to jump in before pulling the tailgate down, and getting into the front passenger seat.

'Will Dad be alright?' Rag asked Peat, as he settled down to support Lachlan's head to stop him rolling around.

'They will do their best for him, Morag – we will all do our best.'

'Laird?' said Russ, from the driver's seat.

'Yes, home, as quickly as we can,' said Wulf climbing into the passenger seat.

The car pulled away, the bug-eyed headlamps lighting a bright path down the dark country road winding between the clustering pine trees.

Muirdoch tapped Wulf on the shoulder, offering him the flask. 'You could do with this too,' he whispered.

Wulf nodded and accepted, sipping a little liquor slowly, before handing it back. 'Finish it,' he said to Muirdoch quietly so the youngsters couldn't hear. 'I have to set that shoulder and stitch your leg when we get back.'

Epilogue

When the station-wagon pulled into the courtyard of the castle there was a crowd of little people headed by Broonie and Gam – several had fresh bandages over minor wounds. They bustled forward with blankets ready to help get Lachlan and the children and Muirdoch out of the car and into the house.

Wulf climbed a little stiffly out of the passenger seat, Russ had quickly come around to hold the car door open. Wulf paused, looked at him, and Broonie, who had come forward to greet The Liosalfar.

'My thanks – to all of you.'

They both bowed from the waist.

'Are they all back, are they safe?'

Broonie shrugged, nodded his head – they're so-so, but ok…

'In with you. Food and rest is what we all need. Have Lachlan put near my rooms. Tomorrow we will take stock and see what we must deal with.'

Lachlan was already being carried into the house, the weary youngsters walked behind him. Russ and Peat helped Muirdoch out; his face now chalk-white, lips pressed together, his jaw set, as he hobbled up the steps and into the castle.

Wulf paused outside for a few moments in the silence, looking around him; virtually everything looked peaceful again now that they had all gone into the house. He straightened his shoulders and looked up into a night sky glittering with familiar stars. He took in a deep breath of still, night air, and then he walked inside after his household, closing and bolting the Keep's doors behind him.

Rag flung her bedroom door open, the bedside light was on and her bed had been turned down. She didn't stop to take her boots off, just threw herself onto the bed. She turned her head – a small fire had been lit in the grate, it flickered comfortingly behind the gleaming brass fire-guard.

Then she noticed the soft toys over her pillows and sat up. She looked around – previously empty shelves were now filled with her beloved toys and ornaments from her old home. The little pukis poked his head out from under the bed and flew up to join Rag, chirruping to be fussed, butting her hand with his head to encourage her to stroke him.

'What happened…?' breathed Rag astonished.

The pukis chirruped and flew around the room, flapping his little dragon wings hard, darting her and there, wanting to show her what he had done and looking for praise.

'You did all this just for me…?' He fluttered back to land on the bed and snuggled up against her. 'You fetched all of my stuff…?'

Pookie chirruped happily and started purring, rubbing his head against her.

'Oh good boy, Pookie. Good boy!'

There was a knock at the bedroom door,

'Come in!'

Boyd opened the door. He walked in and looked around the fire-lit room, astonished by the unexpected arrival of the toys and trinkets… all the stuff he called 'Rag's Junk'.

Rag was grinning from ear to ear. 'Look what Pookie did for me! Now I'm really home!'

THE END

About the Author

Helen Brady lives in a small, ancient town in Warwickshire, sharing her house with a Manx cat called Logan. *The Fabulous Zoo* is her debut novel, the first of a proposed series of five about Rag and Boyd and their travels beyond the Veil.

An avid life-long reader of science-fiction, fantasy and history, Helen's long time influences are Alan Garner, Bernard Cornwell and JRR Tolkien. She has two grown-up children, and when she's not writing, she's a volunteer, sorting costumes as Head of Wardrobe at her local independent theatre.

ragandboyd@hotmail.com

ACKNOWLEDGEMENTS

I'd like to thank Ann for her consistent loyal cheer-leading – she's been a very supportive beta reader since 2004. Also to Helen, a recent good friend on whom I have tried out many styles of writing and she's patiently read all of them and provided enthusiastic constructive feedback.

Thanks to Heddwen and Jonathan at Writing West Midlands, who encouraged me as I turned from scripts to novels.

Thanks to Karla Harris for her proof-reading and picking up the typos when I couldn't see the wood for the trees.

And many thanks to Charlotte Mouncey, who listened to my garbled opinions as to what should be on the book cover and interpreted them beautifully.

LOOK OUT FOR MORAG AND BOYD'S NEXT ADVENTURE

Rag and Boyd: The Elfstone